"Delectable and delicious . . . with mouthwatering recipes."
—*Midwest Book Review*

"Will leave readers feeling as if they have shared a warm cup of tea on Church Street in Charleston."   —*The Mystery Reader*

"A delightful series."   —*Deadly Pleasures Mystery Magazine*

"Enjoyable . . . Childs proves herself skilled at local color, serving up cunning portraits of Southern society and delectable descriptions of dishes."   —*Publishers Weekly*

"Along the way, the author provides enough scrumptious descriptions of teas and baked goods to throw anyone off the killer's scent."   —*Library Journal*

"This mystery series could single-handedly propel the tea shop business in this country to the status of wine bars and bustling coffeehouses."   —*Buon Gusto*

STEEPED IN EVIL

Tea Shop Mystery #15

LAURA CHILDS

BERKLEY PRIME CRIME, NEW YORK

THE BERKLEY PUBLISHING GROUP
Published by the Penguin Group
Penguin Group (USA) LLC
375 Hudson Street, New York, New York 10014

USA • Canada • UK • Ireland • Australia • New Zealand • India • South Africa • China

penguin.com

A Penguin Random House Company

STEEPED IN EVIL

A Berkley Prime Crime Book / published by arrangement with the author

Berkley Prime Crime Books are published by The Berkley Publishing Group.
BERKLEY® PRIME CRIME and the PRIME CRIME logo are
trademarks of Penguin Group (USA) LLC.

For information, address: The Berkley Publishing Group,
a division of Penguin Group (USA) LLC,
375 Hudson Street, New York, New York 10014.

ISBN: 978-0-425-25264-2

PUBLISHING HISTORY
Berkley Prime Crime hardcover edition / March 2014
Berkley Prime Crime mass-market edition / March 2015

PRINTED IN THE UNITED STATES OF AMERICA

10 9 8 7 6 5 4 3 2 1

Cover illustration by Stephanie Henderson.
Cover design by Lesley Worrell.

ACKNOWLEDGMENTS

Heartfelt thanks to Sam, Tom, Amanda, Troy, Bob, Jennie, Dan, and all the fine folks at Berkley Prime Crime who handle design, publicity, copywriting, bookstore sales, and gift sales. A special shout-out to all tea lovers, tea shop owners, bookstore folk, librarians, reviewers, magazine writers, websites, radio stations, and bloggers who have enjoyed the adventures of the Indigo Tea Shop gang and who help me keep it all going. Thank you so very much!

And to you, dear readers, I promise many more mysteries featuring Theodosia, Drayton, Haley, Earl Grey, and the rest of the crazy Charleston cast.

1

Theodosia Browning didn't consider herself a wine connoisseur, since tea was really her forte. Fragrant Darjeelings, malty Assams, and her current favorite, a house-blended orchid plum tea that tickled her fancy as well as her taste buds.

On the other hand, how often did a girl get invited to a fancy wine-tasting party at the very upscale Knighthall Winery?

Rarely. In fact, tonight was a first for Theodosia. And her invitation to this lushly groomed vineyard, located a leisurely drive from Charleston, South Carolina, came at the behest of Drayton Conneley, her right-hand man and tea expert at the Indigo Tea Shop. Luckily for Theodosia, Drayton happened to be a dear friend of Jordan Knight, Knighthall Winery's slightly flamboyant proprietor.

"You see?" said Drayton, grabbing her elbow and steering her toward an enormous trestle table set under a spreading live oak. He was sixty-something and still debonair with a prominent nose and thatch of gray hair. "Jordan man-

aged to produce four completely different varieties of wine."
Wine bottles beckoned like shiny beacons, and attentive
waiters were more than willing to fill glasses. "Amazing,
wouldn't you say?"

"Amazing," Theodosia echoed. She didn't know if four
varieties was a feat worth celebrating, but Drayton certainly
seemed impressed. And the grounds of the winery did look
absolutely magical this September evening, all lit up and
sparkling like a scene from some elegant Austrian fairy tale.
Plantation oaks and pecan trees were iced in silvery lights,
candles floated in a free-form pool, a string quartet played
lively music, and a handsome magician in white tie and tails
amused guests with fluttering, disappearing pigeons and sly
card tricks.

Drayton handed Theodosia a crystal flute filled with
white wine. "This is Knighthall's White Shadow," he told
her. "Although I'd call it more of a Riesling."

Theodosia took a small sip and found the wine to be
utterly delicious. Crisp and aromatic, with hints of apples
and citrus. Not unlike a fine oolong tea. "It's spectacular,"
she replied.

"I told you," said Drayton. "Lots of folks thought it would
be next to impossible to grow grapes out here on Wad-
malow Island, but Jordan's definitely proved them wrong."

If tea plants could grow here and flourish, Theodosia
thought to herself, why not grape vines? Although perhaps
a sandier soil was needed? Wasn't a sandier, rockier soil supposed to prove the true mettle of the grape?

They stepped away from the tasting table and looked
around, enjoying the warmth and excitement of the evening
and the rather excellent people watching.

"I'd say the crème de la crème of Charleston is here in full
force tonight," said Theodosia. Tanned and toned women in
chiffon dresses drifted by, wafting perfumed scents that
hinted at lilies and lilacs. Men in seersucker suits also wan-

dered the elegant grounds, sipping wine as well as an occasional tumbler of bourbon. Of course, Charleston folk being the congenial sort, everyone seemed quite preoccupied with the exchange of air kisses and pleasantries, pretending not to notice if they themselves were being noticed.

"The beautiful people," Drayton mused. "Dressed to the nines just in case a society photographer should happen along." Of course, he was also dazzling in a blue-and-white seersucker suit—a sartorial Southern statement that was punctuated by his trademark red bow tie.

Theodosia would have denied it, of course, practically laughed in your face, but she was also one of the beautiful people. With an abundance of auburn hair that might have inspired a painter like Raphael, creamy English skin, and sparkling blue eyes, she looked like she might have slipped in from another, earlier, century. She was bold yet tactful, filled with dreams and yet practical for her thirty-some years. Her only flaws were that she tended to wear her heart on her sleeve and often rushed in where proverbial angels feared to tread.

"Jordan!" Drayton called out as Jordan Knight, the owner of Knighthall Winery, came up to greet them. "Congratulations on such a fine turnout." He turned to include Theodosia. "And this is Theodosia Browning, I don't believe you two have met."

"Thanks for coming," said Knight as he shook hands with each of them. He was midforties, with a shock of salt-and-pepper hair, watery blue eyes, and a slightly pink complexion. He'd removed his jacket, loosened his tie, and his manner seemed to veer between nervous and ebullient.

"I'm pretty sure I just convinced the owner of the Lady Goodwood Inn to carry my wine," Knight chortled. In his other, more practical life, he was the CEO of Whizzen Software. Knighthall Winery was his most recently established passion.

"Well done," said Drayton, clapping his friend on the back.

"Your winery appears to be thriving," Theodosia told Knight. Being a business owner herself, she knew how difficult it was for a company to succeed, let alone flourish, in today's tough business climate. And the deck was stacked against upstarts even more.

"We're starting to gain some traction," Knight responded. "We have distribution to thirty liquor stores in something like five states. And my son is in the process of helping to negotiate a potentially large deal with a Japanese distributor, as well." Knight gazed about distractedly. "You've met my son, Drew, haven't you?"

Drayton nodded yes. Theodosia shook her head no.

"I'd love to say hello to him," said Drayton. "Is he here tonight?"

"Drew's around here somewhere," said Knight as he cast a quick glance at the large crowd and shrugged. "He's no doubt managing all the behind-the-scenes activity." Now he glanced nervously at his watch.

"Relax," Drayton told him. "This is your big night. Enjoy it!"

Knight grimaced. "I'm a little antsy about my presentation."

"What is that?" Theodosia inquired politely.

"In about five minutes," said Knight, "we're going to do a special barrel tasting of our new cabernet reserve." He flashed a perfunctory smile. "We're calling it Knight Music."

"Catchy," said Theodosia.

"We're pinning all our hopes on this one," said Knight. "Going for broke."

"I'm guessing that several of Charleston's food and wine critics are in attendance tonight?" said Drayton.

Knight nodded. "We invited anybody and everybody who can give us a mention, article, or shout-out. After five years of moving heaven and earth to produce four varieties of muscadine grapes, it's all come down to this one make-or-break moment."

"Good luck to you then," said Theodosia as Knight hurried away.

Theodosia and Drayton edged their way slowly through the crowd, in the direction Jordan had gone. A makeshift stage had been set up just outside a large, hip-roofed barn, and two workers were rolling out an enormous oak barrel. Two Japanese men, both wearing white suits and standing ramrod-stiff, stood nearby, watching intently.

Theodosia gave Drayton a nudge. "Those must be the Japanese distributors your friend Jordan mentioned."

Drayton nodded. "I read a recent article in the *Financial Times* about how the Japanese are suddenly head-over-heels crazy for wine. Particularly the pricier ones."

"*Sake* being so last year," said Theodosia.

"Everything is cyclical," said Drayton, trying to sound practical.

"Except for tea," said Theodosia. "Tea just seems to keep gaining in popularity."

"And aren't we glad for that," said Drayton.

"Excuse me . . . Theodosia?" said a voice at their elbow.

Theodosia turned with a smile and her eyes met those of a good-looking man with piercing green eyes and a mop of curly blond hair. Kind of surfer dude meets buttoned-down lawyer. He was smiling back at her, and with a kind of instinctive knowledge, she realized that she knew him. The man's name was Andrew something. Andrew . . .

"Andrew Turner," said the man, filling in the blank for her, bobbing his head. "We met at my gallery a couple of weeks ago."

"That's right," said Theodosia. "Max brought me to one of your openings—you were featuring all sorts of dynamic, contemporary oil paintings as I recall."

"Where you undoubtedly feasted on cheap white wine

and stuffed cherry tomatoes," said Turner. "The hopeful gallery owner's stock-in-trade."

"I don't recall the wine," said Theodosia, "but I do remember a wonderful painting that you had on display. All reds and purples and golds. Subtle but also very visceral. The artist was . . . James somebody?"

"Richard James," said Turner. "You have a very keen eye. And as luck would have it, that particular piece is still for sale if you're interested."

"Let me think about it," said Theodosia. She hastily introduced Turner to Drayton, then they all paused as a passing waiter stopped with his tray of hors d'oeuvres to offer them mini crab cakes and shrimp wrapped in bacon.

"Why don't you drop by again during the Paint and Palette Art Crawl," Turner suggested. "You know it kicks off this Wednesday."

Theodosia was about to answer, when Drayton quickly shushed them. Jordan Knight was standing on the stage next to an enormous weathered oak barrel. And it looked as if he was about to begin his speech.

The crowd hushed en masse and pressed forward to hear his presentation.

"Thank you all for coming," said Knight. "This is such a proud moment for me." He clasped a hand to his chest in a heartfelt gesture of appreciation. "We've labored long and hard to cultivate grapes here in South Carolina."

There was a spatter of applause.

"And our newest vintage, Knight Music, which you are all about to taste, would never have been possible without the hard work of my manager, Tom Grady, and our many dedicated workers." Jordan extended a hand toward a red-haired woman who stood off to the side. "And, of course, I must thank my wonderful family. My wife, the amazing Pandora Knight, and my son, Drew Knight." He smiled as his eyes searched the crowd for Drew. When he didn't find him, he said, "Though my son seems to be missing in action at the moment."

There was more laughter and guffaws from the crowd.

As Jordan continued his speech, two workers began to tap the large barrel of wine. They fumbled around on the top, trying to get a spigot going, but it didn't seem to be working.

"Of course," said Jordan, playing to the crowd now, "our winery is not without problems—as you can plainly see."

One of the workers tilted the large barrel up onto one edge. The other worker, looking frustrated and brandishing a crowbar, suddenly popped off the round, wooden top. The heavy lid went airborne, spinning in the air like an errant Frisbee, and then hit the stage with a loud bang. At that very same moment, the entire barrel seemed to teeter dangerously.

"Whoa!" Jordan shouted. "Careful there. We're going to sample that fine wine."

But the giant barrel, unbalanced and heavy with wine, was more than the workers could handle. They fought valiantly to right it, but were beginning to lose their grip.

Slowly, the barrel tipped sideways and viscous red liquid began to spill out, sloshing across the stage and spattering the crowd. There were sharp cries of dismay from the guests as everyone tried to jump out of the way.

Jordan Knight scrambled for the barrel in a last-ditch effort to avert total disaster. He leaned down and tried to muscle his shoulder beneath the huge barrel. Unfortunately, the laws of physics had been set into motion and he was clearly too late. The barrel continued to tip, rolling over in slow motion like a sinking ocean liner making a final, dying gasp.

The barrel landed on its side with a deafening crash, and torrents of red wine gushed out like rivers of blood.

Now horrified gasps rose up from the crowd as Jordan Knight seemed to stagger drunkenly. He crumpled to his knees, landing hard, and his entire face seemed to collapse. Then an agonized shriek rose up from his lips, blotting out the music and even the gasps from the crowd.

Curiosity bubbling within her, Theodosia pushed her way through the crowd to see what on earth was going on.

And was completely shocked to see the body of a dead man lying on the stage!

He was curled up, nose to knees, like a pickled fish. His head was tilted forward, his arms clutched close across his chest. The man's skin, what Theodosia could see of it, was practically purple from being submerged inside the barrel of red wine.

Who? and *What?* were the first thoughts that formed like a cartoon bubble deep in Theodosia's brain. And then her eyes flicked over to Jordan Knight, who was kneeling in the spill of wine, his pant legs completely soaked with purple as tears streamed down his face and his arms flailed madly about his head.

From the look of utter devastation on Jordan Knight's face, Theodosia was pretty sure he'd found his missing son.

2

❧

This Sunday morning was infinitely better than the horror Theodosia had witnessed last night. Because, on this sunny day, she and her boyfriend, Max Scofield, were relaxing on the backyard patio of her cottage in the historic district, enjoying a lovely, leisurely brunch. Her dog, Earl Grey, was wandering lazily about, sniffing in the garden, which was still in full and glorious bloom. Fish swam in the tiny little pond, and fuzzy yellow bumblebees hummed and bumped their way from fragrant flower to sweet vine.

Over entrees of crab Benedict and poached asparagus, Theodosia related to Max all the gory details from last night. The rough wooden barrel being canted onto its side. The tremendous glut of wine swooshing out. The splayed-out body of Drew Knight. Then the horrified cries of the guests followed by flashing lights, blatting sirens, and the hurried arrival of the local sheriff.

Max gave a mock shudder. "A body rolling out of a barrel of wine. It sounds like the kind of awful thing Edgar

Allan Poe would write about. Like 'The Cask of Amontillado.' Or in this case, 'The Body in the Barrel.'" Max was tall and wiry, with dark hair, an olive complexion, and a quirky brand of humor. Though it was horror rather than humor that was clearly being expressed at the present time.

"Funny you should bring that up," said Theodosia. "Since good old Edgar Allan once resided right here in Charleston. In fact, he used to stalk the windswept beaches of Sullivan's Island trying to conjure up divine inspiration." She smiled brightly at Max and lifted a platter. "Would you care for another cucumber and cream cheese sandwich?"

"No thanks," said Max, holding up a hand. Her recounting of last night's fiasco had been a little too graphic for his taste.

"Lost your appetite?" said Theodosia.

Max cocked his head at her. Theodosia was more often than not a puzzle to him. She was smart and funny, always highly enterprising, but seemed to possess a quirky fascination for the dark and slightly macabre.

"More tea then?" Theodosia reached for the blue-and-white Chinese teapot and poured refills of tippy Yunnan tea for both of them. It never occurred to her that Max wouldn't want another cup of tea. Everyone she knew pretty much drank their weight in tea, after all.

"Thank you," said Max.

"You know the funny thing about last night?"

"*Is* there a funny thing?" said Max.

"Everyone assumed that Drew Knight *drowned* in that barrel of wine."

Max lifted one eyebrow. "No?" Now he was just this side of interested.

"Drew was shot in the head first and then stuffed into that barrel." Theodosia took a sip of tea to punctuate her sentence. "So he was probably already dead from the gunshot wound."

"How did you discover that little gem?"

"Oh . . . I suppose I overheard the sheriff talking about it. Sheriff Anson. Or one of his deputies."

Max sighed and leaned back in his chair. He was the PR director at the Gibbes Museum and far more interested in ruminating over his plans for the upcoming Art Crawl, which they were helping to sponsor. Between arranging for fine art demonstrations and getting all the galleries on the same page, there was a lot of work to complete in three days' time.

Theodosia picked up a basket of cherry scones and held it out to Max. "Another scone?" As a tea shop owner, she was used to pampering her customers and catering to their whims. Which usually meant offering seconds—and even thirds.

Max groaned. "Theo, sweetheart, I have to fit into my tux this Saturday evening."

She smiled sweetly at him. "You look just fine to me." Then she studied him carefully. "I know you're worried about the Art Crawl. And something else, too?"

"No, I'm just concerned with . . . logistics," said Max. "There's so much going on this coming week, what with the Art Crawl, our museum patrons' dinner, and then the Art Crawl Ball."

"I'm sure it will all go off without a hitch," said Theodosia. She was an optimist, hard worker, and planner of the first magnitude. Which meant that all of her teas, catering gigs, and special events went off with the crisp efficiency of a well-conceived military campaign. It also never occurred to her that other business owners didn't sweat the details as much as she did.

Max picked up a tea sandwich that had been cut into a perfect triangle. "Do you know that Andy Turner is one of the sponsors and he still doesn't have a date?" He took a nibble. "Now that's cutting it close."

"Oh, I meant to tell you . . . I ran into him last night. At the wine tasting." She sighed. "Although now it will probably forever be known as the wine murder."

"Maybe for the next twelve hours," said Max. "And then something else will pop up and the media will be all over *that* story."

"You're probably right," said Theodosia as the cell phone in her pocket hummed a greeting. "Thanks to our relentless twenty-four/seven news cycle, this will all just fade away." She pulled out her phone and said, "This is Theo."

Drayton didn't mince any words. "We need you."

Theodosia frowned. Drayton was being his usual cryptic self. "What are you talking about?" she asked.

"I'm sitting here in my backyard garden talking to Jordan Knight."

"Oh." Theodosia may have sounded calm, but warning bells were suddenly clanging and banging inside her head.

Drayton continued. "And we are in dire need of your assistance."

Theodosia managed a quick glance at Max, who was now perusing the sports section of the *Post and Courier.* Good, he had no idea what they were talking about. Then she said in a slightly strangled whisper, "Really? Me?"

"Yes, you," came Drayton's urgent plea.

"Um . . . what's going on?" She needed to stall Drayton, she needed some time to think.

"I don't believe I'm being particularly obtuse," said Drayton. He let loose a deep sigh. "We need you because you're rather competent when it comes to this type of problem."

"Excuse me?" said Theodosia. Still stalling, but Drayton wasn't buying it.

"You know what I'm referring to," said Drayton. Now there was a distinct *tone* to his voice.

Oh rats, Theodosia thought to herself. *Of course he means good at solving murders. He's asking me to help his friend Jordan Knight.*

She leaned back in her wicker chair, smoothed the skirt of her dress, and thought, *Please . . . no.* Not today, on this lovely, carefree Sunday, when her fella was over for brunch. When they were reading the Sunday paper and just lazing around enjoying the warm weather. In fact, not ever. Because after all the fuss and flurry that happened last time she got involved in a crazy murder investigation, she'd pretty much promised Max that she wouldn't let herself get pulled into yet another one.

Still holding the phone, Theodosia smiled at Max and took a sip of tea. Max looked up, reached for the variety section of the newspaper, and smiled patiently back at her.

"Well," said Drayton, his voice beginning to betray more than a hint of impatience. "Are you coming over here or not?"

Theodosia thought about the ghastly purple body she'd witnessed last night. A truly horrific sight that had turned Jordan Knight's face into a mask of unbearable pain. She swallowed hard and said, "Five minutes, Drayton. Give me five minutes."

Drayton lived a few blocks from Theodosia, also in the heart of Charleston's historic district, in a quaint, 160-year-old home that had once been owned by a prominent Civil War doctor. While her own home was a classic Queen Anne–style cottage, Drayton's home was a single-story, gabled roof home with a narrow brick front and elegant dark blue shutters. There was a side piazza, now screened, and a bumpy, cobblestone walk that led around to his rather verdant backyard.

Theodosia gave a perfunctory knock on the front door, waited a few seconds, and then walked around to the back.

Drayton and Jordan Knight were sitting at a black wrought-iron table, talking in low voices, and sipping cups of tea. The patio was modest at best, gray flagstone with pots of bougainvillea, but the rest of the backyard was a veritable jungle. Tall thickets of bamboo, beds of furry green moss, and large twisted *Taihu* rocks set off Drayton's enormous collection of Japanese bonsai trees to perfection. There were windswept trees that had been tamed and twisted, elegantly pruned junipers and oaks, and even miniature bonsai forests.

When Drayton noticed Theodosia's arrival, he smiled and said, "There's a pot of Assam sitting on the kitchen counter if you'd like. It's organic and from the Kandoli Tea Estate."

"And Drayton has brandy if you'd like something stronger," Jordan Knight called to her.

Theodosia walked into the kitchen, poured herself a cup of tea, and looked around. Drayton's house never failed to amaze her. It was impeccable in its bachelor simplicity, yet housed a stellar collection of French and English antiques. There were no Pottery Barn look-alikes here, just the real deal. She took a quick peek at what appeared to be two new sterling silver flagons sitting on his Hepplewhite cupboard, then she headed out to join the two men. "What's going on?" she asked as she sat down at the table. As if she didn't know.

Jordan Knight gazed at her with a pained expression. His eyes were rimmed in dark circles, tension lines creased his face, and he looked as if he'd slept in his slacks and shirt. "Sheriff Anson hasn't been able to come up with a single suspect."

Theodosia crossed her legs, cleared her throat, and said, in what she hoped was a fairly sympathetic tone, "It's still very early in the investigation."

"I'm not sure there *is* a viable investigation!" said Drayton, looking more than a little indignant.

"Of course there is," said Theodosia. "It's just that . . ." She searched for the right words. "These things take time." She knew instantly that they *weren't* the right words and that they sounded empty. Positively vacuous, in fact.

Jordan Knight rested his elbows heavily on the table and leaned in toward her. "Drayton tells me you're a very clever investigator."

"I've stumbled upon a few answers in the past," said Theodosia, trying to sound noncommittal. "I got lucky."

"You got good," said Drayton. "Which is why I asked you to join us here. And I sincerely do thank you for coming."

Jordan Knight turned to Theodosia, his face crumpled in pain. "After hearing what Drayton had to say about your rather prodigious skills," he said, "I was hoping you might lend us your assistance. Perhaps you could work a little of your amateur investigative magic."

Theodosia shook her head. "It's not magic."

"Whatever it is," said Drayton, lifting a hand. "Call it a knack or a talent or a genius, the fact remains that you're very good at talking to people, extracting information, and figuring things out. You're a good judge of character and personal motivations. Which is why we're hoping you might do us the supreme favor of going back out to Knight-hall Winery to sniff around. Just . . . talk to a few people. See what you come up with."

"Wouldn't I be stepping on Sheriff Anson's toes?" said Theodosia, gazing directly at Jordan Knight. Sheriff Allen Anson and three of his deputies had shown up last night and taken immediate control of the situation. From what she had observed, they'd seemed extremely competent.

"You wouldn't be in anyone's way," said Drayton, answering for him. "Because you'd be running your own personal . . . well, let's call it a discreet inquiry."

"I think a government agency might call that a shadow investigation," said Theodosia.

"I don't care what we *call* it," said Drayton. He directed a sympathetic nod toward Knight. "This poor man is in desperate need of your assistance!"

Knight gave Theodosia a cautious gaze. "Would you be willing to come out? To the winery, I mean? Talk to some of my people, see if you're able to puzzle out any answers?"

"Find a suspect!" put in Drayton.

"Not so fast," said Theodosia. "It doesn't work that way."

Knight lifted a hand and spread his fingers. "Well . . . how *does* it work? You tell me."

"First I'd have to ask you a load of questions," said Theodosia. "And some of them could make you rather uncomfortable. They're questions you might not want to answer."

"Such as?" said Knight.

"Let's start with a few easy questions," said Theodosia. "Such as when was the last time you saw your son? Was it at the party last night?"

Knight nodded eagerly. "Yes, I think so."

"You have to know so," said Theodosia. "You have to be absolutely sure of your answer."

"Well, I'm positive I saw him," said Knight. He furrowed his brow and his eyes drifted sideways as if he were deep in thought. "At least I *think* I did."

"Just think back," said Theodosia. "Let your mind kind of free-associate."

"Now that you mention it," said Knight. "It might have been more like midafternoon?"

"Okay," said Theodosia. "Do you know—did Drew have any enemies?"

Knight snorted. "Hardly. Drew was a good kid. He was well liked by everyone."

Clearly not, Theodosia thought to herself. Someone had disliked Drew sufficiently enough to shoot him in the head and stuff his body into a barrel of wine.

"Did Drew have a girlfriend?"

"Yes," Knight said slowly. "A lovely young woman by the name of Tanya Woodson. She works in fashion. In fact, she's a fairly well-known model."

"How does she figure into all of this?" asked Drayton.

Knight shifted uneasily. "She doesn't."

"Are you sure about that?" asked Theodosia. "Were they living together?"

"Actually, yes," said Knight. "They were staying in the guest house at the winery."

"And how is Tanya taking Drew's death?"

"Not very well," said Knight. "Then again, none of us are. This has been a nightmare experience."

"What's your current business situation?" Theodosia continued, ignoring Knight's obvious discomfort. "Is your company profitable?"

Now Knight really looked unhappy. "My software company, Whizzen, is right in the process of launching Whizgo 3.0." He lifted a hand, teetered it back and forth. "So far we're holding our own."

"And the winery?" said Theodosia.

"That hasn't turned a profit yet," Knight said slowly.

"Who would stand to gain through Drew's murder?" asked Theodosia.

Knight grimaced. "Excuse me?"

"Who would stand to gain through Drew's murder?" Theodosia repeated. "Monetarily or otherwise?"

"Why . . . no one," said Knight.

"Are you sure about that?"

"I'm positive." Knight frowned and directed his gaze at Drayton. "I feel like I've been thrown into the ring with an overzealous sparring partner." He cocked a thumb at Theodosia. "She keeps throwing jabs and uppercuts at me."

"If this is too uncomfortable for you . . ." said Theodosia.

"No, no," said Knight. "Please, let's continue."

"So you mentioned last night that Drew was in charge of coordinating the event?"

"That's right," said Knight. "He was the one responsible

for hiring the outside bartenders, caterers, and entertainers. That sort of thing."

"How big is your regular staff at the winery?" asked Theodosia.

"Six people," said Knight. "We run a pretty tight ship."

"So you had a lot of extra people working there last night. People you really didn't know."

"I didn't think we had to check credentials," said Knight.

"And there were a lot of guests," put in Drayton.

"I'd say a hundred or so," said Theodosia. "Perhaps we could get a copy of your guest list?"

There was the sharp sound of stiletto heels on the tiled kitchen floor, then a woman in a pink skirt suit and floppy white hat stepped out onto the patio.

"Pandora," said Drayton, scrambling to his feet. "Come join us, dear lady." He turned toward Theodosia. "Theo, have you met Pandora Knight? No, I'm sure you two haven't been introduced."

"Nice to meet you," said Theodosia, extending a hand. "And I'm so very sorry about Drew's death and . . . well, the awful circumstances."

"You're very kind," said Pandora. "And it's lovely to finally meet you. Drayton's told us so much about you. And thank you so much for consenting to meet with Jordan like this." She glanced around the table. "I hope you were able to accomplish *something*."

"We're certainly trying," said Drayton. "Giving it our all."

"Anyway," said Pandora, favoring them with a sad smile. "I wanted to wait outside so Jordan could talk freely."

"I've been racking my brain," said Jordan. "Searching my heart and trying to figure out who would have wanted Drew dead!"

"Perhaps if you could try to answer my last question," said Theodosia.

"What was that again?" asked Jordan.

"Who would stand to gain from Drew's death?"

"I can answer that," Pandora snapped. "It would be Georgette Kroft." She delivered her answer with such vehemence that the brim of her hat flip-flopped in her face.

"Who's that?" asked Drayton.

"Georgette owns a rival winery," explained Knight. "Oak Hill Winery."

"Ever since Knighthall went into production," said Pandora, "Georgette's been running around like a maniac, trying to worm her way into every account in Charleston. Attempting to block our every advance."

"Excuse me," said Theodosia. "Do you really think this woman, Georgette Kroft, might have killed Drew?" It sounded far-fetched to her.

"Was she even present last night?" asked Drayton. He thought it was a stretch, too.

Jordan and Pandora Knight gazed at each other for an uncomfortably long time. Then Jordan shook his head and said, "No, I don't believe so."

"She could have been," said Pandora defensively. "We don't know that she wasn't there. It was a bit of a mob scene. A lot of the guests brought guests and I'm positive there were a few crashers."

"I can't believe Georgette had anything to do with this," said Jordan. "She's an aggressive woman, yes, but I doubt she's a killer."

"I beg to differ," said Pandora. "Georgette Kroft's got a mean streak a mile wide. And she's desperate to put her winery on the map. She's in a terrible lather over the competition we're starting to put up against her."

"One more question," said Theodosia, hoping to obtain some concrete information rather than angry innuendos. "The ownership of Knighthall Winery is what? Corporation? Limited partnership?"

"Limited partnership," said Jordan. "That's correct."

"And the partners are?" said Theodosia.

"Myself, of course," said Jordan. "As well as Pandora, Drew, and a private investor."

"The private investor being . . . who?" said Theodosia.

"Alex Burgoyne," said Jordan. "He's a fairly well-known liquor distributor."

"And you all hold equal shares?" said Theodosia.

"Not exactly," said Jordan. "Drew and Burgoyne were in for twenty percent, and Pandora and I each hold thirty percent."

"What's going to happen to Drew's share now?" asked Theodosia. "Is there a provision for that? A buy-sell agreement in place?"

"I have an option to buy those shares," said Pandora.

"I see," said Theodosia. She thought for a minute. "Can either of you think of any other person who might have a grudge against your family?"

Pandora shook her head.

Jordan Knight looked thoughtful. "There's a reporter. A freelance food writer, really, who contributes articles to that awful gossip rag, *Shooting Star.* He seemed to take particular delight in savaging our wine."

"That's a good thought," said Pandora. "I wouldn't put it past him, either."

"Okay," said Theodosia. "You've given me a few things to think about."

While Drayton walked Jordan and Pandora Knight out to their car, Theodosia sat in the garden, contemplating all the information the Knights had given her. As she gazed at Drayton's collection of bonsai, she noted that several of the small trees still had bits of copper wire wound around their twisted branches—bonsai in training.

When Drayton returned, he gave Theodosia a perfunctory smile and said, "Well, that went well."

Theodosia was still pretty much lost in thought. "Did it?" she murmured, half to Drayton, half to herself.

Drayton cocked his head and peered at her over his tortoiseshell half-glasses. "Excuse me, but is there a problem? Did I miss something?"

"Maybe," said Theodosia. "Possibly."

"What on earth are you mumbling about?" said Drayton.

"Pandora is Drew's stepmother, correct?"

"That's right. She's Jordan's third wife."

"The thing is," said Theodosia, "when I asked Jordan who stood to gain from Drew's death, he failed to mention Pandora."

"And you think that's significant?"

"I think it's significant that Pandora can now seize majority control of the winery if she feels like it," said Theodosia.

"Do you think she'd do that? I mean, she has to be terribly upset over Drew's death, right?"

"I don't know," said Theodosia. "If you ask me . . . Pandora didn't seem particularly upset at all."

3

Teakettles chirped and whistled while fragrant aromas perfumed the air this Monday morning. As soon as the clock struck nine, the doors of the Indigo Tea Shop had been unlocked and early bird customers came pouring in. Most were shopkeepers from up and down Church Street and a few were tourists, but all their guests were anxious to kickstart their morning with a fresh-baked scone and a nice hot cuppa.

"It's shaping up to be a very busy week," said Drayton. He was standing behind the front counter, a long black apron draped around his neck, filling teapots with hot water. When the teapots were sufficiently warmed, he dumped out the water and added heaping scoops of loose-leaf tea.

"Mondays are always busy," said Theodosia, glancing around the already half-filled tea shop. "Used to be our week would start out nice and leisurely, slowly building to a crescendo by Saturday. Now we always seem to kick off in high gear."

"That's good, huh?" asked Haley. She'd just dashed out of the kitchen carrying a tray stacked with fresh-baked strawberry scones. "It's because so many more people have discovered tea, right?"

"Or they've discovered us," said Drayton, taking the tray from her.

"Careful when you plate those scones," Haley cautioned. "They're all hot and steamy from the oven." She brushed a hank of stick-straight blond hair from her eager blue eyes and gazed at Theodosia and Drayton. Haley Parker was their young chef and baker *exceptionale.* She was a waif of a martinet who ran her kitchen with cutting-edge precision. Nobody was allowed into the postage stamp–sized kitchen except to pick up an order. And nobody was ever permitted to divulge her recipes to a customer. No matter how hard they begged and pleaded.

Knowing a good thing when they saw it, Theodosia and Drayton were smart enough to take a hands-off approach, stay out of Haley's way, and respect her quirky work demands. Which made their little three-person operation amazingly successful.

"Let's see," said Drayton. "Table two ordered a pot of Darjeeling and scones with Devonshire cream. Table four wants a pot of Assam and, oh dear, is your apple bread ready yet?"

"It'll be out of the oven in two shakes," said Haley. She spun on the heels of her ballet flats and dashed back into the kitchen.

Theodosia grabbed a stack of small floral plates and laid them out on the counter. Drayton quickly placed a scone on each of the plates, along with a tiny silver spoon and a small glass bowl mounded with Devonshire cream.

"Lovely," said Theodosia. She grabbed two of the finished plates and danced her way across the teashop. Drayton followed on her heels carrying steaming pots of tea.

With the mingled aromas of Assam, Darjeeling, oolong,

and Lapsang souchong hanging redolent in the air, Theodosia was of the opinion that taking tea at the Indigo Tea Shop was akin to a marvelous aromatherapy treatment at a first-rate spa. The inhalation of the various teas just seemed to tickle the senses and impart a feeling of profound relaxation and well-being.

Of course, the tea shop was a feast for the eyes, as well. Small tables were graced with white linen tablecloths and matching napkins. Tiny white tea light candles flickered in glass votive holders. Antique sugar bowls, gleaming bone china teacups and saucers, and silver spoons and butter knives were carefully arranged on each table. A single brick wall held antique prints and grapevine wreaths, while tea tins and tea accoutrements were displayed on antique highboys and wooden shelving.

On her way in to work this morning, Theodosia had stopped at the Church Street Farmer's Market and purchased several bunches of purple chrysanthemums. Now those cheery flowers bobbed their shaggy heads in cut-crystal vases.

"I have the guest list from Sunday night," Drayton told Theodosia when they were back at the counter. "Jordan messengered it to me first thing this morning." He reached up and plucked a red Chinese teapot from one of the upper shelves. "I think he's expecting us to sort through the various guests and perhaps talk to some of them."

"If we talk to them," said Theodosia, "they're going to figure out that they're suspects."

That idea brought Drayton up short. He thought for a moment, then said, "Well, isn't that how the police routinely conduct an investigation?"

"Sure it is," said Theodosia. "But the police have actual authority. So most people are nervous about withholding information from them. Besides, if the police don't get the answers they want, they're free to haul people into jail and work them over with a rubber hose."

"They don't really do that," Drayton snorted. "Do they?"

Theodosia smiled faintly. "No. But still. Law enforcement professionals tend to be rather . . . persuasive. They have fairly well-honed skill sets that can often make people drop their guard and cough up pertinent information."

"So do you," said Drayton. "You just go about it in a different manner."

Startled, Theodosia did a kind of double take. "I do? Really? Because I'm not aware of . . . excuse me, *how* do I persuade them?"

Drayton gave her a cryptic smile. "You charm them."

At ten thirty, just when Theodosia was looking out across the tea shop and noticing that there was a single empty table left, Max burst through the front door. And wonder of wonders, he had Andrew Turner, the art dealer, in tow.

"What are you two doing here this fine Monday morning?" Theodosia asked as she led the two men over to the small table by the stone fireplace. She was thrilled to see Max and pleased that he'd seemingly hooked up with Andrew Turner.

"Believe it or not," said Turner, "we're busy putting the final touches on this weekend's Paint and Palette Art Crawl."

"As well as the Art Crawl Ball on Saturday night," said Max. He hooked a thumb and pointed at Turner. "Turns out we're both on that committee."

"That's very generous," said Theodosia. "I mean that you're both giving your time like that."

Turner shrugged. "Ah, we both got roped in."

"I still think it's lovely that the museums and art galleries have put their collective heads together on this," said Theodosia. "It's about time we had something fun like an art crawl. Demystify the whole gallery thing and make art more casual and approachable."

"That's exactly the plan," said Turner. "We've got three

museums and twenty galleries who've agreed to throw open their doors, as well as another ninety-five street vendors who'll be participating."

"And that's not even counting the local bars, restaurants, and food trucks," said Max, "who'll contribute to the whole festival atmosphere."

"I like the sound of that," said Theodosia.

But when she returned with tea, scones, and apple bread for both of them, Max said to her, "*You* should have a food truck."

"Oh no," said Theodosia. She set the tea and goodies in front of them. "That's the absolute last thing I need. Between the tea shop, catering gigs, and a fairly bustling take-out business, we already work a long enough day." She didn't mention that she had to juggle a social life on top of that, as well as enjoy much-needed down time that included jogging, reading, and hanging out with Earl Grey!

"Yeah," said Turner, spreading a dollop of lemon curd onto his scone. "I know the feeling. Overworked, overstressed, and over it totally. Besides being on the committee for the Art Crawl, I'm up to my eyeballs in work at the gallery, and trying to manage a kind of halfhearted search for a new home."

"He's on the lookout for one of the big, historical ones," said Max, sounding more than a little impressed. "Preferably something with Italianate or Georgian architecture."

"The problem is," said Turner, "there's not much inventory available right now."

"That's the thing of it," said Theodosia as she poured a stream of rich English breakfast tea into their teacups. "There never is. Most of the really grand old homes in Charleston hardly ever show up on the commercial market. They're sold by word of mouth, quietly and discreetly, to friends or relatives."

"Well, if you ever hear of anything," said Turner. He took

a quick sip of tea and gave her a curious glance. "That was some bizarre scene Saturday night, huh?"

Theodosia figured that he'd mention the murder eventually. After all, he'd been one of the horrified bystanders.

"It was awful," said Theodosia. "And poor Drayton's been in a tizzy ever since. He's good friends with Jordan Knight."

"According to the story in this morning's *Post and Courier*," said Max, "there don't seem to be any suspects."

For some reason, this prickled at Theodosia's sense of fair play. "You know what?" she said. "There are always suspects. You just have to know where to look."

"She's right," said Turner. He took a bite of scone and chewed thoughtfully. "If I were an investigator, you know where I'd look?"

Theodosia and Max eyed him with curiosity.

"Where?" Theodosia asked. She noted that Drayton, who was pouring refills at the next table, seemed to be listening closely to their conversation. She wondered who else was, too.

"Those golf course people just down the road from the winery," said Turner. "What's that place called? Plantation Wilds, I think. Anyway, the scuttlebutt on the street is that they've been trying to buy the vineyard property for almost two years. Only Jordan Knight doesn't want to sell."

"Of course he doesn't," said Drayton, joining the conversation now. "Because he's dedicated to cultivating his vineyard." He seemed offended. "Honestly, must every part and parcel of fine property be turned into an overly manicured piece of lawn on which to chase a silly little white ball? Is there that much of a demand?"

"You know," said Turner, "I think there might be."

"The lunch menu," said Drayton, tapping a forefinger against the counter. "Do you have it?"

Theodosia reached into her apron pocket and pulled out

the small index card Haley had handed her a few minutes earlier. "I do."

"Care to share it with me?"

"Let's see," said Theodosia, scanning the menu. "We've got chilled mango soup, citrus salad, and three kinds of tea sandwiches—chicken salad with chutney, vegetable medley, and Black Forest ham with Cheddar cheese. Oh, and brownie bites and lemon bars for dessert."

"Excellent," said Drayton. He reached beneath the counter and grabbed a handful of indigo blue bags. "Do you know we've got something like twenty-two take-out orders for today?"

Theodosia nodded. "That's why Haley's doing three different tea sandwiches along with the brownies and lemon bars. So everything's finger food as well as quick and easy to pack."

"And I'm the one who has to pack it," muttered Drayton. He straightened up and, with a serious expression on his face, said, "Someday you might have to have to think seriously about expanding."

"There isn't any more space," said Theodosia, looking startled. "This is it. The Indigo Tea Shop is a finite space."

"Well . . ." said Drayton.

"No," said Theodosia. "We're not going to move. We're never going to move. It would break my heart to leave this space." Indeed, the little tea shop, a former carriage house with leaded windows, stone fireplace, and pegged wood floors, was a second home to Theodosia. In fact, it had been her home—literally. She'd lived in the upstairs apartment for several years until she'd finally bought her dream cottage. Now Haley was cozily ensconced in the loft upstairs.

"It was just . . . a suggestion," said Drayton.

"What I might consider someday," said Theodosia, "is a second shop."

Now it was Drayton's turn to look horrified. "Are you

serious? You working in one shop and me in another? That would rip the heart and soul out of our operation. We'd lose our purpose, our sense of . . . collegiality."

"Drayton," said Theodosia. "We're just fine right here. We always make a living and quite often a nice profit. Do you really want to break your back for a few more dollars and additional square footage?"

"Not really," said Drayton. "It's just that with so many little tables and our antique cupboards stuffed with jams, jellies, teas, and teacups for sale, we sometimes feel a little bit constrained." He glanced sideways at her. "To say nothing of all the grapevine wreaths hanging on the walls."

Theodosia smiled. "Most of our customers consider that cozy."

Just when lunchtime was as its busiest, Delaine Dish breezed in like a majestic ship under full sail.

"Theo!" she cried. She gave an imperious wave of a wrist that was loaded with jangling gold bangles and tipped her aristocratic nose into the air.

"Delaine," Theodosia replied. Delaine might be her friend, but the woman had the personality disorder of the Mad Hatter. You never knew when she'd show up for tea. And when she did, everything was thrown into a tizzy and their nice sedate tea shop turned into a complete madhouse.

"I've got barely twenty minutes," Delaine announced. "Maybe fifteen. So please please please squeeze me in as fast as you can." Delaine tilted her heart-shaped face toward Theodosia, and her violet eyes blinked rapidly. Smudges of pink colored her cheeks, and her long dark hair was pulled back into an elegant chignon.

"Do you mind sitting at the table by the window?" asked Theodosia.

"Perfect," said Delaine. She was wearing a daffodil yellow skirt suit, the jacket nipped tightly at the waist, and matching stiletto sandals and white gloves. As she pulled her gloves off, she dimpled and said, "I read all about your merry adventures in the newspaper this morning."

"Oh," said Theodosia. "You mean the murder at Knighthall." She was hoping Delaine wouldn't bring that up. Then again, Delaine was a ferocious gossip and social gadabout. So why wouldn't she? Decorum wasn't really her strong suit.

"Sounds like that wine tasting turned rather nasty," said Delaine, settling herself into a chair. "With a dead body and all."

"It was beyond awful," said Theodosia, lingering at her table. "I've never seen anything like it. And Drayton's a good friend of Jordan Knight, so he's particularly upset."

"About the murder or the divorce?"

Theodosia's brows pinched together. "Excuse me? What did you . . ."

Delaine smiled beatifically, as if she were privy to a deep, dark secret. "Oh, you didn't know?"

Theodosia slid into the chair opposite her. "Know what?" she asked.

"Jordan and Pandora are in the throes of a very nasty divorce!" Delaine said in a loud whisper. She seemed to relish her rather startling announcement.

"Are you serious?" said Theodosia. Delaine's words prickled like thorns. Jordan and Pandora were headed for divorce court? With the united front they'd put up yesterday, they certainly could have fooled her. In fact, they *had* fooled her!

"Oh, their marriage is definitely on the skids," said Delaine. "In fact, their entire relationship has deteriorated to the point where they're barely even on speaking terms."

"How do you know that?"

"Please." Delaine rolled her eyes expressively. "Pandora is one of my absolute best customers. Besides knowing her dress size, I happen to be her very close *confidante*." Delaine was the proprietor of Cotton Duck, one of Charleston's premier boutiques. Her selection of cool, comfortable cotton clothing as well as casual silks and evening dresses was practically unparalleled. In fact, business was so gangbusters, Delaine had even added a lingerie shop called Méchante. Which translated to "naughty" in French.

"And you're quite sure about this divorce business?" said Theodosia. She felt taken aback by the news.

"Positive. Ask Pandora if you want. I'm sure she'll be happy to give you an earful." Delaine leaned forward and hissed, "Their marriage was a total disaster. I think Pandora's lucky to get out while she can!"

"Wow," said Theodosia. Yesterday, Pandora had seemed so solicitous and loving to Jordan Knight. And now it turned out it was all an act. Theodosia wondered what else might be an act.

"Theo," said Delaine. "You're coming to my Clothes Horse Races, aren't you?"

"Um, what?" Theodosia was still mulling over the startling news. "When are they again?"

"Tomorrow!" said Delaine. She frowned, and then realized she was frowning. So she poked a delicate finger at the crease between her brows and rubbed gently. "Please tell me you didn't forget. Oh, but you have to come. Our couture fashion show will feature the most magnificent clothes and everyone is going to be bidding like crazy for charity! The proceeds will all go to help fund the Loving Paws Animal Shelter and you know that's such a worthy cause!"

"Of course," said Theodosia, though her mind was still reeling from this unsettling new information about Jordan and Pandora's divorce. She popped up from her chair and said, "How about a small pot of jasmine tea and a citrus salad?"

"Perfect," said Delaine. "No carbs. And if you can rush it right out, I'd really appreciate it."

Back at the front counter, Theodosia couldn't wait to share her news with Drayton. Or maybe he already knew?

"I need to brew another pot of Assam," Drayton muttered as he slid behind the counter. "Those women at table six are drinking tea like it's a frat house chugging contest. They've already gone through three pots."

"Drayton," said Theodosia. "Did you know that Pandora and Jordan are in the throes of a divorce?"

The spoon Drayton had been holding clattered loudly to the counter.

He blinked rapidly, obviously startled, and looked at her with great intensity. "What?"

"Delaine just spilled the beans to me. She said Pandora and Jordan are in the final stages of divorce."

"And you believe her?"

Theodosia lifted a hand and tilted it in a gesture that said maybe yes, maybe no. "She seemed to know quite a bit about it, since Pandora's one of her best customers. And Delaine usually has all the latest gossip. So . . . were you aware of this?"

Drayton's mouth opened and closed silently a couple of times. Obviously this came as a shock to him. "I . . . I had no idea," he finally stammered.

"A situation like this could change things," said Theodosia. "It could change things dramatically."

"Because . . . why?" said Drayton.

"Because there may be an undercurrent of desperation. Especially when it comes to Pandora."

"But I thought . . ." said Drayton, trying to recover. "I

thought Jordan and Pandora were utterly *devoted* to each other. Destined to be together forever!"

Suspicious thoughts were already swirling in Theodosia's head as she replied, "Obviously not."

4

After this morning's news, Theodosia was more determined than ever to figure out what was fact and what was fiction. What was Pandora's true relationship with Jordan? And how had she gotten along with Drew? Had the two of them been friendly? Or had she hated Drew's guts and somehow schemed to get him out of the way?

Theodosia stuck around until their lunch crowd had dwindled to just a handful of customers and Drayton and Haley assured her they could manage afternoon tea service just fine without her. With a backward gaze that was tinged with a small amount of worry, she hopped in her car and sped out to Knighthall Winery.

When she pulled into the winery's parking area, the place had a decidedly different air than it had Saturday night. Gone were the tents and trestle tables; lights no longer sparkled in the trees. In fact, the place looked practically deserted except for a couple of dusty pickup trucks that were parked outside the enormous hip-roofed barn.

Theodosia climbed out of her car and headed for the tasting room, a low, white building that had a discreet OPEN sign propped in the front window.

But just as she was mounting the steps, the door flew open and Pandora came rushing out to greet her.

"You came!" said Pandora, looking pleased. Dressed in slim-fitting designer jeans and a light blue shirt with pearl buttons, she appeared upbeat and friendly. Almost a little too carefree for a woman who was about to bury her murdered stepson.

"I promised Jordan that I'd come, so here I am," said Theodosia.

Pandora grasped her hand and squeezed it. "I can't thank you enough. Drayton says the most wonderful things about you. Sings your praises to high heaven!"

"Really," said Theodosia. "I haven't done anything yet."

"But you will, my dear. I just know you will." She leaned forward and winked. "Drayton tells us you're the second coming of Nancy Drew!"

"I didn't realize he was that enthusiastic," said Theodosia. "And it's all very flattering, but I'd feel slightly more confident if you placed your trust in Sheriff Anson."

Pandora made a dismissive gesture. "Pah! Unfortunately, I have very little faith in Sheriff Anson's abilities. Do you know he hasn't come up with a single lead or suspect?"

Maybe he has, Theodosia thought to herself. *But he just hasn't told you. Maybe* you're *the suspect!*

"You know, Pandora," said Theodosia, "I had no idea that you and Jordan were estranged. I was under the impression, as was Drayton, that the two of you were quite happily married."

"Just a little bump in the road of life," said Pandora, trying to give it a casual, philosophical spin. "Yes, we are getting divorced—the big D. But you didn't come all the way out here to try to patch up our silly little marital spat.

You've gamely agreed to talk to a few of our people. To ask around—dare I say snoop?—and see if you can come up with any of your clever ideas or impressions."

Theodosia knew that Pandora was smoke screening her divorce, so she decided to drop the subject for now.

"I'm curious," said Theodosia. "You mentioned yesterday that you had an option to buy Drew's shares of the winery."

Pandora's smile never faltered. "That's right."

"How exactly did that come about?"

"Why, the boy simply needed money," said Pandora. "He didn't exactly work for a living, though he liked to party. And he did drive a Porsche." She gave a little shrug. "You do the math."

"And you had the cash," said Theodosia. It was a statement, not a question.

"I do have a fairly tidy nest egg set aside, yes. My previous husband was a rather generous man."

"So your relationship with Drew was amicable?"

"Heavens yes," said Pandora. "I loved him like he was my own son!"

"Really," said Theodosia. Now Pandora's smile seemed tight and brittle. So . . . maybe an untruth?

"But I'm keeping you from doing your business," said Pandora, easing away. "While I need to hurry and run a few errands in town." She playfully shook a finger at Theodosia. "I'm definitely going to drop by that tea shop of yours one of these days. You just wait and see!"

Before Pandora could manage a clean getaway, Theodosia said, "How many people did you have working here Sunday night?"

Pandora tilted her head and thought for a minute. "I imagine there were almost three dozen. A few Knighthall employees and the rest from the catering company. Oh, and of course, musicians and parking valets, too."

"And Drew had been in charge of—"

"You know what?" Pandora said, interrupting. "You really should speak to Tom Grady, our general manager. He's the one who can best answer your questions."

Interesting, Theodosia thought. *She doesn't really want to talk to me.*

"And I'd find Mr. Grady . . . where?"

"That way," said Pandora, hooking a thumb and pointing toward the barn. "His office is that way."

Tom Grady wasn't thrilled to meet her, either. He was tall, lean, and taciturn—a man of few words with a chiseled, suntanned face and a head full of curly gray hair. He wore faded blue jeans and a T-shirt that said, LIFE IS A CABERNET.

"You're here why?" Grady asked Theodosia.

"Jordan Knight asked me to look into things."

Grady stood behind a gray metal desk in his bare-bones office, his arms folded protectively across his chest. "You some kind of investigator?"

"Just a friend," said Theodosia.

"I don't know what you want from me," he said.

"How about if you show me around?" Theodosia suggested. "And I'll just ask a few questions."

Grady's eyebrows shot up. "You want to see the operation?" Now he sounded a little less hostile.

"Sure. I'd love to."

"Okay then." He came around his desk and slipped out the door. "Down this way. Here's where it all takes place."

Theodosia followed Grady past a half-dozen gigantic stainless steel vats into the heart of the building. She was immediately greeted by the prickly, spicy, almost heady scent of fermenting grapes.

"Watch your step," Grady warned. "Don't go slipping in any grape goo."

"In the winemaking process," said Theodosia. "What exactly happens first?"

"Well, we've got thirty acres under cultivation," said Grady. "And we're smack-dab in the middle of harvest time. So what happens is this—the grapes are carefully harvested by hand and then placed in small plastic tubs."

"Okay."

Grady led her to an enormous stainless steel tank. "Once all the grapes have been washed, destemmed, and crushed, they end up in fermentation tanks."

"How long does fermentation usually take?"

"Two or three weeks, depending. Then we do the pressing and set the juice aside for additional fermentation. Our white wine gets transferred into a number of smaller tanks while red wine goes into oak barrels."

Theodosia flinched. "Like the kind that . . ."

"Yes," said Grady, gazing at her. "I'm afraid so."

"And those barrels are stacked where?"

Grady indicated the four walls where large oak barrels, exactly like the one Drew came sloshing out of Saturday night, were stacked floor to ceiling. "Anywhere. Everywhere. Knighthall Winery started out doing white and blush wines, but more recently we've been focusing mostly on reds. So we've been experimenting with aging times. Winemaking may be a science, but there's a lot of artistry involved, too."

"Going back to the unfortunate events of Saturday night," said Theodosia. "That wine barrel had obviously been tampered with." She glanced down at the concrete floor and noticed the number of drains. Had Drew been shot right here? In the production center? Had his blood sloshed down one of these drains? The idea unnerved her.

"Yes, the barrel had been tampered with," said Grady. "But I really don't know how. That particular barrel had been earmarked and set aside for the barrel tasting."

Theodosia decided that maybe the killer *wanted* Drew's

dead body to be rudely displayed. "Did any tours go through here on Sunday afternoon?" she asked.

Grady shook his head. "Nope. In fact, there haven't been any tours for the last two weeks, what with the harvest being under way."

Theodosia thought for a minute. "What can you tell me about the people who own the golf course down the road?"

"Plantation Wilds?" said Grady. "Nice place. Supposed to be a bit pricey to join, though. Some of the managing partners were guests here Sunday night."

That notion startled Theodosia. "Seriously? I thought there was bad blood between Jordan Knight and the golf course people."

"There had been," said Grady. "The golf course people kept making offers on this property and Mr. Knight kept refusing. In fact, things got kind of heated. Anyway, I suppose the invitations were intended as a sort of peace offering."

"Extended by Jordan Knight?"

"That's right."

"When the golf course people were trying to negotiate to buy this place, did any of the partners want to accept their offer? Perhaps Pandora or Drew?"

"I'm not sure," said Grady. "You'd have to ask them."

Theodosia decided to take another approach. "I understand there were quite a few people working here Sunday night. Musicians, bartenders, caterers, the waiters who were passing around the hors d'oeuvres . . ."

"I didn't have much to do with that. Just handed out purchase orders and collected invoices."

"Who did the catering?" said Theodosia.

"That was handled by Crabs and Dabs, a small local restaurant just down the road from us. As you can imagine, their specialty is crab and other seafood. They fry up a killer crab cake and serve it with a real nice aioli sauce."

"Good to know. And the servers?"

"All the bartenders and servers came highly recommended by Virtuoso Staffing."

Theodosia wondered if anyone had talked to Virtuoso Staffing yet, and she made a mental note to do so.

"In your opinion," said Theodosia, "do you think Drew's murder will hurt your winery's credibility? Or put another way, will this undermine its financial stability?"

Grady glanced down and shuffled a toe along the nubby concrete. "I don't know that it's going to make a whole heck of a lot of difference either way. This place hasn't been all that profitable."

"Jordan Knight had mentioned to me that there were financial concerns. But he seemed quite optimistic that Knighthall Winery was about to turn a corner."

This time Grady met her gaze full on. "First I've heard of that. Seems to me if Mr. Knight wanted to nudge this company into the black, he would have done that deal with Mr. Tanaka."

Theodosia shook her head. "What deal? Who's Tanaka?"

"One of the Japanese guys who was here Sunday night."

Theodosia did recall a pair of Japanese men who'd been guests at the party. "Yes, Jordan Knight did mention that he was working on a distribution deal. So why wouldn't that still be on the table?"

"Because the rumor is, Mr. Tanaka was more interested in becoming a partner than just a distributor. My impression was that his company, Higashi Golden Brands, wanted to manage the entire operation."

"You mean take over the winery?" said Theodosia.

"Call it a takeover, a partnership, whatever you want. Basically, the Japanese investors would have infused a serious amount of much-needed capital into this operation." He hesitated. "And they'd probably have been a lot more aggressive with sales and marketing."

"So venture capital in exchange for partial ownership,"

said Theodosia. "That's fairly interesting." She was per-
turbed that neither Jordan nor Pandora had mentioned any
of this to her.

"Is Mr. Tanaka still around?" Theodosia wondered. "Can
that deal be salvaged?"

"I don't know if he's still here or if he's gone back to Japan
with his associate," said Grady. "But if *something* doesn't
change fairly soon, I may not be here for long, either." He
turned and stepped over to a large sliding door. There was
the sound of ball bearings moving smoothly on rollers, then
the door slid open to reveal a picture-perfect view of the
vineyard and surrounding lands.

Theodosia studied him carefully. "It sounds to me like
you might be looking for another job."

Grady ducked outside into the sunlight. "Let's just say
I'm going to keep my options open."

Theodosia followed him out. "Just a couple more questions," she told him.

He put up a hand to shield his eyes from the sun. "Yeah?"

"How well did you know Drew?"

"We got along okay."

"Do you know what else was going on in Drew's life?
Was he worried about something? Was he in any sort of
trouble? Financial or otherwise?"

"Not that I was aware of," said Grady. "But you could
probably ask his girlfriend—she might know."

"Is she here right now?"

"Should be. She's usually hanging out at the cottage."

"That's right. I understand Drew lived right here on the
property."

Grady nodded.

"So he was close to his work."

This time Grady offered a grunt. "If that's what you
want to call it."

"Drew wasn't involved in the day-to-day operations?"

Theodosia knew Pandora's take on the matter; now she wanted to hear Grady's opinion.

"Let's just say Drew preferred to deal with what he called the aesthetics of the operation."

"I'm not sure I understand," said Theodosia.

"Drew enjoyed drinking wine and designing wine labels. Pretty much in that order. Although I have to say his designs weren't half bad. I guess he might have put in a year or so at the Charleston College of Art and Design."

"Hmm," said Theodosia. She gazed at the grounds, so lovely with the sun angling down upon the leafy vines, neat rows of peach trees nearby, and a sliver of shimmering pond off in the distance. "And Drew's cottage is where?"

"Back that way," said Grady, gesturing a paw. "You take the path past the big white house, where Mr. Knight lives."

"But not Pandora?"

"No," said Grady. He gazed off into the distance. "She never liked it out here. She's always stayed in town."

The cottage Drew had been living in was ramshackle cute. A compact, one-story building with a peaked roof whose wooden exterior had been weathered into a lovely silver-gray by the elements. A tangle of morning glories and honeysuckles swarmed up the sides, and a pro forma picket fence defined the entry.

Theodosia stepped onto a small front porch and rapped her knuckles against the door. "Hello? Anybody home?" she called out. There was no answer, no movement inside. She peered through a dusty triangle of window, saw no one, waited a decorous minute or two, then reached down and turned the knob. The door wasn't locked so it swung open immediately with a low creak. She took a step inside. "Hello?"

The cottage was basically set up like a small apartment. A living room with a faded red-and-gold Chinese rug covered the hardwood floor, a pair of high-backed chairs, and a leather sofa faced a stone fireplace that was flanked with bookshelves. A galley kitchen was on the opposite side of the room, and through a doorway, Theodosia could see a small bedroom. A suitcase was open on the bed.

Just to the left of a small dining table was a contemporary-looking desk that held a large iMac. Theodosia wandered over and saw a pile of papers along with a stack of white foam core squares that had been cut into a ten-by-ten-inch size. Having worked in marketing and design for a number of years, she knew exactly what these were. They had to be the wine labels Drew had designed. Printed out from his color laser printer and mounted individually. Undoubtedly for presentation purposes.

She picked up one of the label designs. It was a label for a wine called First Blush, and the design featured bouncy type above a loose sketch of a woman with rosy round circles of pink on her cheeks. Cute. Theodosia shuffled through the rest of the stack. There were also labels for wines called Summer Sangria, Red Zone, and Knight Music. Theodosia balanced this last label in her hands, studying it. It was simple and elegant, a line drawing of a small lion crouched atop a violin against a sepia-tone background. Fine, copperplate typography spelled out KNIGHT MUSIC and, in a smaller font, KNIGHTHALL WINERY. She knew this was the biggie. This was the wine Jordan had said he was betting the farm on.

Theodosia set down the labels and let her eyes rove across the top of the desk. There were dog-eared issues of *The Wine Spectator* and *Wine Enthusiast*, a Mason jar filled with corks, a jumble of papers, and a spiral-bound desk calendar. She pushed aside some of the loose papers so she could study any notes or notations on what she presumed was Drew's calendar. She glanced at today's date as well as last Sunday's date and didn't see any notes at all. She turned back to the previous week, found only a yellow Post-it note with the words *green alien* scrawled on it.

Just as Theodosia was about to search the desk drawers, the front door flew open, footsteps pounded across the floor, and an angry voice screeched, "What do you think you're *doing* in here!"

5

~❦~

Theodosia's initial impression of the woman was a tangle of honey blond hair, flashing amber eyes, and impossibly long legs.

The model, Theodosia decided. *This has to be the model.*

"Who are you?" the young woman demanded in a strident tone. She took three more quick steps and, hands planted firmly on her nonexistent hips, crowded up against Theodosia. "How *dare* you paw through my things!"

Theodosia stood her ground impassively. "Your things? Are you sure about that?"

The girl pressed her full pouty lips together and gathered her anger into a burst of kinetic energy. "I don't know who you are but I want you to get out!" For added emphasis, she flung out an arm and indicated the door.

"I'm Theodosia Browning," Theodosia said, not budging an inch from her spot. "Jordan Knight asked me to drop by and talk to you." She offered a faint smile. "I'm guessing you're Drew's girlfriend."

The girl, who must have been used to intimidating people because of her beauty or tall stature, sputtered in frustration. "Yes, I'm his girlfriend. Of course I'm his girlfriend."

"You are . . ." Theodosia fished for her name. "Trisha?"

"Tanya," said the girl. "Tanya Woodson."

"My condolences," said Theodosia. "This must be a very difficult time for you."

"Yes, it is," said Tanya. Although she still seemed to be more angry than grief stricken.

"Do you mind if I ask you a few questions?"

Tanya rolled her eyes and let loose a heavy sigh. "You're just like that stupid Pandora—you want me to play nice."

"That might be helpful."

"So what do you want?"

"Tell me," said Theodosia, "this past Sunday . . . when was the last time you saw Drew?"

Tanya stared at her. "I don't know, I don't remember," she said in a petulant tone. "Look, I've been through all of this with that rather unattractive sheriff."

"Try to recall the time if you can," said Theodosia. "It could be a great help."

Tanya wrinkled her pert nose. "Maybe . . . two in the afternoon?"

"And you saw Drew where?" asked Theodosia.

"I went outside to take a look at the tables and tents and everything, then I ducked behind the barn to come back here and get ready for the party."

"Um . . . Drew was standing next to the barn talking to one of those Japanese guys."

"Was it Mr. Tanaka?"

"I guess that's his name."

"And that's the very last time you saw Drew alive?"

Tears suddenly swam in Tanya's eyes. "Yes," she said in a small voice.

"I realize you may not be able to answer this," said Theodosia. "But could you tell me anything about Pandora's relationship with Drew?"

"Of course I can," said Tanya. "They hated each other!"

Theodosia tried to mask her surprise. "Are you sure about that?"

"From the moment I first started seeing Drew, Pandora was always on his case. She was always harping about him not doing an honest day's work, telling him he really had to pitch in and help."

"And did he?"

"That's what's so weird," said Tanya. "In the last couple of months, Pandora backed off totally. It was almost as if she *didn't* want him involved in the winery."

"And how did Drew feel about that?"

"I think he talked to his father about it, but . . ." She shrugged. "Not much came of it. I think the old man's kind of browbeaten by Pandora, too. Lately, she's been a lot more involved in the winery. I guess she feels like it's her show."

Theodosia looked past Tanya at the plush surroundings of the cozy apartment. "I take it you're going to continue living here?"

"In this dump?" said Tanya. "Not hardly!"

"You *are* here by the good graces of Jordan and Pandora Knight," Theodosia reminded her.

Tanya's look of anger turned to one of scorn. "Good graces?" she spat out. "Hah!"

Her curiosity heightened now, Theodosia stared at the girl. What was going on? Could there be even more turmoil?

Turned out there was.

"A couple of hours ago," said Tanya, "I had a rather one-sided discussion with the evil stepmother. She of the brassy blond hair, dark roots, and too much Botox."

Theodosia barely nodded.

"And then," said Tanya, her face suddenly contorted with rage, "she threw me out!"

Theodosia strode anxiously toward the back door of the tasting room. Nothing seemed to add up thus far, and she was still anxious to get some answers. Correction, she was going to demand some answers!

As she pulled open the screen door, she literally ran smack-dab into Jordan Knight.

"You!" said Theodosia. "You're just the person I need to talk to!"

Jordan stared back at her blankly. His face was slack, his hair was unkempt, and his gestures seemed slow and wooden.

"I didn't mean to bark at you," Theodosia told him quickly. She was shocked at how bad he looked. Did he even remember that he had begged her to come out here? Because he looked completely dazed. Just . . . very out of it.

Then Jordan shook his head and seemed to pull himself back to the here and now. "Why don't you come in here," he said, gesturing toward a doorway. "Come into my office."

Jordan led Theodosia into a good-sized office that had a large wooden desk, comfy leather visitors' chairs, and an antique parson's table that held dozens of bottles of wine. Overhead, crystal wineglasses sparkled in a custom-built wooden rack. Settling herself in a chair, Theodosia waited as Jordan eased himself down slowly behind his desk.

"I think it's really just hit me," Jordan said in a strangled voice. "That Drew is truly . . . that he's gone."

Pity welled up inside Theodosia. She'd lost both parents herself, her mother when she was young, her father when she was in college. And she knew firsthand how the death of a loved one could leave you feeling shaken and orphaned.

"Again," said Theodosia. "I'm very sorry for your loss."

"Thank you," said Jordan. "And I do appreciate your

coming here today. I hope you've been able to view our operation and develop some initial impressions."

"Somewhat," said Theodosia. "Though I can't say that I've picked up any concrete facts or answers. Truth be told, I keep running into situations that lead to more questions."

Jordan's brow furrowed. "Such as?"

"For one thing," said Theodosia, "I wish you'd have been more forthcoming about your divorce from Pandora."

Jordan waved a hand. "Our problems have nothing to do with—"

"Don't say that," Theodosia snapped. "You don't know that at all."

Jordan rocked back in his chair. "What are you implying? That Pandora had a hand in Drew's death?" He seemed shocked and more than a little angry. "No." He shook his head. "That would never happen! No matter how much the two of them were at loggerheads, she'd never put Drew in jeopardy."

"But there could be an indirect influencer," said Theodosia. "Some strange twist or permutation that we don't know about."

Jordan looked stunned. "I can't imagine what that could be."

"Look, relationships around here seem awfully strained. Between you and Pandora, Pandora and Tanya . . . why, even your manager, Tom Grady, is nervous and on edge. And what I'd really like to know is—what is going on with Mr. Tanaka?"

"Nothing's going on," said Jordan. "He's a distributor. Here to lock down a business agreement. Hopefully we'll have that hammered out and signed by the end of this week."

"So he's still here?"

"Of course he's still here."

"I understand Mr. Tanaka pitched you and Pandora on the idea of becoming an actual partner?" said Theodosia.

"That was brought up only in passing," said Jordan. "There was never a serious discussion about it. If you've learned anything about me so far, you know that I'd never turn this place over to someone else. Knighthall Winery is my passion!"

"I was under the impression that Higashi Golden Brands was willing to give Knighthall a much-needed infusion of cash."

"They're a very successful company," said Jordan. "But I assure you, they're never going to own a piece of this winery."

"Mr. Knight," said Theodosia, almost formally now. "Were you and your son at odds over this deal?"

"Not at all."

"What about you and Pandora?"

Jordan drew breath. "Pandora did like the idea. But even though we've had a troubled marriage, she understood that I was against selling out. So it was really only ever dinner table chatter."

"How would you characterize your relationship with the people at the Plantation Wilds golf course?"

"With Donny Hedges, the owner? Fairly amicable."

"But they've been trying to buy you out," said Theodosia.

"No," said Knight. "They've been trying to buy my land. Big difference."

"And you don't want to sell."

"Absolutely not. I've poured my heart and soul into this winery. Do you know how difficult it is to cultivate grapes in this kind of heat and humidity? It's a viticulturist's nightmare. But now, with Knight Music, we're on the verge of having a breakout wine . . . so no, I don't want to sell. I *never* want to sell."

Just as Theodosia was about to climb into her Jeep, a black-and-tan cruiser slid into the space next to her. A few moments later, Sheriff Allen Anson climbed out. He was a big man. Barrel-chested, square-jawed, and flat-footed. He wore a khaki uniform, black boots, and a modified Smokey Bear hat. He was fully armed, and his gold star shone like he'd just polished it that morning. Anson stood there for a few moments, looking around, casually adjusting his belt. Then, like the periscope on a U-boat that was sighting in on its prey, he turned to look at Theodosia.

With a start, Theodosia decided this might be a lucky break for her. She scrambled out of her car, came around the back, and said in her friendliest manner, "Good afternoon, Sheriff."

Sheriff Anson peered at her from behind his mirrored sunglasses. "Who are you?" He wore both a pistol and a Taser on a belt that sported an enormous silver buckle embellished with what could either be a cicada bug or a cootie.

Theodosia stuck out a hand. She figured maybe she could disarm him with her friendliness. Or at least worm a grudging smile out of him. "I'm Theodosia Browning. Jordan Knight asked me to come out and look into things around here."

"Look into things," Sheriff Anson repeated in a flat tone. "What the Sam Hill is that supposed to mean?"

Theodosia decided she'd get further with the good sheriff if she didn't utter the word *investigation*. So instead she said, "Just try to get a handle on who might have murdered Drew."

Sheriff Anson's lips twitched. "That's funny," he said, his voice a gravelly rumble. "I thought that's what *I* was supposed to be doing."

"I don't mean to step on any toes . . ."

Anson frowned at her. "No?"

"Would if be possible to ask you a few questions?"

This time he managed a faint smile. "No."

Driving back to Charleston proper, Theodosia called the Indigo Tea Shop on her cell phone. *Be there, somebody*, she muttered to herself. *Please answer.*

Luckily, she managed to catch Haley just as she was getting ready to lock up.

"Hey!" said Haley in her usual upbeat fashion. "How'd it go at Knighthall? Did you solve the murder mystery yet?"

"Hardly," said Theodosia. "But I do have a quick question for you."

"Shoot."

"Do you know anyone who works at Virtuoso Staffing?"

"I'm guessing they're the one who provided the servers and bartenders for the ill-fated wine event?"

"That's right."

"Well, sure," said Haley. "I know Linda Hemmings, the manager. You know her, too. Don't you remember? Linda's the one we worked with when we needed a couple of extra warm bodies for that swanky party we catered at the Heritage Society last winter."

"Okay, now I remember," said Theodosia. "So Virtuoso's office is where?"

"Not that far from the tea shop," said Haley. "On George Street, a few doors down from Gilder's Art Supply."

"Got it," said Theodosia.

Linda Hemmings remembered Theodosia and Haley quite favorably. But she was understandably upset. "We talked to one of Sheriff Anson's men yesterday," she told Theodosia. "And two investigators from SLED who dropped by this morning." SLED was the South Carolina Law Enforcement Division.

They were standing in the outer office of Virtuoso Staffing. Photos of smiling black-coated waiters serving food and drinks at wedding receptions and formal garden parties lined the walls. Theodosia decided the waiters looked like they were having a much better time than the guests. Although to be fair, the pictures had probably been staged.

"The people you sent out to Knighthall Winery," said Theodosia. "These were all people that you know and trust?"

"Sure," said Linda. "They're all good people." Linda was medium height, skinny as a rail, and had a sharp nose and long brown hair with a couple of blue streaks in it. She looked like she might have been a sort of hippie in her younger days.

"So they're basically your employees?" said Theodosia. She wasn't sure how the arrangement worked. If they were employees or freelancers.

"Not really employees per se," said Linda. "More like contract help."

"So the waiters and bartenders don't work for you full-time."

Linda shook her head. "Most of the personnel we place have jobs elsewhere in the hospitality industry. This is just a way for them to earn a little extra cash." She studied Theodosia with some intensity. "And it's good for us, too. That way we don't have to stress over payroll."

"Were you present at the winery on Sunday night?"

"No, I wasn't," said Linda. "But Janet was there."

"Is it okay if I talk to Janet?" asked Theodosia.

"Sure," said Linda. "No problem. Come on." They walked down a short hallway where two offices, really cubicles, were jam-packed with computers, printers, copiers, and all the other equipment a small business can't live without.

Janet D'Lisio turned out to be the office manager. A red-haired dynamo with a quick smile and an extra twenty pounds on her.

"So you were at Knighthall on Sunday night," said Theodosia. "You saw the barrel crack open and—"

"And that poor boy come flopping out!" exclaimed Janet. She shook her head and put a hand to her forehead as if reliving the memory, of recalling Drew's dead body, was just too painful for her. "It was awful! Just a terrible shock to everyone."

"Especially to his family," said Theodosia. "Which is why I'm asking questions," she explained. "I'm looking into things on their behalf."

"Oh, okay," said Linda.

"And you had how many people working there that night?" Theodosia asked.

"I can tell you exactly," said Janet. She hit a few keys on her computer, studied her screen, and said, "Fourteen contract workers. Six bartenders, five servers to handle the hors d'oeuvres, two car park valets, and me to supervise."

"And everyone was hard at work doing their job?" said Theodosia.

"Pretty much everyone was working their buns off that night," said Janet. "Except for . . ."

"Who?" said Linda. "What?"

Janet rolled her eyes Linda's way. "Carl. He was . . . what would you call it? A little off his game that night."

Linda frowned. "Really? Carl Van Deusen? He's usually a pretty good worker."

"What happened?" Theodosia asked.

"For one thing," said Janet, "he disappeared for a while." She grimaced, as if she really didn't want to tell tales out of school. "I think he might have been drinking."

"*That's* certainly against policy," said Linda.

Janet shrugged. "Well, it was a winery and there were, like, *hundreds* of open bottles of wine floating around. You know how tempting something like that can be."

"What's the background on this Carl person?" Theodosia asked.

"Carl Van Deusen," Linda repeated. "He normally works as a waiter at Smalley's Bistro. But he likes to freelance with us every once in a while. I think he's hoping to make some contacts and score a better job."

Theodosia pulled a notebook out of her purse. "What's his number?" she asked. "Where exactly does he work again?"

6

❧

Smalley's Bistro was a cute storefront restaurant with a shingled overhang and a redbrick façade, tucked between Longitude Books and the Glad Hands Pottery Shop. There was a valet parking stand out front, but no attendant in sight. No problem. Theodosia found a spot at a nearby parking meter and walked back to the restaurant.

The front door was unlocked but nobody was minding the host's station yet. Theodosia edged her way in and called out, "Hello? Anybody here?" The décor was predominantly red and black and the place smelled of roast chicken, garlic, and tomato sauce. A salsified version of Demi Lovato's "Heart Attack" played over the speakers.

A tall, skinny busboy carrying a tray of clean glasses came crashing through a swinging door. "We're not open yet," he told her. "But if you'd like to make a reservation, I can call the manager."

"I'm looking for Carl Van Deusen," Theodosia told him. "One of your waiters. Do you know if he's here?"

"Um . . . maybe." The busboy wiggled his shoulders as he shifted his heavy load. "I *think* Carl's on tonight, but I'm not completely sure. Do you want me to find out?"

"That would be great."

The busboy set his tray of glasses down on the bar. "I'll have to run back to the locker room."

"Thanks."

Theodosia waited a good three or four minutes before a slightly chubby, dark-haired man came hustling toward her.

"Carl?" she said.

"No, I'm Philip Rusk, the manager." Rusk's voice carried a warning tone and his eyebrows seemed to be permanently raised and frozen into a disapproving arc. "Perhaps I can help you?"

"I was looking for Carl Van Deusen," said Theodosia.

"May I ask for what reason?"

"For personal reasons."

"Carl is on the clock right now," said the manager, obviously trying to brush her aside. "So I'm afraid he's unable to entertain visitors."

"Look, I get that you're busy setting up for dinner. But this won't take long, I promise."

"I'm sorry," said Rusk "But it's really quite impossible."

Theodosia held up a hand. "Five minutes, okay? No, not even five minutes. One minute. Please?"

Carl Van Deusen appeared a few minutes later. He was a tall, redheaded fellow in his late twenties. Big shoulders, a spattering of freckles across a friendly, open face, and muscular arms. Like he probably worked out a fair amount.

"Mr. Rusk said you wanted to see me?"

Something in Theodosia's memory clicked and she had a fleeting impression of Carl serving her a canapé two nights ago. "That's right," she told him. "I wanted to talk to you about Saturday night."

"What about it?" he asked, instantly on guard.

"For one thing," said Theodosia, "you were there."

"So were a lot of people." Carl frowned. "Who are you?"

"I'm Theodosia Browning, a friend of Jordan Knight's family. I'm kind of looking into things for him."

"Well . . . good." This time Carl sniffled and wiped at his nose.

"Something wrong?"

Carl's jaw worked nervously and his throat seemed constricted. "That was a bad scene," Carl said finally.

"I'm wondering if you knew Drew," said Theodosia.

Carl gave a slow nod. "I knew him." A loud clatter of dishes caused Carl to flinch and glance over his shoulder.

"You two were friends?"

"We were friendly," said Carl.

"I've also been talking to Linda and Janet over at Virtuoso Staffing," said Theodosia.

Carl stuffed his hands into the pockets of his white waiter's jacket. "Okay."

"They tell me you might have been drinking that night."

"Me?" Carl took a step back, as if utterly gob-smacked by her accusation. As if the notion of having a drink would've never occurred to him. "No way. That's strictly against policy."

"It wouldn't be the first time policy was kicked to the curb," said Theodosia.

Carl just stared at her.

Theodosia decided to jump right in. "You don't know anything about Drew's death, do you?"

Carl looked suddenly uneasy. "I really don't . . ." he mumbled.

"I think you might."

Carl shook his head vehemently and said, "Uh-uh," just as the door from the kitchen swung open and Rusk, looking officious and annoyed, bustled toward them.

"This conversation is over," Rusk announced in an annoyed bray. "Van Deusen, you're needed in the back room. And you, Miss Whatever-your-business-is, your time is definitely up!"

Twenty minutes later, still smarting from practically being physically ejected from Smalley's Bistro, Theodosia arrived home. She kicked off her shoes, let Earl Grey out into the backyard, and brewed herself a pot of chamomile tea. Then she sat down at her kitchen table and called Drayton.

"I was just doing some much-needed trimming on my bonsai trees," he told her. "Refining that tamarack forest you like so much."

Theodosia recalled a lovely arrangement of miniature tamarack trees in a large, shallow blue dish. Moss covered the floor of the tiny "forest," and there was a winding path of small stones. "That is a lovely piece," she told him.

"So tell me, what happened at Knighthall?"

"Do you want the short version or the dreadfully long version?"

"Mmn, that bad?"

"Drayton, those people do not get along with each other at all. They're a totally dysfunctional family and, I think, dysfunctional business."

"That's unfortunate. But I still want to hear about it."

Over the course of the next ten minutes, Theodosia gave Drayton a slightly abridged version of her afternoon at Knighthall, her stop at Virtuoso Staffing, and her meeting with Carl Van Deusen.

When she'd finished, she said, "You see how weird things are? How broken down communication seems to be?"

"But you seem to have uncovered a valuable cache of information," said Drayton. "That's the one saving grace."

"I have information, yes," said Theodosia. "Suspects, no."

"What kind of vibes did you get off this Van Deusen fellow? Is he a possible suspect?"

"Hard to tell," said Theodosia. "Van Deusen seemed upset over Drew's death, but who knows? They could have been crocodile tears."

"And the girlfriend?" said Drayton. "She's kind of a wild card in all of this."

"I'm on the fence concerning her," said Theodosia. "Somehow she doesn't seem like the kind of person who'd shoot Drew in the head and stuff his dead body in a barrel of wine."

"You're saying that because she's a woman?"

"I'm saying that because she strikes me as the type who wouldn't want to get her hands dirty."

"Still," said Drayton, "you never know. Even a fashion model can have an irrational, angry side."

"Probably because they never eat," said Theodosia.

Theodosia changed into a T-shirt, leggings, and tennis shoes. Then she busied herself in the kitchen, dicing an onion and a tomato, slicing a ripe avocado, and tossing it all into her Cuisinart along with a splash of chicken stock, cilantro, and a generous dollop of sour cream. She whirred her ingredients for a couple of minutes, then poured her thick, green masterpiece into an aluminum bowl and stuck it in the refrigerator. There. When she came back from her run with Earl Grey, she'd have a nice bowl of chilled avocado soup waiting for her.

"C'mon, big guy," Theodosia called out to Earl Grey. He was a Dalbrador, part Dalmatian, part Labrador, who was constantly sniffing around the backyard, always on the lookout for marauding raccoons. There'd been problems in the past—fish had been stolen—and Earl Grey, though gentle in nature, seemed to be itching for a rematch with the little masked bandits.

Theodosia snapped a leash onto his collar, gave a final glance back at her yard, and headed off down the narrow back alley.

The back alleys were one of the things Theodosia dearly cherished about her hometown of Charleston. They were cool, quiet, hidden places—narrow little byways that were often only wide enough for one or two people. Some of the best known were Philadelphia Alley, Unity Alley, Lodge Alley, and Longitude Lane. If you were a tourist, you might be lucky to stumble upon one or two. But only if you took a chance and did a little creative exploration.

Nestled between Church Street and State Street was Philadelphia Alley, one of Theodosia's favorites. Originally named Cow Alley probably because it was a holding pen for livestock, the narrow, walled lane soon picked up the name Duelers Alley. With its high walls and limited access at either end, it became the perfect spot for conflicts to be resolved and chivalry and honor to prevail. Although Theodosia didn't think there was much honor in bleeding to death on bumpy cobblestones just so you could save face or prove your point.

Still, it was a cozy little romp and very fun. Flora and fauna cascaded down the brick walls that closed in on either side of them, and there was even a cutout in the wall that led straight to the graveyard at St. Philip's Church!

Fog was beginning to steal in from the churning Atlantic, so the air in the historic district, always highly atmospheric to begin with, was starting to develop a slight haze. The air felt damp and close, and lampposts suddenly appeared a little fuzzy, as if being photographed through a soft focus lens.

A quick jog back across Church Street and Theodosia and her fine companion were suddenly keeping pace down

Stoll's Alley. This narrow crevice of an alley, with its brick pathway and earthy scents, was one of her favorites. It was a teleporter to an earlier, magical time and featured a reward at the end of it—a lovely courtyard filled with moss and ferns.

Theodosia smiled to herself. The alleys weren't quite as majestic as running through White Point Gardens with the Atlantic surging in to stir up the ions. But if you were looking for peace and quiet, and didn't mind glancing over your shoulder because you often had the niggling sense there might be a ghost or apparition following in your footsteps, then exploring back-alleys was clearly the way to go!

As she jogged back down her block in full-on dusk, her little cottage finally came into sight. And what a cottage it was. The exterior was adorable and semiquirky, a classic Tudor-style cottage that was asymmetrical in design with rough cedar tiles that replicated a thatched roof. The front of the cottage featured arched doors, cross gables, and a small turret. Lush tendrils of ivy curled their way up the walls. A couple of years ago, when she signed the papers to buy it, she even found out it had a name—Hazelhurst.

As focused as she was on getting home, Theodosia was still surprised when she noticed lights blazing in the enormous house that sat next door to hers. It had belonged to Dougan Granville, Delaine's onetime fiancé who had been murdered a few months ago.

Was someone showing the house to a prospective buyer? Was someone about to buy it? Or had they bought it already?

Theodosia slowed her stride as three figures meandered down the mansion's front walk. She heard lively chatter and a peal of laughter ring out. And suddenly realized that she recognized one of those voices. It belonged to Maggie Twining, the woman who'd served as her realtor not so long ago. Theodosia waited with Earl Grey on the sidewalk, watching as Maggie bade good night to her clients. Then she stepped forward to greet her.

Maggie was thrilled by their impromptu meeting.

"Theodosia!" she cried. "How fun to see you again!" She shifted her leather briefcase and extended a hand for Earl Grey to sniff. "And your lovely dog, too." Maggie had a friendly, open face surrounded by a tumble of gray hair and wore a pair of narrow, turquoise glasses on a chain around her neck. Her navy-and-white-striped suit was sturdy but stylish.

"It looks like you just showed the Granville mansion," said Theodosia. "Tell me, am I about to have new neighbors?" She was more than a little curious. And nervous, too. Who would they turn out to be? "You weren't showing it to the Rattlings, were you?" Frank and Sarah Rattling were a pair of quasi-strange innkeepers that she'd had a run-in with recently.

Maggie glanced down the street at the couple she'd just bade good-bye to. "No, this was a young couple, Lou and Margaret Blankenship."

Theodosia followed her gaze. She saw that they were in their early thirties at best and were just climbing into a slightly dented car.

"There's no way they can afford this place," Maggie told Theodosia, as if reading her mind. "They're just lookers, curiosity seekers. A waste of time. I could have stayed home, snarfed a bag of Chips Ahoy, and watched *Dancing with the Stars*." She smiled. "Or I suppose I could have dropped by your place and probably enjoyed *petit fours* and fancy little crab salad tea sandwiches."

"Anytime you want," said Theodosia. "So how has business been for you lately?" Earl Grey strained at his leash, already bored with their conversation.

"Slow but steady," said Maggie. "Nothing earth-shattering,

though. Not like a few years ago when the banks were practically throwing money at buyers."

"I didn't realize you even had this listing," said Theodosia.

"I don't have an exclusive," said Maggie. "But this place, the Kingstree Mansion, is listed with Sutter Realty, my brokerage firm. Between you and me, I'd love to sell this white elephant if I could. The commission would keep me in cat food for five years!" Maggie had three beautiful cats, two Manx and one Siamese, that she loved and adored.

"You know," said Theodosia, "I might have a potential client for you."

"Be still, my heart," said Maggie. "Who is it? Do I know him? Or her?"

"Do you know Andrew Turner, the fellow who owns The Turner Gallery over by Church Street and Hopper?"

"Sure," said Maggie, nodding. She paused and then said, "Well, I don't know him *personally*, but I know the place. I'm at least familiar with the gallery."

"I'm sorry I don't have his phone number . . ."

Maggie quickly held up a hand. "Not a problem. I can find that easily enough." She peered at Theodosia. "And you're sure this Mr. Turner is in the market for a house? A really grand house like this one?" By *grand*, Maggie meant expensive.

Theodosia nodded. "He just mentioned it to me this morning."

Back home again, Theodosia took a quick shower and wrapped herself in a terrycloth robe. She grabbed her laptop and padded barefoot downstairs to the kitchen. The chilled avocado soup was delicious. It was nice and creamy and the flavors of all the ingredients had melded together beautifully. As she ate, she tapped along on her computer.

Checking the news, the stock market, and her Facebook page. Then, just to satisfy her curiosity, just because it had stuck in her mind and was nagging at her, she Googled the words *green alien*.

Surprisingly, there were all sorts of weird things with the moniker *green alien*.

For one thing, there was a sweet mixed drink made with Midori and lime juice. Theodosia wrinkled her nose as she perused the mixology instructions. It didn't sound all that appealing.

Another hit turned up a green tongue ring. Okay. That was fairly strange. And there were about a hundred websites all selling T-shirts with alien depictions on them.

Theodosia sat back and let the term *green alien* rumble through her brain. And decided it was either complete nonsense, or something decidedly comic book–like. Such as *The Green Lantern* or *Iron Man* or *Batman*. But as a clue, it didn't seem to take her anywhere meaningful. So probably, it didn't mean anything at all.

7

❧

Theodosia folded a linen napkin into a bishop's crown and set it next to a Shelley chintz teacup. For some reason, Drayton had decided to pull one of their fancier sets of china out of storage today and use it on the tables. So, of course, once that was all laid out, it pretty much cried out for an elegantly folded napkin as well as sterling silver teaspoons. And even though Drayton was watching her like a hawk, she felt a certain sense of pride in using some of their nicer things, too.

"It's looking very good over there," Drayton called. He was standing behind the front counter, pouring hot water into a Brown Betty teapot. Making a pot of Irish breakfast tea for them so they could fortify themselves before opening up for business this bright and sunny Tuesday morning.

"I think you're just practicing for the Downton Abbey tea tomorrow," said Theodosia.

"Hah," said Drayton. "A dress rehearsal of sorts." The

corners of his mouth twitched up in a mischievous smile. "Could be, could be."

With the light streaming in and the tables sparkling like a chandelier of cut crystal, Theodosia joined Drayton at the front counter. There she once again ran through her impressions concerning her visit to Knighthall Winery yesterday afternoon.

"I know I already told you all this," said Theodosia.

"That's okay," said Drayton. "Run through it again. Maybe something will jump out at us."

So she told him about her encounter with the rather blasé Pandora, her tour with Grady, and the fact that she'd also talked with Tanya, Jordan, and Sheriff Anson.

"Oh, and did I mention that I stopped by Virtuoso Staffing, too?" said Theodosia. "Talked to the two ladies who run it and then paid a visit to Carl Van Deusen, one of the waiters who were working at the wine tasting."

"Why did you want to speak with this Van Deusen person?" Drayton asked. He poured out a cup of tea for her and said, "Taste that."

"Probably because the Virtuoso people indicated that he was acting a little strange."

"Did you find him strange?"

Theodosia took a sip of tea. "Mmn, excellent. No, I found him to be fairly normal. I think he and Drew might have been acquaintances." She took another sip of tea. "No, I think they might have been friends."

"You sure about that?" asked Drayton.

"I am for now," said Theodosia.

Drayton gazed out across the tea room, a look of general satisfaction on his face. "I spoke with Jordan last night. Right after I talked to you."

"He called you?"

"Yes, he did. He said he was sorry that he hadn't been

more helpful to you. That he wasn't in a better frame of mind."

"He's been through a lot," said Theodosia. She couldn't imagine losing a son like that. She'd once read, in *Psychology Today* or *Prevention,* that a parent losing a child was one of the worst traumas the human heart could endure.

"Anyway," said Drayton, "Jordan said he'd be willing to talk to you again tomorrow morning."

"At the memorial service?" said Theodosia, surprised.

"Well, afterwards anyway," said Drayton. He patted his bow tie and gazed at Theodosia with hooded eyes. "I know we asked you to look into things, but do you think you should perhaps get in touch with Detective Tidwell, too?" Burt Tidwell was the departmental head of Robbery-Homicide with the Charleston Police Department. He and Theodosia shared a grudging admiration for each other, one that had developed after they'd been thrown together on a couple of strange murder cases.

"This is completely out of Tidwell's jurisdiction," said Theodosia. "If I even broach the subject of Drew's murder, all he'll do is warn me to back off."

Drayton looked suddenly glum. "Maybe you should. Back off, I mean. I've been thinking about what you told me—all the personal hassles and problems that the family seems to be having. Maybe I dragged you into something that's just a little too convoluted." He paused. "A little too dangerous."

"I hear what you're saying, but I don't *think* I'm in any danger. It doesn't feel that way. Besides . . ."

"Besides what?" said Drayton.

"I have to admit my curiosity is piqued."

Drayton nodded. "Mine, too. The people at Knighthall are turning out to be—"

"Fairly strange ducks," finished Theodosia. "Like characters in a B movie."

"I was going to say practically Shakespearian," said Drayton.

Theodosia wondered if she should mention green alien to Drayton, dismissed the idea, then thought, why not? What did she have to lose?

"Does green alien mean anything to you?"

"Green what?" said Drayton. Now he seemed preoccupied with deciding on one of his morning tea choices. Harney & Son's Uva Highlands or Adagio's Fujian Baroque.

"Alien," said Theodosia.

"Alien," said Haley, coming up behind them. "I've always been crazy about that movie!" She struck a quick kung-fu pose. "Sigourney Weaver and her cat Jonesy fighting off the slivering, slavering monster."

Theodosia and Drayton just stared at her. They'd never seen a Haley action figure before.

"Actually," Haley continued, "I pretty much love anything that smacks of sci-fi."

"Ghastly," said Drayton, offering a disapproving look.

"Not just alien," Theodosia said to Haley now. *"Green* alien. Does that particular phrase strike a chord with you?"

Haley gave a bright smile. "Maybe Ridley Scott's been tapped to direct a new movie? Another sequel?"

"Somehow," said Theodosia, "I don't think that's it."

"Do you want me to kind of ask around?" said Haley.

"It's probably some new musical group," said Drayton.

"Techno punk," said Haley as Drayton rolled his eyes.

"Okay," said Theodosia. She'd just checked her watch and decided she had enough time to restock the shelves with some of her T-Bath products.

A couple of years ago, Theodosia had put on her entrepreneur's cap and developed an entire line of bath and skin care products infused with various blends of tea. Now her T-Bath line included such delicious-sounding fare as Oolong Bubble Bath, Ginger and Chamomile Facial Mist,

Lemon Verbena Hand Lotion, and Chamomile Calming Lotion. And she was currently working with her manufacturer on a recipe that included hibiscus and honey. So probably a body lotion called Hibiscus and Honey Butter.

She stacked the bottles and jars on the antique highboy, tucked a few gingham tea cozies next to them, and finished off her display area by adding a few more jars of DuBose Bees Honey. There, it was looking very presentable.

"Excuse me," said Drayton. "But before we open our door and get inundated with customers, could we please take these last five minutes to run through our plans for tomorrow's Downton Abbey tea?"

"Fine with me," said Theodosia. She dusted her hands together and went over to the celadon green velvet curtains that separated the tea room from the kitchen and back office. Parting the curtains, she called out, "Haley?"

"You presence is required," Drayton called out loudly.

Two seconds later, Haley popped out, wiping her hands on a red-checkered towel.

"You're using your Heritage Society orator's voice," said Haley. "This must be important."

"Everything we do here is important," said Drayton.

"Well . . . sure, dude," said Haley, sounding more Valley Girl than South Carolina native.

"Drayton wants to review the menu for the Downton Abbey tea," said Theodosia.

"Oh that," said Haley, waving a hand, satisfied that nothing major was amiss. "Nothing's changed since I shared my menu ideas with him."

"Then kindly share them with Theodosia, as well," said Drayton.

"Okay," said Haley. "We'll be serving Mrs. Patmore's Smoked Salmon Tea Sandwiches, Lady Crawley's Cucumber Dreams, and Mr. Carson's Crumpets."

"Did you just make this up?" said Theodosia.

Haley nodded happily. "Yeah, pretty much."

"Well, people are going to *love* this," said Theodosia. "They're especially going to want the recipes."

"Well . . . I don't know about that," said Haley, looking askance. She hated any talk of divulging her recipes. In fact, she treated them like top secret government documents. "We'll have to see."

"Shall we stick to the business at hand?" said Drayton.

"You mentioned once that you might do a fruit trifle?" said Theodosia.

"Probably strawberries, blueberries, and raspberries," said Haley. "Particularly since most of the berries are still in season."

"Not here," said Drayton.

"Well . . . somewhere," said Haley. "Plus I'm going to bake a couple batches of Banbury tarts."

Drayton looked puzzled. "I don't recall anyone named Banbury in the show's cast of characters."

"There isn't," said Haley. "The tarts are actually named after the town of Banbury in Oxfordshire. They're butter tarts filled with figs, candied peel, raisins, and walnuts. Really yummy. Oh, and I'm doing dark chocolate cupcakes with a touch of brandy and then decorating them with herringbone frosting designs to underscore our very tally-ho British theme."

"Everything sounds wonderful," said Theodosia. "If there's anything I can do to help in the kitchen . . ."

Haley held up a hand.

"I know, I know," said Theodosia. "But I thought I'd make the offer." She turned to Drayton. "And what about your tea selections?"

"As you know," said Drayton, "black tea is the tea of choice throughout the United Kingdom. And it's generally drunk with milk and sugar. So we need something strong and hearty to stand up to those particular additives."

"So what were you thinking?" asked Theodosia.

"Possibly an English breakfast tea or a Goomtee Garden Darjeeling," said Drayton.

"I think that will be perfect," said Theodosia.

"We'll use the Coalport china and the Garnet Rose silver," said Drayton.

"What about centerpieces?" Theodosia asked.

"The flowers are on order from Floradora," said Drayton, "and I have a few other special tidbits that will be delivered first thing tomorrow morning."

"Care to elaborate on that?" asked Haley.

"No," said Drayton. "I think I'll let it remain a surprise."

They opened their doors then, and guests began tumbling in. Haley had baked her special jammy scones stuffed with strawberry jam, along with loaves of zucchini bread. And Drayton had added a rose petal tea to his morning repertoire.

By midmorning, just when things were beginning to hum at a fever pitch, Andrew Turner walked through the door.

"Mr. Turner!" said Theodosia. His dropping in was a surprise indeed. Especially since he'd just been in yesterday and she'd mentioned him to Maggie last night.

Turner grinned and held up a hand. "Call me Andrew, please. Andy would be even better."

"I'm surprised to see you again so soon," said Theodosia. Somehow she hadn't pegged him for a tea drinker.

Turned out, she was wrong.

"Are you kidding?" said Turner. "I can't stay away—I think I've become a tea convert. Especially after that delicious English breakfast tea that you served yesterday."

"Then we're delighted to have you."

"I have another confession to make," Turner said, inching a little closer to her.

Theodosia peered at him. "What's that?"

Turner scrunched up his face. "I'm hopelessly addicted to your scones."

"Ah," said Theodosia. "We have a self-help group for that."

Turner looked suddenly puzzled. "You do?"

"Absolutely. You just come in and help yourself."

Turner pointed a finger at her. "You are good. And you're cute. I get what Max sees in you!"

Theodosia blushed, a little at a loss for words. Thank goodness Turner didn't seem to notice as she led him to a table.

"Oh, say," he said as he slid into his seat. "I almost forgot. I wanted to thank you for giving me a line on that house. Your realtor friend Maggie Twining? She called me first thing this morning."

Now Theodosia's embarrassment was replaced by a small twinge of worry. "I wasn't sure if you'd be interested in that place, since it's monstrously huge. In fact, you'd probably just rattle around inside. But it recently came on the market and I have to say it meets all your criteria. At least I think it does."

"That's okay," said Turner. "I'm definitely on the lookout for a much larger home. It would be particularly useful for entertaining clients. And as you can imagine, I need wall space—acres of wall space!"

"That house has wall space galore," said Theodosia. She could vividly recall the dozens of oil paintings in gilded frames that had graced the walls when Dougan Granville lived there.

"Maggie's offered to give me a private showing tonight." Turner chuckled. "She's quite the bundle of energy."

"She really is," agreed Theodosia.

Turned nodded. "Apparently there's a big brokers' open

house scheduled for Thursday afternoon, so Maggie's getting me in for a kind of sneak peak." He paused. "She seems like a lady who really knows her stuff."

"And she's persuasive," said Theodosia. "So watch out!"

Drayton, who'd been pouring tea at the next table, came over to join them.

"Am I to understand that you have your eye on the mansion next door to Theodosia?"

Turner nodded happily. "Yes, and I'm told it even has a name. The Kingstree Mansion. I'm going to take a look at it tonight."

"That's a fantastic home," said Drayton. "Been on the Spring Home and Garden Tour for as long as I can remember. I hope that if you do purchase the place, you'll want to continue the tradition." He touched a finger to his bow tie. "Nothing like tradition, I always say."

"If I buy it," said Turner, "if I can *afford* that monster house, I promise that it will remain on the tour."

"Excellent," said Drayton. "Good to know."

Turner looked suddenly serious. "Have either of you heard anything more about the murder at Knighthall? Do you know if the police have anyone in custody yet? I'm afraid I haven't been following the news."

"Not only do they not have anyone in custody," said Drayton, sounding outraged, "they don't have any suspects."

"That's awful!" said Turner. "A really sad state of affairs."

"Which is why I asked Theo here to look into things."

"Just as an outside, impartial observer," Theodosia hastened to explain.

"I think that's a smart idea," said Turner. "From what I know about Jordan and Pandora, they're basically nice people. Maybe a little misguided at times, maybe at each other's throats on occasion, but they mean well. And they certainly don't deserve to have their son—or stepson as the case may be—murdered in cold blood!"

"How do you know Jordan and Pandora?" Drayton asked.

"Oh, maybe a year or so ago they wandered into my gallery," said Turner. "We got into a rousing discussion about Chuck Close and Damien Hurst and then I ended up trading them a small Wilhelm Bach sculpture for five cases of cabernet."

"That's not such a bad deal," said Theodosia.

"Actually, I was fairly pleased," said Turner. "Since it turned out to be lovely wine. And then, over the past couple of months, Pandora kind of sweet-talked me into handling some of Drew's paintings and sketches in my gallery. You see, every October, I have what I call my newbie show." He smiled. "Well, that's not what I *really* call it. The promotional title I use is *New Artists of Note*, since it's all about showcasing new artists. Anyway, the art-buying public gets to see fresh talent, and young artists who are trying to break out receive valuable exposure that they wouldn't ordinarily get."

"I love that," said Theodosia. "You're very kind to give young artists such a helping hand."

"Aw, it's not that big a deal," said Turner.

"Sure it is," said Theodosia. "You're helping to nurture young talent. Not a lot of people take time to do that these days."

"The thing is," said Turner, "Drew wasn't a bad artist. He showed a lot of promise."

"I think he did, too. I saw some of the wine labels he designed. Not bad."

"Not bad at all," agreed Turner.

8

❧

Noontime rolled around and the tea shop got even busier.

"Where are the salads? Where are the salads?" Drayton cried. "I've got tables waiting!"

Theodosia came hurrying out of the kitchen, carrying a large silver tray that held a half-dozen beautifully plated salads.

"They're right here," she said. "A mix of summer greens with honey Dijon dressing. Just as Haley promised."

Drayton poked a finger at one of the salads. "What on earth is that leafy little garnish?"

"A sprig of thyme," said Theodosia.

"Looks like Haley paid a visit to the farmer's market again."

"I think she does every morning," said Theodosia. "She's such a stickler for fresh ingredients."

Drayton grabbed the tray from Theodosia. "Just as long as she doesn't try to make us over into one of those trendy

California farm-to-table restaurants where they serve thistle salads and wheat juice shooters."

Theodosia grinned at him. "You know, that doesn't sound all that bad."

"Oh please," said Drayton, darting away.

But the rest of Haley's menu was traditional tea shop fare. Tea sandwiches of mozzarella cheese and tomato spread, as well as a prosciutto and roasted red pepper sandwich. Then there was her white Cheddar cheese *croque monsieur,* which was really just French for grilled cheese sandwich, and a luscious maple-flavored French toast casserole for dessert.

Theodosia delivered luncheons, poured tea, chatted with a few of their regulars, and helped Drayton pack up their take-out orders. And just as she was returning to the counter, a teapot in each hand, Max came rushing in.

"Hey there," Max said to Theodosia. "Got time for a five-minute break?"

Theodosia raised a single eyebrow and glanced at the crowded tea room. "Uh . . . not really."

He edged closer to the counter. "I guess you're kind of busy, huh? Well, can you talk while you work?"

"For you . . . yes." She grabbed a cookie from a plate and slid it across the counter to him. "Your buddy Andrew Turner was just in here an hour or so ago."

"He was?" said Max. He took a bite of cookie then threw her a funny look, half questioning, half expectant. "Um . . . he didn't ask you for a date or anything like that, did he?"

For the second time that morning, Theodosia blushed. "No, of course not. He just came in for tea and scones." She shrugged. "It was all perfectly neighborly."

"Well good," said Max, taking another bite. "He's a nice-looking guy so I'd hate to . . . I don't know . . . have to beat him off with a tube of cadmium red or something."

"Very funny," said Theodosia. "In fact, I kind of set him up with a realtor. Maggie Twining."

"For a date?" said Max.

"For a house," said Theodosia. "That big one next to me."

"The one Dougan Granville owned?"

"That's right. It's finally up for sale."

"Then I guess Turner is pretty serious about buying a big place," said Max.

Theodosia scanned the take-out boxes that were packed and piled on the front counter. "You're here to pick up your order, right?"

Max gave a slow wink. "Unless you have something better in mind."

"And the order's under your name?"

"Oh, I see," said Max. "We're going to pretend we're not really snuggle bunnies. Instead we're going to act very proper and businesslike. Okay, yes. Yes, it's under my name."

"How many box lunches?" Theodosia was searching the counter, checking labels that were taped to a dozen or so boxes.

"Six."

"Here they are," said Theodosia. She bent down, grabbed a large indigo blue shopping bag, and stacked the boxes inside. "Put it on your tab or on the museum's tab?"

Max cocked his head. "Please."

"Okay then, the museum's tab," said Theodosia, making a notation. She looked up, smiled at him because he was giving her one of his trademark crooked smiles, and said, "Hey, cutie, can I fix you a cuppa to go?"

"Why not," said Max.

He leaned forward as Theodosia grabbed a teapot and poured a generous amount of Keemun tea into an indigo blue cup.

"Hey," he said.

She snapped the lid on the cup and handed it to him. "Hey what?"

"How much are you getting involved in this winery thing?"

Uh-oh. "I'm just helping Drayton out. Asking around."

"That's a nice noncommittal answer, but what is your role really?" said Max. "Just helping Drayton out? Which I don't believe for one minute. Or investigating a brutal murder?"

"Last I heard" said Theodosia, "Sheriff Anson was the one who was tracking down suspects and asking the hard questions."

Max stared at her. "And you're sure he's the only one doing that?"

She gave him a cagey smile. "Call the good sheriff himself if you don't believe me."

"Oh, I'm sure Sheriff Anson is up to his hips in crime fighting," said Max. "What I'm not so sure about is how involved *you* are."

"Like I said, I'm just asking a few questions, keeping my eyes and ears open."

"I worry about you," said Max. "You've got this crazy headstrong instinct that compels you to get involved in sticky situations."

"You think I rush into things?" said Theodosia.

Max nodded slowly. "Where angels fear to tread."

Theodosia reached out and touched his hand. "I'll be careful. I promise."

"I want to believe you."

Theodosia decided it was time to change the subject. "We're still on for the Art Crawl tomorrow night?"

"Count on it," said Max.

"Great, because I still need something to hang in my dining room. A nice painting or print. Something splashy."

"Aren't you lucky that you have your own personal art consultant going along with you?"

Theodosia gathered up Max's bag and handed it to him. Then she gave him a slow wink. "Luck had nothing to do with it, cutie."

When lunch had finally dwindled to a dull roar, Theodosia ducked into her office to change. She knew Delaine would have a conniption if she showed up in a T-shirt, slacks, and ballet flats. So, against her personal rules that governed comfort, convenience, and basic happiness, she changed into a black sheath dress and shucked her feet into a pair of high-heeled sandals. Then she plopped down at her desk and dug out a sliver of a cracked mirror from the top drawer. She added a smidge of Chanel's Rose Sand lip gloss and a touch of black mascara.

There, that should meet the minimum daily requirement of glam.

Her cell phone shrilled abruptly and Theodosia grabbed it, hoping against hope that it was Delaine calling to offer some sort of pardon.

But it was Angie Congdon, proprietor of the Featherbed House B and B, which was located a few blocks away.

"Angie, hi!" said Theodosia.

"I'm just calling to see if you're still coming Friday night," said Angie. "I know I sent you an invitation for our open house, but I thought a personal call might be in order, too."

"It's on my calendar," said Theodosia. "I wouldn't miss it."

"Good," said Angie. "I'm anxious for you to see all the changes we made here."

"I hear a major addition."

"That's right," said Angie. "A reboot."

"Featherbed House 3.0." Theodosia laughed. "But you kept all the geese, didn't you? I mean, everybody *loves* your geese!" Angie had an enormous collection of ceramic, stuffed, and wooden geese.

"I'd never let my little darlings go," said Angie. "This is their home!"

"See you Friday," said Theodosia as she clicked off.

Okay, where was I?

Oh. My hair.

Theodosia's auburn hair, always full to begin with, had poufed out heroically today. Heat, humidity, and the constant steam from chirping, burbling tea kettles had contributed to an angelic halo that most women would kill for.

All except Theodosia.

Always a little self-conscious about her hair, she ran a brush through it, trying to tame the curls and waves and puffs. Then she gave a sigh, patted it down, and hoped for the best. Dashing out the back door, she fired up her Jeep and headed for Cotton Duck.

So, of course, when she pulled up in front of Delaine's boutique, there were two youthful valets who were busy parking cars. One had just hopped into a white Mercedes and pulled away, while the other was handing a ticket to a woman who'd just climbed out of an enormous BMW that could have doubled for a Sherman tank.

And then there's my Jeep, thought Theodosia. A few bumps and dings, not the most glamorous mode of transportation. But she loved the crazy thing. It took her off road, roaring and rollicking deep into the woods of her aunt Libby's farm to search for morels in spring and to gather tender dandelion shoots, clover, and wild watercress in high summer.

She pulled up to the front door, climbed out, and smiled at the young valet.

"Boss ride," he murmured as he handed her a ticket.

"I think so," she answered back. And then Theodosia ratcheted up her courage and pushed her way into Cotton Duck.

The first thing that greeted her was the thump-bump-thump of eardrum-busting techno music. The next thing was the enormous jostling crowd. There was, quite literally, a sea of well-dressed women who, by some mysterious circumstance, all seemed to know one another. They jabbered away, grabbed for programs, and exchanged air kisses. As Theodosia stood there, a little nonplussed and looking around, she couldn't help but notice that the shop looked fantastic. Delaine had pushed her racks of dresses, slacks, tunics, and tops to one side of the store to make room for an actual runway. It was approximately a foot high and covered in shiny white Mylar. A string of miniature klieg lights had been suspended above it. On either side of the runway were rows of pristine white wooden folding chairs. There was a champagne bar set up just to Theodosia's left, and of course, enormous baskets of flowers graced every available surface.

"Theo!" called Delaine. She glided to Theodosia's side like a predatory cat. "What do you think of my décor?" She gave a little toss of her head, and her gold chandelier earrings tinkled like wind chimes.

"Gorgeous," Theodosia told her. "Very impressive." Delaine herself was decked out in a long black column of crepe de chine. One bare arm and shoulder were exposed as well as her pink lacquered toenails peeping out from a pair of cage booties.

"You see?" Delaine purred. "I've arranged my runway the same way my favorite couture houses do it—you know, Chanel, Dior, Lanvin. With the front row reserved for my absolute best customers and friends!"

Theodosia glanced around at all the well-heeled customers in their designer dresses and skirt suits and took a gulp. She was thankful she'd done her little presto-chango act and worn a presentable dress.

"You'd better grab a flute of champagne from the bar and find your seat," Delaine instructed. "The show is set to kick off in just a couple of minutes." Then she placed a hand on Theodosia's forearm and squeezed gently. "I think you'll be delighted to find yourself seated in the front row!"

"I'm thrilled," Theodosia responded. Really, she didn't care where she sat, but she was happy to go along with this front row business for Delaine's sake. This entire afternoon—an amalgam of fashion, music, drinks, and craziness—was an elaborate package deal. And she not only had to buy into it, but was expected to bid—generously at that—on some of the clothes.

Oh well.

Theodosia made her way to the bar and grabbed a glass of champagne from a young, hunky-looking bartender. Just as she was headed for the front row, her cell phone rang. Dipping a hand into her bag, she scooped it out and checked her screen. *Indigo Tea Shop.* Uh-oh, a problem?

"Hello?"

"Theo, it's Haley."

"Is everything okay?" *Please tell me the tea shop didn't blow up.*

"Just peachy," said Haley. "But I checked on that thing for you."

"Thing," said Theodosia.

"You know. Green alien."

"Okay."

"You remember that sort of Goth guy I used to go out with? Heinrich?"

"I remember." Theodosia remembered Haley's friend as having more metal in his lips, eyebrow, and ear than a custom hot rod.

"Well," said Haley, "he's kind of counterculture, so I figured he might know something."

"About the green alien reference," said Theodosia. *Come on, spit it out.*

"It means . . ." Haley dropped her voice. "A kind of heroin."

"What? Are you serious?"

"Cross my heart."

"Okay," said Theodosia. "Wow. Talk to you later . . . and thanks."

She stood stock-still in the sea of women and thought about the ramifications of this. Was Drew using heroin? Had he been a drug addict? Did that have something to do with why he was killed?

The overhead lights blinked once, a warning for everyone to hurry up and find their seats.

Still pondering the significance of green alien, Theodosia slipped between the runway and the first row of chairs, searching for the chair with her name pinned to the back, trying not to bump the knees of the women who were already seated. And just as she spotted her chair, a hand reached up to stop her.

Theodosia glanced down and put a game smile on her face, ready to say hello. But she didn't recognize this woman whose hand was clamped tightly about her wrist. A woman with a broad, squarish face, sparkling eyes, and an enormous reddish-orange beehive hairdo. Talk about your Southern tradition of big hair—she made Theodosia look like an amateur!

Then the woman smiled and said in a fairly assertive tone, "You don't know who I am, do you?"

Theodosia was searching her brain, trying to put a name to this face. Was this a customer from her tea shop? A friend of Delaine's? When she wasn't able to retrieve the woman's name from her internal database, she gave a smile and a resigned shrug and said, "I'm very sorry . . ."

The woman continued to grin up at her. "I'm Georgette Kroft from Oak Hill Winery."

9

❧

"*Oh my goodness!*" said Theodosia. She was so startled, the words just seemed to burst from her mouth.

"I don't think *goodness* is quite the right word, darlin'," Georgette drawled in response. "In fact, I'll bet you've been told that I'm the devil incarnate." She released Theodosia's hand and waited for her to settle into the chair next to her.

"I haven't heard anything quite *that* bad," said Theodosia. Now that she'd recovered from her initial shock, she was curious to learn something about this woman whom Pandora really had demonized.

"I'll just bet," said Georgette, "that Jordan and Pandora Knight asked you to take a hard look at me. Am I right? I bet they pointed their irate little fingers at me and said, 'She's the killer!'"

Instead of answering yes or no, Theodosia said, "How do you know I've been talking to the Knights? That they've asked me to look into things for them?"

"I have my ways," said Georgette. "And let's face it, now

that we're sitting here having our friendly little tête-à-tête, you *are* curious about me, aren't you? You really do want to know if I'm such a big bad monster?"

Theodosia decided to meet Georgette's tumble of words head-on. "As a matter of fact, I do."

"Well, the simple fact of the matter is, they've got their undies in a twist all because I made an offer on Knighthall Winery. A rather generous one at that, considering the circumstances."

"Those circumstances being . . . what?" Theodosia asked.

"Oh, how about the fact that their winery is a losing proposition and Jordan Knight doesn't really know what he's doing?"

"Jordan Knight seems to be under the impression that you acted quite aggressively toward him," said Theodosia.

Georgette considered this for a moment, then her mouth twitched and a smile worked its way across her broad face. "That's probably because I *am* aggressive. How else do you become a success in business?"

"Is *your* winery a success?" Theodosia wasn't being impudent; she was just plain curious. She found this woman a fascinating study in brashness and bravado.

"I'd say so," Georgette said in measured tones. "We produced almost five hundred thousand bottles last year and practically doubled production this year."

"That sounds pretty amazing. You have that many orders?"

"We do," said Georgette. "It seems we're the flavor of the mouth here in South Carolina." She looked rather pleased and added, "North Carolina and Georgia, too."

"You must have excellent distribution," said Theodosia. She decided to keep Georgette talking and learn as much as she could from her.

"I've built a crackerjack sales force that's opening more and more accounts every day."

"Then it sounds like you've got your hands full."

"You got that right," said Georgette. "Some days I don't know if I'm coming or going."

"Then why would you want to take on Knighthall Winery, too? Why on earth did you make them an offer?"

Georgette glanced down at her program, then back at Theodosia. "I didn't want to buy the winery per se. It was the vineyard I was after, simple as that. More grape production equals more wine equals more bottles for me to sell."

Keep her talking, keep her talking, Theodosia told herself. Luckily, Georgette was cooperating nicely.

Besides," Georgette continued, "I think Pandora was rather pleased with the offer I made."

This was news to Theodosia. "You think so?" As far as she could recall, the Knights had made it sound like Georgette was trying to negotiate a hostile takeover.

"In fact, I'm fairly sure that Pandora's had a belly full of the wine business."

"What are you saying?" said Theodosia. "That Pandora wants out?"

Georgette nodded. "My guess is that Pandora would like to *cash out.* That she's sick to death of the whole thing. Think about it—she's endured five years of nursing so-so harvests, of struggling to gain traction in a tough market, and negotiating with the bank for additional time to pay off their loans."

"I had no idea things were that bad," said Theodosia.

Georgette uttered a sharp bark. "Bad? They're terrible out there! Pandora is divorcing Jordan and is probably going to take him to the cleaners. And face it, she certainly never got along with Drew."

"What you're telling me is . . . interesting," said Theodosia. Actually, it was enlightening!

"It's a mess out there at Knighthall," said Georgette. "Even Tom Grady is thinking about moving on."

"Would you hire him?"

Georgette's eyes slid away from her just as the lights dimmed and a riff of music filled the air. And Theodosia realized that Georgette had indeed talked to Grady. In fact, Grady had probably confided to Georgette that she was the one looking into things. Okay, so a direct pipeline to Georgette. She'd have to be a little careful here.

"Grady's a good manager," Georgette said as she leafed nonchalantly through her program. "He understands viti-culture inside and out. I could probably find a place for him at Oak Hill."

Sudden applause drowned out anything more Georgette had to say. Then a spotlight flicked on, the music dipped low, and Delaine walked out onto the runway. She paused in the bright circle of light, looked around, and put a microphone up to her mouth.

"Friends," Delaine began, "I'm absolute *thrilled* that so many of you turned out for my annual Clothes Horse Races. As you know, many of your favorite designers have donated some amazing fall preview items for you to appreciate and bid on. So enjoy the show, pick out a few garments, and please be generous. All of the money earned here today will go to the Loving Paws Animal Shelter. So remember, there are sweet dogs and kitties who are counting on you!"

With that, the room went dark. The crowd seemed to hold its collective breath until the music crashed on and the lights came on. They were colorful and incredibly bright, focused directly on the Mylar runway. The music was the DJ's mash-up of Marilyn Manson's version of "You're So Vain" and Beyoncé's "Run the World."

And then the dizzying parade of models began. The first few models wore filmy, flimsy cottons and silks, the kind of flowing slacks and dresses that you could enjoy and wear right now. Then the show segued into a more autumnal theme, with gilded jackets, skintight pants, flowing skirts, and lightweight suede. The models pranced their way down the runway like Tennessee walking horses, lifting their knees unnaturally high as they remained aloof and unsmiling.

The next grouping of fashion featured evening wear. Black lace gowns, burgundy and dark green dresses, and even some smoking jackets, all worn with multiple strands of beads and opera-length pearls.

To Theodosia's eyes, the fashion show was glitzy, high-energy, and fast-paced. Lots of expensive clothes showed off to perfection by a bevy of attractive, underfed young women.

"Will you look at that ruffled cocktail dress," said Georgette. "Really amazing."

Theodosia turned her attention to the waves of blue ruffles that made up the short flouncy skirt, and then was stunned beyond belief when her eyes traveled upward and she suddenly recognized the model! It was Tanya Woodson. Drew's girlfriend. Or ex-girlfriend, as matters now stood.

Sitting through the rest of the show was difficult for Theodosia. She squirmed and fidgeted, thinking about how strange it was to run into Georgette Kroft and then to see Tanya walking the runway!

When the show came to its grand conclusion, lights blazing and music blasting, all the models came back out and took their final walk down the runway and back. Then Delaine reappeared to make a final plea. She was carrying a little white dog with a curly coat and shiny oil spot eyes.

"Please," she said, holding the wiggling little dog up for the crowd to see, "fall in love with some of the amazing pieces you've just seen here and fall in love with this little guy, too. Then dig deep into your pocketbook and buy. And remember, every penny goes to charity!"

"I just have to have that ruffled cocktail dress," Georgette enthused as she jumped to her feet. "What about you, Theodosia? Did you pick out a few things that you just have to have?"

"Absolutely," said Theodosia, though she really hadn't. She

had one eye trained on the runway, watching the models—Tanya in particular—and saw that they were all now carrying little order sheets. Instructed, no doubt, by Delaine to circulate through the crowds, which were surging back toward the champagne bar and all the racks of clothes.

"In fact, I'm going to put my order in right now," said Theodosia.

"You go, girl," said Georgette.

Theodosia jumped up on the runway, ran to the end of it, and jumped down, pretty much heading off the surging crowd. "Tanya! Tanya!" she called after the waiflike model.

Tanya heard her name called, glanced around, and saw Theodosia. A frown flickered across her face. Not anger, just annoyance. As if Theodosia were a pesky mosquito buzzing about her head.

"What?" Tanya mouthed.

Theodosia continued to push her way through the crowd until she was face-to-face with Tanya. Well, at least face-to-collarbone, since the girl was so doggone tall.

"I need to talk to you," said Theodosia.

"Now what's your problem?" said a petulant Tanya. "Look, I really can't talk right now. I'm supposed to be working, can't you see that?"

But Theodosia wasn't about to take no for an answer. "This won't take long. I just need to ask you a couple of questions."

Tanya's mouth twisted into an unhappy pout. "What?"

"What does *green alien* mean to you?"

Tanya's eyes widened slightly, but she kept her calm. "I have no idea."

"Think hard."

"It's means *nothing* to me!"

"Think harder."

Tanya started to turn away.

"Had Drew been using drugs?" Theodosia asked.

Tanya hesitated, and then turned back. Her face had the harried, frightened look of a trapped animal.

"He was, wasn't he?" said Theodosia. Then, before Tanya could say anything, she added, "It must have been heartbreaking for you. I know you loved him very much."

Now tears sparkled in Tanya's eyes. "Drew tried to . . . managed to . . . clean up in treatment. But then he . . . stumbled."

"Drew started using again?"

Tanya gave an imperceptible nod. "I loved Drew, but he was struggling. He went through drug treatment two separate times."

"Recently?" said Theodosia.

Tanya nodded again.

"Do you think he was using drugs last Sunday? The day he was . . . um, the day he died?"

"I don't know, maybe."

"You lived with him," said Theodosia. "So you must have known if he was still using."

"He . . ."

"Excuse me!" said Delaine. "Theodosia, you haven't bid on a single item of clothing yet. And *you* . . ." She turned blazing eyes on Tanya. "You need to circulate, young lady, and help hustle up some serious sales. I know someone's going to want to purchase that lovely cocktail dress you're wearing!"

Theodosia watched as Tanya eased away from them and melted into the crowd. A smile was pasted back on her face but she still looked achingly sad. As if she'd lost the love of her life. Which she probably had.

And who had been responsible? Theodosia wondered. A disgruntled drug dealer who hadn't been paid? Or something a whole lot more sinister?

"Theo!" said Delaine, a reprimanding tone in her voice. "Are you even *looking* at the clothes? Have you even heard a word I said?"

"I like the dress you're wearing," Theodosia blurted out. She figured she had to say something.

"You do?" Delaine squealed. "That's fantastic. In fact, it might be the perfect dress for you to wear to the Art Crawl Ball this Saturday night! Of course, I'm wearing a sample size, while you're . . . shall we say a size or two larger."

"Thanks a lot," said Theodosia. Just because she ate carbs and didn't starve herself with juice fasts and master cleanses . . . well, she didn't need to be pilloried for it!

"But you are so in luck!" Delaine simpered. "I have that dress in another size and I'm positive it will fit you perfectly. Of course, I can't go rummaging through my inventory right now, dear, because my guests are still here and my poor head is buzzing with a *hundred* different things that I simply must do. But I promise I'll find your gown and drop it by your house tonight."

"*Theodosia.*" *Theodosia was* trying to make her escape, but now Georgette was at her elbow. "I was wondering . . . I'm having a small wine-tasting party Thursday night at Oak Hill and I was thinking you might like to attend."

"Really?" Theodosia was completely taken aback. This invitation had come zooming out of left field. After all, they'd only met.

"Yes, really," said Georgette. "You seem like a very nice person. And I'd like you to come to an understanding that I am, too." She smiled broadly. "Besides, I have an ulterior motive."

"What's that?" Theodosia couldn't imagine what it could be.

Georgette's eyes danced with mirth. "One of these days perhaps you and I could put our heads together and plan some sort of joint tea and wine tasting." She hesitated. "Tea and wine. Twine."

"Twine," said Theodosia. "That's an interesting idea." She wasn't sure it was, but she figured she owed Georgette a polite response.

"Then you'll come?" asked Georgette.

"Sure. I'd like to very much."

"Bring a friend if you want. A date, a plus one, or whatever people are calling it these days. Of course, my wine tasting won't be as fancy-shmancy as the one at Knighthall. Just a few friends and neighbors drinking wine and enjoying some barbecued chicken and ribs. No beautiful people, no paparazzi."

And hopefully no murder, Theodosia thought to herself.

After retrieving her car from the valet, Theodosia drove back to the Indigo Tea Shop, dodging down a few back alleys, trying to avoid the late afternoon traffic. When she arrived, she was pleased to find that Drayton was still there. He was wearing a long black apron and wielding a broom, poking at an insignificant amount of crumbs under one of the tables. When he heard her come in through the back, he stopped his cleaning, and looked a little startled.

"You're back," he said.

"Yes, I am," Theodosia told him breathlessly. "Because I have news. News with a capital *N!*"

"What's up?" said Drayton.

Theodosia tossed her bag onto one of the bare tables. "Number one, your good friend Jordan Knight failed to disclose some critical information about his son."

"What are you talking about?"

She kicked off her shoes. "Drew Knight did a stint in spin dry."

Drayton's face went completely blank. "What on earth is *that* supposed to mean?"

"Translation," said Theodosia. "Drew went through drug treatment. In fact, he scooted through twice."

Drayton's brows shot up. "Seriously? Just recently?"

"I got the impression that . . . yes. That his last stint in rehab was fairly recent."

Drayton looked stunned. "I had no idea. How on earth did you find this out?"

"Tanya the stick woman told me."

"The model?"

"Yup," said Theodosia. She was more than a little worked up now. "She was one of the models at Delaine's show today. And you know what else? Haley found out that *green alien* is slang for heroin."

"Seriously?" said Drayton. He looked dumbfounded.

"Anyway, the crux of the matter is, Jordan and Pandora haven't been giving us all the facts. How on earth are we supposed to solve this murder if we don't have all the facts!"

"Well, we technically weren't supposed to *solve* it," Drayton said slowly.

But Theodosia was on a tear. "Hear me out, please, because I've been noodling this around." She rose up on her toes and came down. "What if Drew's murder had nothing at all to do with Pandora or Jordan or their silly winery? Or even the golf course people or Georgette Kroft at Oak Hill? What if Drew was killed because a drug deal went bad?"

Drayton cocked his head at her. "How so?"

"What if Drew absconded with some drugs or stiffed his dealer or something like that? And then the drug dealer wanted to, *had* to, kill Drew to make an example of him!"

Drayton stared at her. "That sounds utterly preposterous."

"No," said Theodosia, shaking her head. "It sounds like reality. Sadly, that's how the world operates these days. That's the kind of story that's blasted at us in newspaper and TV headlines all the time!"

Drayton leaned his broom against a chair and faced her, sadness evident on his face. "You're telling me I live in the bubble of this perfect little tea shop and don't always consider that real evil can intrude."

"None of us want to think about it intruding," said Theodosia. "Because it's always painful. But now, knowing what we do . . ." She shrugged. "Really, Drew's death . . . it could be as simple as that. As *stupid* as that."

"I suppose you're right," said Drayton. He was slowly coming around to her way of thinking.

"So the important thing," Theodosia continued, "is to get Jordan and Pandora to really truly level with us. That's if they still want our help."

"I think they do," said Drayton. "No . . . I *know* they do. Jordan called me a couple of hours ago, right after you left. He was in agony—I could hear it in his voice."

"What did he want?"

"I think he mostly wanted to talk, to hear a friendly voice. Of course, we were busy and I was barely able to give him two minutes. But I did ask him about the golf course people. And interestingly enough, it turns out that I know one of them."

"Who is that?"

"Donny Hedges."

Theodosia thought for a moment. "I think Jordan might have mentioned that name to me when I was out there yesterday."

"Well, I'm acquainted with Hedges because he used to serve on the board of directors at the Opera Society."

"Do you know Hedges well enough to go talk to him?"

"I think I do. Although he might not be very happy when he finds out why we're there."

"Still," said Theodosia, "if we're going to be thorough, we should go see him."

"Maybe we could drive out to Plantation Wilds tomorrow afternoon, after we finish with the Downton Abbey tea.

Miss Dimple will be here helping out, so she can stick around for the cleanup, too. Yes, I think we have to talk to Hedges, if only to clear our mind."

"Or clear him as a suspect," said Theodosia. "Okay, I've also got a kind of surprise invitation for you."

"What's that?"

"I ran into Georgette Kroft today at Delaine's show. And Georgette invited me to her wine-tasting party Thursday night at Oak Hill."

Surprise lit Drayton's face. "No! Just like that?"

"No, not just like that," said Theodosia. "First we circled each other like a pair of Komodo dragons ready to snap each other's heads off, then we decided to make nice."

"Seriously?"

"Actually, it wasn't all that dramatic. But strangely enough, I found Georgette to be a rather reasonable and respectable person. Which is another reason why I think we should accept her invitation."

"You don't think she's a killer?"

Theodosia hesitated. "I suppose there's an outside chance. I mean . . . nothing about this case is crystal clear."

Drayton swiped the back of his hand across his mouth. "Going to Oak Hill and snooping around really could be construed as part of our investigation, don't you think?"

"It really could," agreed Theodosia. "Along with drinking wine."

"In that case," said Drayton, "I think we should go."

10

❧

Theodosia loved her little cottage. When she approached it from the street, the gabled roof, cobblestone walk, and tumble of ivy always set her heart to racing. When she was cozied up inside, her heart slowed to a warm and satisfied pitty-pat.

The living room featured a rustic beamed ceiling, polished parquet floor, and brick fireplace set into a wall of beveled cypress panels. Tucked around a small coffee table, her chintz sofa and damask chairs made for a cozy seating arrangement. In the small but adequate foyer, hunter green walls were hung with antique brass sconces and the floor was red brick.

Her kitchen, however, left something to be desired. The appliances were old but adequate, the linoleum floor not so good, and the cabinets just plain awful. Unfortunately, the kitchen wasn't something that could be corrected piece by piece. Two general contractors had told her that the kitchen renovations should really be done in one fell swoop and she believed them. Max was of the same opinion, so there you go.

Still, as Theodosia sat at her kitchen table, picking through a stack of photos, thinking about creating a couple of scrapbook pages of past themed teas, the overall feeling in the kitchen was one of hominess and comfort. Her collection of teapots helped foster that impression, of course, as well as her perfect little kitchen table. She'd found it in an antique shop over in Goose Creek. A lovely traditional-style mahogany table that had some real age on it. She'd teamed it with a pair of Hepplewhite chairs that still needed refinishing. Of course, the grandness of the ensemble was tempered somewhat by the presence of Earl Grey's enormous dog bed stuffed beneath it. Still, it was his house, too. So what could you do?

Bang, bang, bang!

Earl Grey stuck his head out from what he considered his dog cave and gazed up at her. He wanted to know who on earth was banging away at their back door. Should he get up and woof, do his homeland security routine, or just stay curled up and chill?

"It's Delaine," Theodosia told him. "She said she'd drop by tonight with my evening gown."

Bang, bang, bang!

"Yup, that's definitely Delaine," Theodosia said again. Always impatient, always in an all-fired hurry. She decided she'd better let Delaine in before she tried to bundle up her gown and stuff it through the dog door.

Theodosia hurried to her back door and pulled it open.

"Good heavens!" cried Delaine. "What on earth are you doing cooped up inside your house on a gorgeous night like this? Do you know there's going to be a full moon tonight? Really, you should be outside on the patio enjoying the soft twilight and your lovely garden."

"Nice to see you, too," said Theodosia.

Delaine thrust a large black garment bag into her hands. "Here's your gown, in the perfect size, exactly as promised." She looked around for Earl Grey, stretched a hand out, and just like that, Earl Grey sauntered over to greet her.

If Delaine was brusque and officious with people, she was the polar opposite when it came to cats and dogs. Then she had patience, love, and empathy to spare. And animals responded amazingly well to her. Case in point, Earl Grey was suddenly rolling over on his back, legs akimbo, to get his tummy scratched.

"He loves that," said Theodosia.

"Of course he does. Dominic and Domino love getting tickled, too." Those were Delaine's two Siamese cats that she was head over heels in love with. She considered them a cuter version of children and even had a meow ringtone on her cell phone.

"Would you like a glass of lemonade or sweet tea?" Theodosia asked.

"Mmn," said Delaine, considering. "I think the lemonade."

"Coming right up."

Delaine eyed Theodosia's outfit carefully. "Excuse me, but are you actually wearing *spandex*?" She said it with scorn, as if Theodosia were dressed in long skirts and pantaloons, like Nellie in *Little House on the Prairie*.

"I was about to go for a *run*," Theodosia told her. She poured two glasses of lemonade and then they all trooped outside to sit on the patio. Delaine took a sip of her drink, sighed deeply, and seemed to suddenly let go and collapse in on herself.

Theodosia saw the tiredness etched on her face and reflected in her body language. "You must be exhausted after today."

"I'm brain dead and my feet are killing me," said Delaine.

"But I have to say it was all worth it. After expenses, we raised almost twenty-two thousand dollars."

Theodosia gave a low whistle. "That's very impressive for just an afternoon show."

"And thank goodness the event people I hired are doing the teardown and cleanup at my shop. I don't think I could bear to spend one more moment facing down all that glittery Mylar."

"But it looked great on the runway," said Theodosia.

"It did." Delaine massaged the back of her neck as she glanced around at the garden. "I see most of your plantings finally took hold." Her brows pinched together. "It's not like you have a green thumb or anything."

"Just lucky to have a favorable climate," said Theodosia. Her backyard had been decidedly straggly and bereft of landscaping. Under Delaine's goading, she'd put in dozens of new trees, shrubs, and plants. Now she knew that if she wasn't careful to keep things pruned, the plants would grow and creep and turn the place into a veritable jungle. Then again, Delaine might like that. She'd consider it exotic and verdant.

Delaine tilted her head back, looked sideways, and then did a sort of surprised double take.

"Eep!" Her lips pursed together and she emitted a shrill sound like a little mouse.

"Now what's wrong?" asked Theodosia.

Delaine was staring fixedly across the brick wall that separated Theodosia's cottage from Dougan Granville's former home. "I just got startled because there are . . ." She put a hand to her heart. "There are *lights* burning in Dougan's old house!"

"Oh," said Theodosia. "Not to worry. There's a showing tonight."

Delaine's face crumpled a little. "Oh no."

"The realtor . . . I'm sorry. I probably should have mentioned it to you."

"No," said Delaine. She waved a hand in front of her face. "It's okay. Really."

"Are you sure? We can go back inside if this is going to upset you."

Delaine gave a quick shake of her head. "It's just that thinking about poor Dougan still makes me very sad."

"I'm sure it does," said Theodosia. "It takes time to recover from that kind of heartbreak." Dougan Granville had been murdered on what would have been Delaine's wedding day.

Delaine dropped her head forward and let her shoulders sag. "Yes, it does take time." She sighed. "Probably a *lot* of time."

"Hey!" an exuberant male voice called out. "Hey, Theodosia!"

Earl Grey raised his head and let loose a suspicious *woof*.

"My goodness," said Delaine, lifting her head, suddenly alert. "I think someone is shouting your name over that fence." She wrinkled her nose. "I'd have to say that's rather rude."

There was the distinct sound of crunching gravel and a rustle of leaves, and then Andrew Turner's head poked inquisitively over the fence.

"Hey there!" Theodosia called back. She lifted a hand in a friendly wave.

"Oops, sorry," said Turner as soon as he noticed Delaine sitting next to her on the patio. "I had no idea you had company. Sorry. I didn't mean to intrude or go all Peeping Tom on you."

"No problem," said Theodosia. "Why don't you come on over."

Turner's head disappeared and they could hear footsteps scuffing against cement as he darted out into the alley.

Then a few seconds later he strolled through Theodosia's back gate, a big smile on his handsome face. As Theodosia quickly made introductions, to Delaine and to Earl Grey, she noticed that, halfway through all the pleasantries, Delaine seemed to have brightened considerably.

"So lovely to meet you," Delaine murmured. "You've been . . . ah . . . touring the house next door?"

"Yes, I have," said Turner. "And it's absolutely gorgeous."

"It's stunning," said Delaine. "Oh course, the previous owner did have some decorating help."

"The realtor mentioned the designers at Popple Hill," said Turner.

"As well as *others* who gave creative input," Delaine said pointedly.

"You're sure that house isn't too big for you?" said Theodosia.

"It's roomy, I'll give it that," said Turner. He glanced toward Delaine and studied her for a long moment. "Delaine Dish . . . I know a Hughes Dish from over near Goose Creek. Is he any relation to you?"

Delaine's eyes crinkled as she nodded. "Oh yes, cousin Hughes. He's what you might call a shirttail relative. A second cousin once removed."

"Anyway," said Turner, still focused in on Delaine, "your cousin, once removed that he is, bought a print from my gallery."

"Andrew is the proprietor of The Turner Gallery," Theodosia explained. "Over on Hopper Street."

"Of course," said Delaine. A dreamy look had spread across her face. Suddenly her tension lines were erased and she didn't look quite so exhausted. In fact, she looked downright pert.

Turner persisted. "So, um, is Dish your *married* name?"

Delaine dimpled prettily and her eyes lit up as if South

Carolina Electric & Gas had just thrown their master switch. "I'm not married," she said in a breathy voice.

"Ah," said Turner. He gave it the kind of inflection that indicated keen interest. "Now isn't that a piece of luck."

Theodosia looked from Turner to Delaine. They seemed to be gazing at each other with curiosity, eagerness, and a tiny bit of hunger thrown in for good measure.

"Mr. Turner," said Theodosia. "Can I interest you in a glass of lemonade?" She studied the two of them still smiling intently at each other, pretty much ignoring her. "Or maybe I should break out a bottle of wine?" *And leave the two of you alone?*

Delaine was the first one to break the spell. "Theo, darling," she said, "I'd love to stay and chat with you and your charming friend, but I'm afraid I'll have to take a rain check." Her eyes wandered back to Turner's face. "I'd *adore* the chance to stay and get better acquainted, but I have two more dresses I promised to deliver this evening."

"Of course," said Theodosia. "Another time then."

"We'll definitely make it another time," said Turner.

"I'd like that very much," said Delaine. "It's been . . . delightful to meet you, Mr. Turner."

"Andrew. Please, call me Andrew."

Delaine gathered up her clutch purse and tottered across the patio on sky-high stilettos. She stopped at the back gate, waggled her fingers at him, and said, "And you can call me anytime!"

"She seems awfully nice," said Turner. He was still staring at the rustic wooden gate as if hoping that Delaine might materialize once again. But she didn't. "Do you know—and I hope you don't think this is too forward on my part—but do you know if your friend Delaine has a date for the Art Crawl Ball?"

"I don't believe she does," said Theodosia. She was about to tell Turner that Delaine was in mourning. That her fiancé had been murdered only a few short months ago. Then she bit her tongue and decided not to. Because, really, Delaine had her moments of sadness. But had she been in full-bore sackcloth and ashes mourning? No, she had not. That just wasn't Delaine's style or way of thinking.

"Do you think it would be presumptuous if I invited her to the Art Crawl Ball?" Turner seemed to be fumbling his words a bit. "No, I guess what I'm really saying is, do you think it's too *late* to ask her to the Art Crawl Ball? Because I certainly don't want to insult her with a last-minute invitation." He gave a rueful smile. "Some women can be kind of prickly about that."

"I don't think Delaine would be one bit insulted," Theodosia told him. Truth be told, she knew that Delaine would be over-the-moon thrilled by Turner's invitation. Delaine had even confessed to her last week that she was dying to go to the ball.

"So you think she'd go with me?"

"I think," said Theodosia, "that if you called Delaine at five o'clock on Saturday afternoon, she'd still say yes."

"That's all I needed to hear!"

Theodosia strolled with him to the back gate. "You really like the house?" she asked.

Turned nodded. "It's amazing. Just what I've been looking for. Thanks for kind of introducing us."

"You're welcome."

Turner turned to her, a look of concern on his face. "You're going to the funeral tomorrow?"

Theodosia nodded. "Yes, both Drayton and I are going."

"Me, too," said Turner. He shook his head. "The whole murder is just so . . . bizarre. I mean, this was really just a kid. He wasn't even involved in the business all that much."

"It's very strange," Theodosia agreed.

"And there aren't even any suspects?"

"None that I know of," said Theodosia.

Turner seemed almost down. "Just a shame," he lamented. "A darned shame."

Theodosia thought she might wander next door and say hi to Maggie Twining. But when she saw that the house was dark, she decided to just go for her run.

Once she and Earl Grey got out onto the street, she saw that Delaine had been right. There was a full moon tonight. Silver beams dappled the leaves and cast a moon glow on the streets.

It was late, almost ten o'clock, and Theodosia rarely went out this late for a run. But she'd continued to ponder the murder long after Andrew Turner had left, and she felt a little unsettled. Also, her talk with Georgette Kroft had left her wondering if the woman really was a viable suspect. And her encounter with Tanya had left her feeling oddly sad. The young woman had obviously loved Drew, but had probably been covering for him, too.

Enabling was what professionals called it.

Theodosia wondered if Jordan Knight had enabled his son, too. Had he known about Drew's drug problems? Had he simply turned a blind eye to his son's drug addiction? If so, that was heartbreaking, to say the least.

Earl Grey gave a tug on his leash, as if trying to pull Theodosia's attention back to him.

"You're right," she told him. "I've got to let this thing go for a while. Enjoy the evening and your fine canine company."

Earl Grey tossed his head in agreement.

"So what's it going to be tonight? A jog through White Point Gardens?"

Those were the magic words. Earl Grey tugged again and they were off. Down King Street and headed for the Battery. They ran through the dark night past palatial homes tricked out with pillars, columns, and balustrades, sitting shoulder to shoulder with each other like rich dowagers in their fancy lace and diamonds. Lights twinkled in the windows and Theodosia caught fragments of elegant libraries, crystal chandeliers, and cozy dining rooms.

Then they were at the park, running beneath a canopy of trees that seemed to stretch forever. A stiff breeze hinted at salt, enormous waves, and high adventure as the water rushed in from the Atlantic to pound the shoreline with its oyster shell beach.

It was a good night just to enjoy being alive. To run like the wind and feel your leg muscles warming to the beat.

They turned down Lenwood and slowed their pace, back among the houses now, heading for home. It was full-on dark now, and the old-fashioned round street lamps looked like a string of rosary beads stretching down the cobblestone street.

Nobody was out tonight. No other joggers, dog walkers, or strolling tourists. Probably, Theodosia decided, all the tourists were snugged inside the B and B's and historic inns, sipping their wine, planning their itinerary for tomorrow.

A dark car slid by on the cross street ahead of her. Slowed for a moment, then kept going. Probably tourists rolling in late.

When she hit Tradd Street, Theodosia hooked a right and jogged past the Morgan-Albemarle Home. It was one of Charleston's oldest landmarks, still occupied by Albemarle descendants, and once a year, during the autumn Lamplighter Tour, they graciously threw open their doors for public tours.

She was halfway down Tradd, now heading for home, when another car slid by her. Theodosia wasn't sure, but she thought it might be the same car she'd seen just a few minutes ago.

She felt a small prickle of apprehension work its way up

her spine. She was never frightened when she was out alone at night, but she was always mindful. Charleston tended to be a peaceable city. Then again, she'd just been witness to a murder a couple of days ago.

Picking up the pace, Theodosia and Earl Grey sprinted the last couple of blocks, blasted down their alley, and arrived at their back gate. With no further feelings of uneasiness whatsoever.

In the kitchen, Earl Grey headed for his water dish and Theodosia grabbed a bottle of spring water. It had been a good run, a chance to blow out the carbon and unwind after kind of a crazy day. She took another slug of water and headed upstairs. Now the big question was—hot, steamy shower or bubbly bath? She grabbed a beige cotton robe out of her closet, what she called her spa robe, and stopped in her tracks.

Something up here felt funny. But what?

She frowned, sniffed, and looked around. Something felt . . . different. As if the air had been stirred up, the ions had shifted.

Theodosia stiffened. Had someone come into her house while she and Earl Grey had been out running? Could that happen? *Had* that happened?

Shivering now, even though she was still warm from her run, Theodosia padded back downstairs. She started at the back of her house and worked her way to the front, checking to make sure the doors were locked, double checking the windows.

Like every woman who lived alone, she had dark, creepy thoughts and secret worries that lurked in the deep recess of her mind. Ax murderers, maniacs in ripped straitjackets, zombies. Well, maybe not zombies.

One of the windows in her living room was unlatched. *Whoa.*

But nobody would dare enter her house from the street

side, would they? Wouldn't they get hung up in the rhododendrons and spine-tipped Spanish yucca? Wouldn't they
be noticed immediately if they crawled though her front
window?

"Earl Grey." Theodosia said it calmly and quietly. Her
dog was at her side in a heartbeat, lifting his muzzle and
looking up at her, sensing her concern.

"Good dog. Take a look around, will you?"

Earl Grey padded through the dining room and into the
kitchen. She heard rustling and snuffling for a few minutes,
and then he came pacing back to her. He cocked his head
and threw her a questioning glance, as if to say, "Are you
still worried?"

"Let's go upstairs, fella," she said. "Time for bed." She
had a funeral to attend tomorrow morning so she still had
to pick out some suitable, somber clothing. And then, of
course, there was their Downton Abbey tea. All in all, a
very busy day.

In her bedroom, Theodosia ambled into the turret annex
she used as her reading room. Her laptop computer was sitting on top of a small spinet desk and she decided to do a
quick check of her e-mail. But when she sat down at the
desk, something seemed off. A stack of papers looked like it
had been shifted. A small drawer was slightly open.

Theodosia racked her brain. *Did I do this? In my haste and
hurry, did I leave things like this?*

She hoped so, because the alternative was much too
frightening to contemplate.

Touching a hand to her cheek, Theodosia stroked it gently as she finally let her mind travel in that direction.

Then she dropped a finger to her track pad and called up
her search history.

Turned out the last thing she'd been searching for was
green alien.

Had someone snuck into her house, looked around, had

the nerve to come into her bedroom, and stumbled upon her computer? And then, for some bizarre reason, checked her search history?

The thought chilled her to the bone. Maybe she was over-reacting, maybe she was just being paranoid. But first she decided to check her locks again.

11

~❧~

Magnolia Cemetery, located on the banks of the Cooper River, was the oldest public cemetery in Charleston. Always a place of beauty, peace, and prayer, today it was also a place of great sadness. Long shafts of sunlight filtered down through overhead trees and bounced off Drew Knight's silver metal casket as it rested on a carved wooden bier.

Theodosia and Drayton, seated in the last row of rickety black metal chairs, bowed their heads as the minister, in his somber black suit, said his final words and prayers over Drew's casket. Never having met Drew, except for that horribly unfortunate scene at the winery, Theodosia was still aware of the palpable sorrow that was felt by all the mourners.

"Rest in peace," chanted the minister.

"And let perpetual light shine upon him," responded the mourners.

Theodosia glanced around. Drew's family was sitting in the first row: Jordan, Pandora, and a few aunts, uncles, and cousins. Tom Grady and several of the workers occupied the second row. The girlfriend, Tanya, was also in attendance, but she wasn't sitting in the first row with the family. She had been relegated to the fourth row, the minor leagues of mourning. Dressed in a low-cut black dress that looked more appropriate for the cocktail hour than a funeral, Tanya also sported a large ring with a bright blue stone. Theodosia wondered if that might have been a gift from Drew.

Theodosia also spotted Frederick Welborne, manager at the Lady Goodwood Inn, as well as Andrew Turner crowded in among the mourners. Theodosia thought it was awfully kind on Turner's part. She also found it particularly charitable that he still planned to include Drew Knight's work in his art show. It meant that a small, creative spark of Drew would live on.

Something in Theodosia's peripheral vision made her crank her head to the left. And there, standing against an enormous live oak, almost on the periphery, was Carl Van Deusen. She wondered how well Van Deusen and Drew had known each other. Had they been best buds or just friendly acquaintances?

And, good grief, there was Bill Glass, the sleazy editor/owner of the local gossip rag *Shooting Star.* He was creeping along the perimeter, taking pictures of the mourners. What on earth? Did the man not understand propriety at all? Theodosia glared at Glass. She was so incensed she was ready to spring to her feet and block his next shot. Then Drayton nudged her gently and she reluctantly turned her focus back to the service.

There were a few more gently mumbled blessings and then the minister led everyone in a final song, "How Great Thou Art." Their voices rose in a shaky *a cappella,* blending together in disjointed harmony.

And then, the service concluded, Jordan Knight stood up and stumbled toward the casket. In his hands he clutched a wreath of grapevine that had been woven with a dozen white roses. As he placed it atop his son's casket and bowed his head, his shoulders shook with emotion.

"This is awful," Drayton whispered to Theodosia. "I feel so bad for him. So . . . helpless."

She nodded back as several more relatives clustered around the casket, placing flowers, touching it reverently, and bowing their heads to give it a final kiss.

And then, just like that, the service was over. It really was, as the good book professed, a case of dust to dust. A life had been snuffed out in an instant and now it was being returned to the earth, to take its place in the great continuum of time.

"Do you think we should hurry back to the tea shop?" asked Drayton. He was nervous about their Downton Abbey tea today. "Or do we have time to go through the . . . what would you call it? Receiving line?" He shook his head. "No, that can't be right. Condolence line? That sounds awfully strange, too."

Theodosia slipped her arm through his. "Let's just go tell them how sorry we are one more time."

But as they waited in line, Bill Glass came shlumping along. A camera was carelessly strung around his neck, and he held another one in his hand.

"Glass!" said Theodosia. "What are *you* doing here?"

Bill Glass gave her a sharp look and a sharklike grin. With his slicked-back hair and shiny suit, he reminded her of a sleazy used car salesman.

"This is my kind of event," Glass told her. "A smattering of society duffs, a few tears, a fancy coffin. Makes for good copy."

"That's just awful!" said Drayton.

But Theodosia decided to take full advantage of bumping into him. "I understand you have a reporter working for you who writes food and wine reviews?"

"Yeah," said Glass. "Harvey Flagg. Why? You looking for a choice review?"

"Not particularly," said Theodosia. "But Jordan Knight seems to think your Mr. Flagg has an ax to grind against his winery." She knew investigating the reporter Flagg was a long shot, but decided it was still worth pursuing.

"Not that I know of," said Glass as if this was the first he'd heard. "Flagg's a good guy. Knowledgeable when it comes to local restaurants, a good writer, fairly decent photographer, too."

"I've met him," said Drayton. "He's not a good guy."

"Aw, give him a chance," said Glass. "In fact, I'll even send him over to your place." He smirked. "He can come over today if that's what you want."

"That's not a good idea," said Drayton. "We're terribly busy today."

"We're having a special themed tea," Theodosia explained. "A Downton Abbey tea."

"That's perfect then," said Glass. "A trendy, upscale event like that is just the sort of thing my readers will enjoy. We'll cover it!"

"Oh no!" said Drayton, beginning to sputter.

But Theodosia held up a hand and said, "It's not a good idea."

"Come on," Glass urged.

"Well . . . Flagg would have to promise not to get in the way," Theodosia said with some reluctance.

"He'll be a mouse in the corner," said Glass. "Believe me, it won't be a problem."

As Glass moved off to pester someone else, Drayton turned to her. "Are you sure about this? I don't like the idea of that Flagg fellow just showing up."

"Look at it this way," said Theodosia. "It'll give us a chance to do a kind of assessment of him."

"You mean try to determine if he might be the killer?" said Drayton.

Theodosia sighed. "Well, when you put it that way . . ."

They took their place in line, speaking briefly to several of the relatives, and then moving along until they finally reached Pandora.

"I'm hopping mad!" Pandora cried the moment she saw them. "I talked to Sheriff Anson early this morning and he had absolutely *nothing* new for us. Between you and me, I think the man's an indolent fool! He's done next to nothing to solve this case!"

"I'm sure he's doing something," Theodosia put in. She was aware that Pandora's outburst had caused several heads to turn.

Pandora shook her head. "I don't believe he's even bothered to talk to the golf course people or that awful Georgette Kroft at Oak Hill."

"They're still on our list," Drayton assured her. "We're still committed to checking them out."

"You know," said Theodosia, "I really hate to bring this up. But Drew's drug use . . . it could be an issue." How to phrase this delicately? "It could be related to this case."

Interestingly enough, Pandora gave a resigned nod. "Yes, the boy did have a terrible problem. Even though Jordan never wanted to admit it."

"If Drew was still using drugs," said Theodosia, "it could have put him in contact with all sorts of desperate and unsavory people." She knew it also would have helped if she and Jordan had been honest about this in the first place.

"And desperate people do desperate things," said Pandora. "I'm fully cognizant of that."

"You've spoken with Sheriff Anson about the possibility of drugs being involved?" asked Drayton.

"Yes, I did mention it to him," said Pandora. She glanced

around and lowered her voice. "You know, I was the one who urged Drew to enter a treatment center in the first place."

"That was very courageous of you to intercede," said Drayton. "It couldn't have been easy."

"Believe me, it wasn't," said Pandora. "Talking to Drew about his drug use was like unleashing some crazy kind of hurricane. But I know I did the right thing when I pushed him into treatment. Even though Jordan and that awful, skanky girlfriend were no help at all."

"What's going on with Tanya?" asked Theodosia. "I know she's here today . . . but is she still living in the cottage at the winery?"

"No, thank goodness," said Pandora. "She's finally moved out." She rolled her eyes. "Of course, Drew's Porsche is missing, too, so I certainly wouldn't put it past her. She's a schemer, that one!"

Theodosia and Drayton made their way through the condolence line until they finally reached Jordan Knight. He stood next to Drew's casket, his head bowed, looking like a man who'd lost everything. His watery blue eyes were bloodshot, his skin looked dry and papery, his suit hung limply on his frame.

"I'm so very sorry," said Drayton. He put a hand on Jordan's shoulder and squeezed gently.

"My sympathies," Theodosia whispered. She'd uttered those same words so many times this past week, it felt like rote.

"Please know," Drayton told Jordan, "that justice *will* be served."

But Jordan seemed more despondent that ever before. "I don't know what's going to happen now," he told them in a halting, choked-up voice. "Now that Drew is gone." His head swiveled in a half turn to gaze at the casket and his eyes filled with tears. "Please, if there's *anything* you can do." He stared directly at Theodosia now.

"Really," she whispered. "I am trying."

"We were just talking to Pandora," said Drayton. "And Theodosia here brought up Drew's drug use."

Jordan stiffened, as if he'd been poked with a hot wire.

"We're terribly sorry to bring it up," said Theodosia, jumping in. "But it could be related to Drew's death. A drug dealer, someone he met in treatment . . ."

"Drug treatment," Jordan spat out. "That was particularly useful."

"I'm sure something positive came of it," Theodosia said gently.

"I understand Pandora was the one who convinced Drew to go?" said Drayton.

A harsh look came across Jordan's face and the muscles in his jaw tensed. "Now that Drew is gone, Pandora is starting to work me over again."

"What on earth do you mean?" said Drayton, looking perplexed.

"My soon-to-be-ex-wife is trying to convince me that selling part of the winery to Mr. Tanaka is the smartest smart way to go," said Jordan.

"Is Mr. Tanaka still in town?" Theodosia asked. This came as a huge surprise to her. She assumed the offer from Higashi Golden Brands was old news.

"Yes, of course he's still here!" said Jordan. "Hanging around and forever whispering in Pandora's ear. And now that Pandora can exercise her right to own the majority of shares, she's bent on trying to railroad me." He held up his hand and clenched his fist. "But I swear I'll never let my vineyard go!"

"Absolutely not," said Drayton. "Not after all your hard work."

But Jordan's bravado was short lived. "And even if we

don't sell out," he continued, "Pandora keeps pushing for more red wine production. No more whites, only reds!"

Perhaps that's what sells best," said Theodosia. She didn't think red wine or white wine was really the issue here. What mattered was resolving a murder amid a bunch of grieving people who seemed to enjoy savaging each other.

"That was uncomfortable," said Drayton as he and Theodosia walked slowly back to their car. They passed a tall obelisk and picked their way between two rows of ancient stone tablets.

"Look here," said Drayton, pointing. "The grave of Confederate General Micah Jenkins. Of course, there are lots of soldiers buried here from both sides, Union and Confederate."

"Sad," said Theodosia.

"All wars are a terrible waste," said Drayton. "Magnolia Cemetery seems to be the final resting place for pride, privilege, and sacrifice."

"Don't forget," said Theodosia. "There are also plenty of politicians, pirates, bootleggers, and madams buried here."

"An equal opportunity piece of real estate," agreed Drayton.

Just as they rounded a stone mausoleum with four tall pillars, they saw Pandora talking to someone. Her voice was raised in anger and she was shaking an index finger, looking generally unhappy and out of sorts.

As they drew closer, they saw that she'd buttonholed Andrew Turner and that the two of them seemed to be involved in a heated argument. Or at least Pandora was.

Pandora gazed at Turner and said, "You wouldn't, would you?"

"Of course not!" Turner replied vehemently. "You know me better than that!"

Then, in a surprising move, Pandora stood on her tiptoes and put her arms around Turner, giving him a hug. A moment later, she dashed off.

Turner turned and saw Theodosia and Drayton looking at him with questioning looks on both their faces.

Theodosia lifted an eyebrow. "A problem?" she asked.

Turner looked a little embarrassed. "What can I say? Pandora was afraid that I was going to drop Drew's work from my upcoming show."

"Are you?" said Theodosia.

"Oh no, of course not," said Turner. "There's no way I'd drop Drew. His work is still perfectly deserving to be in the show. I told her that." He nodded, as if to himself, and murmured, "It's only fair."

Theodosia suddenly made up her mind that Andrew Turner might just be the perfect new boyfriend for Delaine. He was kind, considerate, and probably even sweet to his mother.

"You're very kind," she told him.

"Ah," said Turner, "I feel sorry for Pandora. I try to give her business advice from time to time, too. I think Jordan likes the *idea* of making wine, but he's not so much into the sales and marketing part."

"Are they floundering?" Theodosia asked.

Turner frowned. "Yes, they seem to be. Somewhat anyway."

"Then it's very kind of you to give Pandora some business advice, too," said Theodosia as they walked out of the cemetery. She understood firsthand how difficult it was to be a small business owner. When she'd left her marketing job to open the Indigo Tea Shop, she'd had to figure out a laundry list of tasks. Like dealing with leases, payroll, quarterly taxes, inventory, and cash flow. And then there was the day-to-day worry of pleasing customers, staging events, and constantly testing and updating menus. She figured the wine business had to be ten times harder.

Turner walked to his car, a blue Audi that was parked three car lengths behind Theodosia's Jeep. Just as he was getting in, he turned and said, "Oh, hey, I called your friend Delaine."

"What did she say?" Theodosia called back as she pulled open the driver's side door.

A smile lit Turner's face. "She said yes!"

Drayton climbed into the passenger seat, pulled his seat belt across, and immediately began drumming his fingers on the dashboard. "We're late."

Theodosia started her engine. "We're not late."

"We stayed too long. Probably shouldn't have hung around to offer condolences again."

"We'll be okay." Theodosia pulled out into traffic, drove about two hundred feet, and hit her brakes.

"What on earth . . ." was Drayton's startled response as she slalomed her car to the curb.

"Just one minute," said Theodosia, holding up a finger.

"Honestly, we don't have a minute!"

"We do for this," said Theodosia. "Did you see who that was?" The girl who just climbed into the yellow taxi cab?"

"No idea," said Drayton.

"That was Tanya, Drew's girlfriend," said Theodosia. "I need to ask her something." She was already clambering out of the car. Then she made a mad dash across the street, causing a bright green VW bug to swerve around her, all the while calling out, "Wait! Please wait!"

The cab driver, who was almost ready to pull away from the curb, did indeed heed her cry.

Theodosia rushed over to the cab, bent down, and pulled open the back door of the cab. "Hey there," she said to Tanya.

Tanya gazed at her, a fierce light glowing in her eyes. "What do *you* want?"

"I was just wondering how you're doing," said Theodosia.

"Fine," said Tanya, though her lips barely moved.

"One quick question," said Theodosia.

"What's that?"

"Do you know where Drew's Porsche is?"

"No," said Tanya.

"Did you take it?"

"Of course not."

"Did you sell it?" asked Theodosia.

"No. And that's more than one question."

Frustrated, Theodosia said, "Are you sure you don't know where it is?"

A nasty smile played at Tanya's lips. "If you're so smart, why don't you figure that out yourself!"

12

❧

"Oh my goodness," said Theodosia, the minute she and Drayton arrived at the tea shop. "You put tables out on the sidewalk."

"We had to," said Haley. She met them at the door, looking harried and a little nervous. "We got a whole bunch more calls this morning asking for reservations." She thought for a moment. "No, more like *demanding* reservations."

"That's amazing," said Drayton. "And we didn't even have to advertise."

"Just word of mouth," said Haley. "Which shows you how popular these themed teas really are."

"Particularly a Downton Abbey tea," said Theodosia.

"Is Miss. Dimple here?" asked Drayton. He was busy pulling off his jacket and draping an apron around his neck. What he called his tea brewing apron.

"I'm here," called a screechy little voice. Then Miss. Dimple, the tiny plump dynamo who also served as their bookkeeper, came toddling out from the back room. "And I'm so glad you asked me to come and help." Barely five feet tall with a cap of pinkish-blond curls, Miss Dimple was seventy-something but filled with excitement, a sweet-sour wit, and a sharp brand of humor. She was like the Energizer Bunny crossed with your crazy old aunt.

"Who set up the outside tables?" Drayton asked. He glanced at the diminutive Miss Dimple. "You certainly didn't."

Haley held up her right arm and flexed her lithe bicep. "I did. I'm not as scrawny as I look."

"I should say not," said Drayton, clearly impressed. Then he snapped back into work mode. "I take it our luncheon entrées are mostly prepped and ready?"

Haley nodded. "We're in good shape. The kitchen is stuffed to the rafters, but we're ready to rock and roll."

"Tables are set?" Drayton cast a speculative glance at the tea room, where candles flickered and tableware gleamed.

"We just said good-bye to our last morning customer something like twenty minutes ago," said Haley. "And then we barred the door and really hustled our buns to get everything ready."

"We put out the Garnet Rose sterling silver and the Coalport cups and saucers just as you requested," said Miss Dimple. "And I have to say, that tea ware, with the gilded, fluted edges and pink ribbon and botanical designs, is quite spectacular."

"And your friend Mr. Woodrow, from Basically British Antiques, showed up with a couple boxes of stuff that you asked for on loan," said Haley. "So we just kind of arranged the glass decanters and bronze sculptures and pottery and things on the various tables. Tried to make it all look like a pretty still life in an English manor home."

"I particularly love the bronze horse and jockey sculpture and the ceramic bulldog," said Miss Dimple. "They make perfect centerpieces. Very British Empire."

"Yes," said Drayton, surveying their handiwork and finally letting a small smile work its way onto his face. "It all imparts a sort of 'Rule, Britannia!' look and feel."

"You know what?" said Haley, suddenly grinning at Miss Dimple. "It just hit me. You're the spitting image of Mrs. Patmore."

Miss Dimple looked mystified. "Who on earth is that?"

"Come on," said Haley, giggling. "You know. The head cook on *Downton Abbey*."

"Oh her!" said Miss Dimple. She waved a chubby hand. "You sweet silly girl, I don't look anything remotely like her!"

But Haley's remark had set Theodosia and Drayton to giggling as well. Because Miss Dimple looked very much like Mrs. Patmore!

At twelve o'clock sharp, you'd have thought Big Ben itself had bonged out welcoming chimes to come and get it. Because at that precise moment, a throng of eager tea goers clustered at the Indigo Tea Shop's front door, ready for the Downton Abbey tea to begin.

Theodosia and Drayton quickly snapped to, checking their reservation sheet, welcoming all the various parties, and seating them at their reserved tables. Then they hustled back to the front counter to grab the tea that Drayton had set to brewing.

Happily, a lot of familiar faces had showed up for this special luncheon. Delaine was there, of course, bringing along her sister, Nadine, as well as two other friends.

In fact, as Theodosia glanced around, she saw that easily two-thirds of the tables were occupied by Indigo Tea Shop regulars. Timothy Neville, the crusty, long-reigning director of Charleston's Heritage Society, had showed up with two guests in tow. And Brooke Carter Crocket, the jeweler who ran Heart's Desire, had rounded up a group of friends and was seated outside on what they now considered the front patio.

As Miss Dimple circulated with a teapot in each hand, Theodosia and Drayton greeted each of their guests. In her spare time (*what* spare time?) Haley had created cute little paper petal envelopes with squares of English toffee tucked inside as favors. Once those were sufficiently oohed and ahed over, Theodosia's team quickly moved into place and delivered their first course—Lady Crawley's fruit trifle. Drizzled with honey-lemon dressing, this mélange of cake, pudding, strawberries, raspberries, and blueberries proved to be a huge hit, drawing several requests for recipes.

Once the fruit trifle had been enjoyed by all, and had disappeared all too quickly, Theodosia and Miss Dimple each brought out a large silver tray. Each tray was heaped with apricot scones as well as Haley's own version of Mr. Carson's Crumpets. Guests could choose one or the other— or even both. And wisely, most chose both. Frothy dollops of Devonshire cream and satin puddles of lemon curd served as tasty accompaniments.

Their third course consisted of tea sandwiches, an area in which Haley had clearly outdone herself. Each table received a three-tiered stand laden with small finger sandwiches that included fillings of curried chicken, cucumber and cream cheese, crab salad, and smoked salmon.

When these were brought out, all the guests seemed to pause happily and let loose a collective "Ahhhh." Which gave Theodosia, Drayton, and Miss Dimple a little breathing space, too.

"It's going very well," Theodosia whispered to Drayton as she slipped between tables with a fresh pot of Assam.

"Don't be fooled," he whispered back. "It's controlled chaos."

As Theodosia stopped to pour refills for Delaine and her guests, Delaine was all a-twitter.

"You'll never guess who called me last night," Delaine said to Theodosia. Dressed in a bright blue dress, she was grinning from ear to ear, and the feather on her matching blue hat bobbed and dipped with each excited jerk and motion.

"No," said Theodosia, "I probably can't guess." She knew darned well that Andrew Turner had followed through on his promise to call Delaine. Really, the man had been practically smitten!

"That darling Andrew Turner called me!" Delaine announced loudly to Theodosia and anyone else who was remotely within earshot. "He invited me to be his date for the Art Crawl Ball!"

"Isn't that lovely," Nadine simpered. She was Delaine's older sister, practically a spitting image of her except for a sharper jaw—and a sharper tongue. "But hasn't your invitation come awfully late? Is that really socially acceptable?"

Delaine was too excited about her upcoming date to be drawn into a silly hissy fit with her sister. "That's because we just *met,* dear," she explained in a saccharine tone. "Because Theodosia just *introduced* us last night!"

"How sweet," said Nadine, though she didn't display one bit of joy for her sister.

"A gallery owner," said one of Delaine's friends at the table. "Good for you. Keep your heels high and your standards even higher!"

"Now I'm going to have to conjure up a gown to wear," Delaine went on. Then she giggled happily.

"Good thing I own an entire shop filled with fabulous ball gowns."

"Then I'm sure you'll find something wonderful to wear," agreed Theodosia.

"Are you still going to do your lips?" asked Nadine.

"Excuse me?" said Theodosia. Just what would Delaine do to her lips?

"Hoping to," said Delaine. She pulled a jeweled compact from her bag and studied her pouty red lips. "For some reason I'm losing a little fullness in my upper lip."

"Turtle lips," proclaimed Nadine. The two other women stared pointedly at Delaine's lips.

"You have nothing of the sort!" said Theodosia. Delaine's lips looked just fine to her. Then again, her own lips looked fine. Didn't they?

"Oh!" said Delaine, as if something else had just occurred to her. She snapped her compact shut and said, "I've decided to donate a lovely designer handbag and scarf to the Art Crawl Ball's silent auction." She gazed at Theodosia. "You should donate something, too, Theo. I think it would be quite appropriate. Maybe you could put together a basket filled with some of your sweet little lotions and potions."

"You mean my T-Bath products?" said Theodosia.

"Or you could create a lovely tea party in a basket," said Delaine. "You do that so well. With all your teas and jams and jellies and whatnot."

"Something to think about," said Theodosia, who already had a plan in place to donate a basket.

When the last course, the dessert course, was served, Theodosia really did heave a huge sigh of relief.

"Oh joy," she told Drayton. "We're coming down to the home stretch."

"And our guests are loving it," said Drayton.

Haley peeked her head out of the kitchen. "Are they really?" she asked in a stage whisper. "How do they like the desserts?" She'd knocked herself out with all the food, but was especially proud of her Banbury tarts, shortbread, and cupcakes topped with frosting that had been etched and cross-hatched to resemble British tweed.

Drayton put his thumb and forefinger together and gave

her the okay sign. "Trust me," he told her, "our guests are delighted. They're riding a veritable sugar high."

"So there's not that much for us to do anymore," said Theodosia. "Except circulate and pour refills."

"Theodosia!" Timothy Neville's voice rang out, strong and imperious, belying his octogenarian status.

Theodosia was at his table in a heartbeat. "Yes? More tea for all of you?"

Timothy smiled at her. A grin that stretched across his thin face and made her think of a Hans Holbein painting she'd seen of an old English aristocrat.

"Now that you have a moment," said Timothy, "I want to introduce you to my guests. This is Sally and Roger Shepherd."

"Nice to meet you," said Theodosia. She smiled. "Nice to have a little *time* to meet you now that I'm not flying around like a crazed banshee."

"Sally and Roger are major donors to the Heritage Society," Timothy explained. From the proud way he said it, Theodosia knew they were probably big buck donors.

"It's been a lovely tea," said Sally, smiling up at Theodosia.

"We're real *Downton Abbey* fans," said Roger. "So this has been a rare treat for us."

"And everything has been flawless," Sally marveled. "Not just the food, but the service and flowers and décor, too. Really, as good or better than tea at the Connaught in London."

"Or Le Marais in Paris," said Roger.

"We try very hard to make everything special," said Theodosia. And from the praise she was receiving, it looked like they'd succeeded.

Timothy Neville, always a fan of British antiques, said, "That lovely china you used today. It's Coalport, correct?"

Drayton overheard him and quickly stopped at the table.

"Indeed it is," said Drayton, pleased. "You see that lovely fluted edge and swath of pink ribbon? Hand-painted, of course." He and Timothy were longtime friends, as well as antique lovers and history buffs. And Drayton had served on the Heritage Society's board of directors for as long as anyone could remember.

Then Timothy introduced Drayton to the Shepherds, whom, it turned out, Drayton already knew. And Theodosia made a grand dash to the front counter, where, wonder of wonders, customers were requesting take-home orders of scones and were also buying multiple tins of tea.

Another thirty minutes later and the tea room was beginning to empty out. A few guests lingered at tables, while Haley and Miss Dimple quietly cleared dishes from the tables that had been vacated.

Timothy's guests, the Shepherds, had since departed, but Timothy was immersed in conversation with Drayton.

As Theodosia slid by him, Drayton said, "Theo. A moment?"

Theodosia stopped. "Yes?"

"I was just filling Timothy in about Knighthall Winery."

Theodosia was taken aback. "Concerning . . . what exactly?"

Timothy's ancient face creased in a knowing smile. "He was telling me about your investigation."

"It's not really—" began Theodosia.

"Tut tut," said Timothy. "Let's not be coy. We both know where your rather prodigious talents lie."

"Okay," said Theodosia. *Whatever. Hard to pull the wool over Timothy's eyes.*

"Timothy is rather knowledgeable when it comes to fine wine," said Drayton.

"I'm not sure I'd classify Knighthall Winery's product as fine wine," said Theodosia. "I think it retails for something like twelve dollars a bottle."

"Still," said Drayton. "Timothy lends a certain perspective."

"And that is?" said Theodosia, casting an inquisitive glance at Timothy.

"A tough row to hoe," said Timothy, carefully enunciating each word. "There have been several South Carolina wineries that have limped along and managed to produce a few good years. But of the eight or nine startups this state has seen, about half have closed."

"That kind of track record doesn't bode well for Knighthall," said Theodosia.

"I think," said Timothy, "from what Drayton's told me, they've got bigger problems than growing grapes in a former tobacco field in hundred-degree weather."

"We've got to do these dishes by hand," said Haley. She was up to her armpits in sudsy water, scrubbing and rinsing, handing off clean plates to Miss Dimple.

"I appreciate that," said Drayton. "Since those dishes are quite delicate." He was lounging in the doorway to the kitchen, his back propped against the doorjamb, sipping a well-deserved cup of tea.

"Did you know that your bow tie is all crooked?" said Miss Dimple.

Drayton didn't rise to the bait. "If that's the only thing that's askew about me, I'd say I came out of this luncheon relatively unscathed."

"It really was a success, wasn't it," said Theodosia.

Drayton turned to face her. "It was a triumph! And not only that, that awful Harvey Flagg was a no-show. So we really lucked out."

"I'm just glad we're closed for the rest of the afternoon," said Haley. "Otherwise I'd for sure go bonkers."

"Is there even any food left?" asked Drayton.

"Barely a few crumbs," said Haley. "What they didn't eat at lunch, they purchased for takeout. Leftover sandwiches, scones, crumpets, you name it. I think I could have bagged up the crusts and auctioned them off."

"Now, now," said Miss Dimple. "You told me I could take some of the crusts home with me so I can feed the neighborhood ducks."

"Are you guys going to pack up all those British antiques we borrowed for centerpieces?" Haley asked.

"Actually," said Drayton, "I was hoping you and Miss Dimple could handle that. Theodosia and I have an errand we have to attend do."

"We can pack everything up," said Miss Dimple. "No problem. We saved all the boxes and bubble wrap, even though some of it got popped." She grinned. "No matter how old I get, I can never resist bubble wrap."

But Haley wasn't quite as accommodating. "Errands," she said with a snort. "Hah! I bet you two are off on another weird, creepy-crawly mystery mission!"

13

❧

It may have been a mystery mission, but it wasn't particularly weird or creepy-crawly.

"This is gorgeous," said Drayton as they drove through the stone pillars that marked the front entrance for Plantation Wilds. "Look at how amazingly green everything is. It looks almost artificial. Like the turf you see on football fields."

"When you hire a cadre of agronomists and greens keepers who endlessly cut, mow, water, and fertilize, this is the kind of grass you eventually end up with," said Theodosia.

"Still," said Drayton, "it's very impressive."

"Drayton, you act like you've never visited a golf course before."

Drayton lifted his chin just a notch. "Actually . . . I haven't."

Theodosia followed along the road, which swept around several of the fairways and greens, stopping at one point to allow several golf carts to trundle across the road in front of her. Then she continued on to the clubhouse.

Built to resemble an old South Carolina rice plantation,

the clubhouse was painted pale yellow with white trim and featured a high, slanted roof, a wide porch on three sides, and a two-story portico.

"This is nice, too," said Drayton as two valets in golf shirts and knickers quickly sprang to attention and pulled open their car doors.

"Maybe you'll get so inspired you'll decide to take up golf," Theodosia joked as they headed into the clubhouse.

"What . . . me?" said Drayton. "Oh no, I don't think I'm the sporting type at all."

"Could've fooled me," said Theodosia.

They quickly located the business office and told the young fellow at the front desk that they were there to see Donny Hedges.

"You're sure you made an appointment?" Theodosia asked under her breath.

Drayton nodded. "We should be all set."

Three minutes later, they were ushered into Donny Hedges's office.

Hedges was tall and muscular, with a suntanned face and a grip like a professional wrestler. He was probably in his midfifties, but had the physique of a man ten years younger. Basically, he looked like he belonged at a golf club.

"Donny," said Drayton, extending his hand. "Wonderful to see you again."

"Drayton, welcome," said Hedges. The walls of his office were decorated in a green-and-white-plaid wallpaper, and antique gold clubs were displayed in a glass case.

Drayton quickly introduced Theodosia, then they all gazed out the windows of Hedges's corner office, which offered a spectacular view of the superbly manicured golf course and, in particular, the eighteenth hole.

"This looks like a great course," Theodosia told Hedges. There was a beehive of activity going on down below. Golf carts disgorging golfers, caddies unloading clubs, workers speeding around in more industrial-looking carts.

"Do you play golf?" Hedges asked her. "I know Drayton doesn't, but you look like you might play an occasional round or two."

"I do play," said Theodosia.

"Do you have a favorite course?" asked Hedges. He gestured for them to take a seat in the armchairs that faced his desk.

"I'm fairly partial to Palmetto Dunes at Hilton Head."

"A fine course," said Hedges. "But perhaps we might persuade you to play here sometime."

"I'd like that very much," said Theodosia.

"Hey," Hedges said to Drayton. "The Met's doing *La Bohème* this season."

"So I understand," said Drayton.

Hedges smiled at Theodosia. "Are you an opera fan, too?"

"Love it," said Theodosia.

"Donny," said Drayton, leaning forward in his chair and getting down to business now. "I explained a little bit about what I was after when we spoke on the phone."

"The mess at Knighthall Winery," said Hedges. He made a grimace and said, "Shocking, just shocking. When that poor boy came spilling out . . . well, I've never been so shocked in my entire life. Do you know . . . are the authorities any closer to catching his killer?"

"There are a few suspects," said Drayton.

This was Theodosia's cue to jump in. "Jordan and Pandora Knight seem to think that you and your board of directors are bent on engineering some sort of hostile takeover of their land." She didn't tell him that Pandora had out and out accused him of murdering Drew. Better to ease into things.

"I made a couple of *offers* on their land," said Hedges. He blinked and looked up thoughtfully. "Last one was maybe a year or so ago?"

"But nothing recently," said Drayton.

"No," said Hedges. "They made it pretty clear they weren't interested in selling."

"But you were interested in buying," said Theodosia. She was curious as to just how interested he was.

"Oh yeah," said Hedges. "Knighthall has a good-sized parcel of land, not all of it under cultivation. And since it adjoins Plantation Wilds, it would've made for an ideal situation."

"You'd build another golf course?" said Drayton.

"Two or three if I could," said Hedges. "Then we could enlarge the clubhouse and put up a condo development, too." He grinned happily, as if relishing the idea. "Golfers just love condos."

"I'm wondering," said Theodosia, "if you've had any interaction with Jordan or Pandora Knight recently. Something they might have construed as angry or hostile?"

Hedges looked blank. Then a look of dark suspicion came across his face. "Wait a minute. Do those two fruitcakes think *I* had something to do with that kid's death?"

Drayton looked nervous, so Theodosia answered for him. "It's come up in conversation."

"Hey!" said Hedges, sounding outraged. "I'm a legitimate businessman here, not some crazy killer." He slapped a hand down hard on his desk. "And I don't go around hiring hit men, if that's what you're asking."

"I'm sorry," said Theodosia, "but that kind of is what we're asking."

"I was as shocked as everyone else," said Hedges. He focused his angry gaze on Drayton. "Drayton, you *know* me! We served on the Opera Society together!"

"Apologies," said Drayton. "We didn't mean to upset you."

"Well, you did," said Hedges. His right hand reached out

and grabbed a bright yellow sponge rubber golf ball off his desk. Squeezing it hard, he said, "Honestly, I hope other people aren't thinking the same thing . . . gossiping about me."

"They're not," said Theodosia. "I promise. This came only from Pandora Knight."

Hedges still wasn't convinced. "You're sure about that?"

"You have my word," said Drayton.

"Ah . . . jeez," said Hedges. He touched a hand to his heart. "Pandora never liked me . . . so I'd hate to have people talking."

"They're not," Drayton assured him.

"We're sorry to have upset you," said Theodosia. "Really, you have our sincere apologies."

"So why are you even *asking* questions like that?" said Hedges. He was still very upset.

"We're trying to help Jordan Knight," said Drayton.

"Help him?" said Hedges. "Help him how?"

"By trying to find the killer," said Theodosia.

"Well, that went well," said Drayton, once they were back in the car.

"Ah . . . not," said Theodosia. "I sure hope it hasn't destroyed your friendship."

"Shredded it a little," said Drayton as they drove along. "But there are probably a few pieces still intact."

"Maybe you were right," said Theodosia. She slowed to let a golf cart scuttle across in front of her, the golfers laughing and joking, oblivious to her courtesy.

"About what?"

"When you said that maybe we should just let this go."

"Yes, but . . . excuse me, this doesn't sound like you," said Drayton. "You're never one to capitulate."

"I know," said Theodosia. "But this . . . this wanton tirade of accusations that keep spewing out of Jordan and

Pandora. I mean, no wonder Sheriff Anson is playing it so close to the vest. They've probably assaulted him with all kinds of crazy theories."

"He's a professional," said Drayton. "I'm sure he's able to sort through them."

"Maybe," said Theodosia. "And maybe they have him running around in circles, but not homing in on the real killer."

"You make it sound as if they don't want the killer found."

"Not at all," said Theodosia. "I just think they're so mired in grief and anger that they're grasping at straws." They exited the Plantation Wilds property and hooked a left onto County Road 4.

"Going to go right past Knighthall Winery," said Drayton.

"You know what?" said Theodosia. "Why don't we drop by and pay them a surprise visit."

"For what purpose?" Drayton asked. "To ask Jordan Knight some more questions?"

"Not questions per se. Just . . . well, I'd like to get him talking about Drew again. See how much he really knew about the drugs and things."

"You might be opening up a can of worms," said Drayton.

"I think it's already open," said Theodosia.

But when they rolled into the winery, the place looked practically deserted. Not a single car in the visitors' parking lot, a CLOSED sign hanging in the window of the tasting room.

"Nobody home," said Drayton.

"There has to be somebody around."

They climbed out and stood for a moment. The hot sun lasered down on them while a subtle breeze allowed a modicum of cool. A nearby *clunk-thunk* drew their attention. Two workers had just emerged from the large barn, one older man, one young man barely out of his teens. Each was struggling under a large piece of equipment. Theodosia thought they looked like pumps of some sort.

"Excuse me," said Theodosia. "Is Jordan Knight around?"

The workers stopped in their tracks and set their loads down. "I don't think so," the older one said.

"How about Pandora?" called Drayton.

"I'm not sure," said the older worker. "Maybe I can help you?"

"Is Tom Grady around?" Theodosia asked.

Both workers nodded.

"He should be. At least he was an hour ago," said the younger one. Theodosia recognized him as the unfortunate fellow who'd pried the lid off the barrel last Sunday. She wondered how these guys fit into the puzzle, if at all.

"Maybe we should just wander around the grounds," said Drayton. "See if we stumble upon him."

"Let's try his office first," said Theodosia.

They walked inside the enormous barn and were immediately hit by the rich aroma of fresh, peppery grapes.

"Quite an interesting scent," said Drayton, wrinkling his nose. "But awfully potent."

"When you own a winery," said Theodosia, "I don't think there's any escaping it."

Tom Grady's office door was closed, so Theodosia knocked on it. When he didn't appear, she called out, "Mr. Grady? Hello?" Still nothing. She looked at Drayton, who shrugged.

"Maybe he's not here," said Drayton. "Maybe he drove into town or something."

"Only one way to find out." Theodosia grasped the doorknob and pushed the door open. Drayton was right. The office was empty, the desk looking orderly. Nobody home.

"So let's just wander around," suggested Drayton. "We'll probably run into Grady if he's here."

They wandered into the interior of the production area,

past the enormous holding tanks, taking care when they stepped over a tangle of plastic hoses that lay on the floor. Then they emerged through the back door.

"This is so lovely and picturesque," said Drayton. He was admiring the same view that Theodosia had found so charming just two days ago. "I can understand why Donny Hedges was so interested in buying this land. Oh, and look at that charming little cottage. Is that where the offices are located?"

"That's where Drew and Tanya had been living," said Theodosia. "The offices are . . ." She gestured to the left. "Over there. In the back half of the tasting room."

"So let's go take a look," said Drayton.

They crossed the back parking lot, dodging around a pickup truck and huge stacks of plastic bins that were stained purple, and walked in the back door.

"Jordan," Drayton called out. "Are you in here?" He paused. "Pandora?"

They strolled into Jordan Knight's office, which, to Theodosia's eyes, didn't look any different than it had on her first visit. Same desk, same chairs, same parson's table crowded with wine bottles.

"Looks like they're having some sort of party," said Drayton, eyeing the bottles.

"I think it's always like that," said Theodosia.

"Just wine tasting, huh? Business as usual."

"I guess," said Theodosia.

They walked through the tasting room, where bottles of wine, corkscrews, and wineglasses were enticingly displayed. There were also racks of T-shirts and caps, all emblazoned with the Knighthall Winery logo. A long, mahogany bar ran the length of the room.

"This breaks my heart," said Drayton. "They have everything in place but not a single customer."

"Chalk it up to the murder," said Theodosia. "Would

you really want to do a wine tasting at a place where the last wine tasting ended in total disaster?"

Drayton looked glum. "I suppose not."

"Besides," Theodosia went on, "they're closed right now. For an indefinite period of time. Jordan told me that. And it was even announced in the newspaper."

"Still . . . this just makes me sad."

"What makes me sad," Theodosia said, "is that we don't have a clue as to what really happened. In fact, nobody seems to."

They walked out the front door then ambled along a brick walkway that led to the actual vineyard. Leafy grape vines twisted and tangled onto thick wires that were stretched between rough wooden posts. Most of the vines had been picked clean, but a few still had bunches of small purple grapes. They were ripe and kind of dusty looking and, Theodosia thought, looked exactly like the photos of grapes that you saw in fancy food and wine magazines.

"I suppose when Knighthall is open," said Drayton, "coming out here to visit the fields is an important part of their wine tour."

"I would imagine so," said Theodosia. They stepped off the walkway and wandered slowly down a row of grapevines. "It's really remarkable, isn't it?" She held out a hand and cupped a bunch of grapes that dangled from a twisty, turny vine. "These tough grapevines have tucked into this soil and managed to produce a rather remarkable crop of fruit."

"Grapes have been grown in hot climates and on rough terrain for countless centuries," said Drayton. "Look at Sicily or parts of Italy and Greece."

"Pretty amazing when you think about it," Theodosia agreed. She was starting to enjoy their little impromptu ramble through the vineyard.

"From what I understand," said Drayton, "wine is all

about *terroir*—the special characteristics of the soil, climate, and aspects of a vineyard. It all contributes to a wine's unique taste."

"You know more about grapes and winemaking than you've let on," said Theodosia. "I'm impressed."

"Oh no, I'm just a voracious reader. It's amazing what one can pick up from books."

"Funny you should mention that," said Theodosia. "That's where I turned when I needed to know more about tea." She smiled. "Before I met you."

"Still," said Drayton, "there's nothing like actual tea tasting to really educate the palate."

"On-the-job training," Theodosia agreed. "Always the best."

They'd wandered right into the heart of the vineyard now, where an occasional cicada buzzed and a few white cabbage butterflies fluttered leisurely.

A blackbird flew past Theodosia and landed on top of one of the thick wooden stakes that held up the vines. His shiny eye surveyed her calmly, then he leaned forward and, neat as you please, plucked a perfect purple-green grape with his beak. Charmed, Theodosia was aware of the rustling of leaves nearby. A welcome breeze? Or—

Drayton interrupted her thought process. "I suppose we should be getting back. There's nothing happening out here."

The words had barely left his mouth when a strange noise started up a few rows over from them. It was a ratcheting, mechanical sound, like a compressor being fired up.

"What on earth?" said Theodosia. The *rata-ta-ta* was growing ever louder! She turned to say something to Drayton, to warn him, and was suddenly hit in the back of the head with a gush of wet liquid. "Drayton!" she screamed.

He gazed at her quizzically just as they were both suddenly enveloped in a thick white cloud.

"What's going on?" Drayton gasped.

Theodosia felt the back of her throat go thick with a dry, powdery substance and knew in an instant what was happening. She grabbed Drayton's hand and gave a hard pull. "Come on!" she cried. "We have to get out of here! I think someone's spraying the grapevines with insecticide!"

Coughing and choking now, they bent forward, trying to scramble away from the terrible toxic cloud. But the motorized sprayer was revving like crazy now, spreading the fumes and clouds everywhere!

Drayton pulled out a hanky and covered his mouth. "I can't see which way to go!" he shrilled.

Theodosia wasn't sure how to escape, either. They seemed enveloped in the heavy gray cloud. It was everywhere! Stumbling, trying to fight a rising tide of panic, she managed a quick glance upward and caught a glint of sun blazing overhead. And knew instinctively that escape meant running to their left. "This way!" she told him in a strangled voice. "Try not to inhale!"

"I'm . . . trying," came Drayton's voice. His breathing sounded weak and labored.

Theodosia urged him forward. "Come on! Run!" She stepped aside and pushed Drayton in front of her. Then she placed her hands squarely in the small of his back and pushed like she'd never pushed before. Choking and sniffling, anger sizzling inside her, she propelled Drayton forward. They were both wheezing now, as if their lungs were on fire. Theodosia's eyes were watering like crazy, and a thin film of tears made it almost impossible to see.

And just when she thought they'd never fight their way free of whatever toxic substance seemed to be following them, they popped out into fresh air and the relative safety of an open field.

"Are you okay? Are you okay?" Theodosia cried over and over. Drayton was no spring chicken anymore. Certainly not at an age when he should be tiptoeing through the toxins! "Can you breathe?" she asked him.

Drayton was choking, but nodding to her as well. Finally, he seemed to catch his breath and was able to gasp out, "I'm okay. Really." He held up a shaking hand. "Don't call 911 on my account."

"I wasn't going to," said Theodosia. "I was going to call the sheriff. I think somebody did that on purpose!" Her terror was quickly being replaced by red-hot anger.

They limped back to the winery and found the two workers inside the barn.

Theodosia stalked over to them, her face flushed pink and contorted with anger. "Did one of you turn on that sprayer?" she shouted. "Did you just spray us with pesticide?"

They gaped at her with wide eyes and dropped jaws.

"Absolutely not," the older one stuttered in surprise. "We've been working on the pumps in here."

"Nobody's in the fields," said the younger one. "Nobody's doing any spraying today."

"Clearly someone has!" Theodosia shouted back. She pointed to Drayton, who was hunched over, looking a sickly white and still pressing his hanky to his mouth. "Do you see this poor man? Someone tried to poison him!"

Concern and a sort of fear filled the older man's face. "No ma'am!" he said. "We wouldn't do that! We don't know anything about that!"

"Accidents don't just happen!" said Theodosia. She grabbed Drayton again and hurried him out of the barn. "Are you really okay?"

He held up a hand. "I'm fine."

"We could stop at the ER," Theodosia continued. "Because you look a little shaky to me."

"Those guys in there are the ones who are shaking," Drayton told her. "You scared them half to death!"

"Good. Because somebody scared *us* to death." She

opened the passenger door and helped Drayton climb in. Then she slammed the door hard, rushed around to the driver's side, and jerked open the door. She was still hopping mad when she started the engine and backed up, grinding her gears and spinning her wheels in a cloud of brown dust.

"Easy, easy," Drayton told her. "We're okay. *I'm* okay."

"You're sure about that?"

Drayton held up both hands. "Yes."

Theodosia took a deep breath and forced herself to calm down. Tried to take slow, deep breaths that would help bring her temper under control. When she finally had her emotions dialed down to a dull roar, she turned to Drayton and said, "Well, at least we know one thing for sure."

Drayton cocked his head at her. "What's that?"

"Knighthall Winery is definitely not organic!"

14

❧

Church Street, normally the province of sedate little galleries, cute gift shops, and charming cafés, was a veritable carnival tonight. The Art Crawl was in full swing, and the street, always a little narrow to begin with, was jam-packed with artists' booths, food trucks, and flower stands. Every half block or so, where two or three food trucks had converged, groupings of tables and chairs had been set up especially for this event. Colored lights had been strung from lamppost to lamppost, and every two blocks there was a featured group of musicians.

"This is spectacular," said Theodosia. She and Max were strolling along, arm in arm, drinking in the booths and the music and the festive atmosphere. She'd showered off the pesticide and changed into a pink sundress and matching low-heeled sandals.

"So much better than last year," agreed Max.

"There must be almost a hundred artists showcased here

in addition to all the galleries that have opened their doors. And a couple thousand people in attendance."

"You see how it pays to advertise?" said Max.

"You know you're preaching to the choir," said Theodosia. She'd spent several years working as an account executive in one of Charleston's major marketing firms. She knew the importance of advertising, PR, media relations, and social media. She knew it could make or break a business or an event. These folks, the Art Crawl committee and their volunteers, had obviously recognized that and pulled out all the stops.

"So how did your Downton Abbey tea go today?" asked Max.

"Wonderful," said Theodosia. "A full house."

"Why am I not surprised?"

"Ah," said Theodosia. She stopped in a photographer's booth for a moment to glance at a lovely color photo of the Angel Oak, a low-country landmark and treasure. "People do enjoy a good themed tea. Whenever we host a chocolate tea, Victorian tea, Valentine's Day tea, or Queen's tea, we get a huge turnout."

Max pulled her closer. "But it's not just the food and tea that pulls them in, is it? Do you think it has something to do with your vision? That you seem to weave some sort of magical spell that combines food and tea with a soothing atmosphere?"

"Well . . . maybe."

"You're reluctant to take credit, aren't you?" said Max. "You're always a little shy about that."

"Really, can we change the subject, please?"

"Sure," said Max. "Would you like to look at some sidewalk art?"

"Yes. Of course," said Theodosia. She smiled up at him as they walked along.

"I mean literally *on* the sidewalk," said Max. He stopped

short and pointed. A young bearded artist was down on his hands and knees, scribbling furiously with colored chalk, creating a painting on the sidewalk.

"That's so neat," said Theodosia, charmed by the artist's talent as well as his enthusiasm. "Look, he's re-created Rainbow Row!" Rainbow Row was a series of colorful historic homes on East Bay Street that had been painted pastel pink, blue, green, and yellow.

"But here's something even better," said Max. He steered her into a jeweler's booth where gold and silver necklaces shimmered and gleamed under pinpoint spotlights.

"Such beautiful pieces," she breathed. Her heart was starting to beat a little faster.

"Look at this one." Max hooked a finger under a necklace and gently lifted it off a black velvet display rack.

Theodosia smiled. It was a tiny little teapot of fourteen-karat gold. Very charming and round and shiny.

"I think this was meant for you."

"Oh no!" Theodosia protested. "You don't have to do that!"

"Sweetheart, I want to," said Max. He undid the clasp and deftly hung it around her neck.

"Wow," said Theodosia. "Thank you so much!" The little necklace felt slithery and tickly and wonderful. And the little teapot came to rest right in the little hollow in her throat. Perfect.

Max had a whispered exchange with the jeweler, and then they were on their way again, bumping through the crowds, taking their time, enjoying the atmosphere as well as their precious time together.

"Look at that," said Theodosia. "There's a whole covey of food trucks parked over there."

"Is that the right word?" asked Max. "Covey? I thought it was covey of quail."

"And exaltation of larks."

"A conspiracy of ravens," said Max, enjoying their game.

"Good one," said Theodosia. "But seriously, I think the term should be a rodeo of food trucks. Since they're a very different species."

"In that case, what can I tempt you with? I assume you haven't eaten yet. At least I hope you haven't."

"Mmn." Theodosia studied the posters and signs that were displayed on the sides of the various food trucks. There was Creole Kitchen, Jasper's BBQ, Huevos on Earth, and Mr. Mollusk's Fried Oysters. As she was trying to decide, she saw someone out of the corner of her eye that caught her attention.

Was it? Could it have been?

Theodosia took a step forward and looked around, eyes narrowed, head swiveling.

"What?" said Max when he saw her glancing around.

"I thought I saw someone I knew."

"A friend?"

"Well, sort of." Then, because he continued to give her a quizzical look, Theodosia said, "I thought I saw Pandora Knight."

"Oh."

Theodosia lifted an eyebrow. The way he'd said it . . . in that flat, slightly disapproving tone . . . told her he wasn't exactly happy.

"I thought that, after the funeral this morning, you were finished with all that nonsense," said Max.

She bit her lip. "It's not exactly nonsense."

"I know Drayton asked for your help," said Max, "but really. Shouldn't you let the police or sheriff, or whatever authority has jurisdiction out there, handle it?"

"Yes, we probably should."

Max stared at her. "But you're not." Now he looked worried and uncomfortable. "Please tell me you're not in over your head."

"I'm not in over my head," said Theodosia. *And I'm sure as heck not going to tell you what happened today with the sprayer,* she decided. *Or what I thought happened last night. Because if I do, you'll probably drag me home and handcuff me to my refrigerator or some equally immovable object.*

"So you just wanted to speak to Pandora?"

Theodosia smiled at Max but felt awful inside. "Yes, something like that." She glanced around. "But . . . I don't see her. So maybe I could have been mistaken."

Max let it drop then, thankfully, and they bought his and hers baskets of deep-fried oysters.

"Good," said Max as tartar sauce dripped down his chin. It came out "Guh" because his mouth was full.

Theodosia took a napkin and dabbed at his face as he gave her a lopsided grin.

Okay, that grin was definitely hard for Theodosia to resist. She *wanted* to tell him more about what was going on, but hesitated. After all, maybe nothing was going on. Maybe it would all play out and Sheriff Anson would figure it all out and get his man. Sure. And pigs were going to sprout wings and fly away.

Two blocks down, their food cravings satisfied, Theodosia and Max turned into The Turner Gallery.

Andrew Turner, dressed casually in white slacks and a pale peach shirt with a white collar and cuffs, was standing front and center, warmly greeting each person who strolled into his gallery. Behind him was a long table with a striking Japanese *ikebana* flower arrangement, along with a delicious array of sushi appetizers and a pot of Japanese tea.

When he caught sight of Theodosia, he beamed and said, "We're serving tea in your honor."

"So I see," said Theodosia.

"And I called your friend Delaine."

Theodosia smiled back at him. "I heard." *Boy, did I ever.*

"She's pretty cute," said Turner. "And so lively, too."

"You have no idea," said Max. He not quite rolled his eyes.

"Anyway," said Turner, "I'm looking forward to getting to know her better at the Art Crawl Ball on Saturday night."

"Ditto," said Theo.

"Excuse me?" said Turner.

"I know Delaine's looking forward to becoming better acquainted with you," said Theodosia. *Was she ever.*

"I'm guessing you put in a good word for me?" said Turner.

"I really didn't have to," Theodosia responded. "You made a very favorable first impression on her all by yourself."

"Nice to know," said Turner. He glanced around at the crowd of people that had wandered into his gallery. "Now if only a few of these fine folks would be favorably impressed as well," he said in a stage whisper.

"Have sales been slow for you so far?" asked Max.

Turner looked thoughtful. "Business was practically glacial at first. Then the crowds started to build and bump along the streets and finally overflow into the shops and galleries. And now I've managed to sell two prints and a painting in just the last hour. Oh, and I've got an art-collecting couple who placed another painting on hold." He looked pleased. "I'm pretty sure they'll be back for it."

"Then it sounds like you're off to a great start," said Theodosia.

"I think so," said Turner. "And this is just the first night. We've got three more nights to go. Frankly, the economy being what it is, I'm thrilled that I've been able to keep the gallery open and actually rack up some fairly decent sales."

"It's been a tough couple of years for a lot of people," said Theodosia.

"Well," said Turner, "I know this Art Crawl is going to be a godsend for a lot of the small businesses up and down the street."

Theodosia glanced out the front window and saw the

crowds surging by. "It's brought out a lot of people so that's fantastic."

"You know," said Turner, "I've still got that Richard James painting you liked so much."

"I know you do," said Theodosia. "I'm just . . . well, I guess I haven't thought about it lately."

"Doesn't hurt to take another look," said Turner. "In fact, usually a second look helps you make up your mind. Yay or nay. Whatever. No pressure from me, seriously."

"Okay," said Theodosia. "I would like to take another look." Max had wandered off and was chatting with some people he knew.

"Cynthia?" Turner raised a hand and waved to a tall, efficient-looking blonde who was dressed all in black and carrying a clipboard. "Can you watch the front door for a couple of minutes?"

"Certainly," Cynthia said, nodding. With her hair twisted into a topknot and her lips a bright red against her pale complexion, she had the regal look and bearing of a Nordic princess.

"My assistant," said Turner.

Theodosia hoped that Delaine didn't suddenly drop by and catch sight of Cynthia. Because she knew Delaine wouldn't be happy. Delaine was awfully touchy when it came to women who were younger, prettier, and thinner than she was.

"Has Cynthia worked for you long?" Theodosia asked.

"A couple of months, off and on," said Turner. "She and her husband moved here recently after the medical products company he works for transferred him."

So Cynthia was married. Good.

"Over here," said Turner. They made their way through a fairly large back room that was literally stuffed with art-work. Sculpture and ceramic pots were crowded on shelves and desks. Paintings were hung on the walls, dozens were leaning up against walls, and another hundred more were jammed in two-feet-by-eight-feet-high wooden cubes that rose all the way to the ceiling.

"You have an amazing inventory," Theodosia marveled.

"A polite way of saying I've got way too much," said Turner. He sighed. "But there are a tremendous number of good artists doing wonderful work, and I am a pushover for a well-painted canvas." He tilted a large seascape forward that was leaning against the wall and reached a hand behind it. "Here it is." He pulled the painting out and propped it up on a wooden crate.

It was maybe three by three-and-a-half feet in dimension, an abstract impressionist painting with subtle blocks of red, gold, and persimmon that hinted at ocean, waves, and sky.

Theodosia studied it and felt something stir within her. She liked it. Correction, she liked it *very* much.

Turner was smiling at her, studying her face and body language. "So what do you think? What's the verdict?"

"It's got a red dot stuck down in the corner," said Theodosia, suddenly worried. "Does that mean this painting's already been sold? Or spoken for?"

"Not in this case. I was holding it for you, just in case you changed your mind."

"I am changing my mind," said Theodosia. "In fact, I'm loving this more and more."

"Wonderful," said Turner. "And I'm sorry the light's so bad in here. Maybe we should——"

Cynthia was suddenly hovering in the doorway. "Andrew? Can you . . . That couple who was so interested in the Jackson Nestor painting just came back and made an offer on it." She gave him a questioning look.

"One moment," Turner said to her.

Theodosia waved a hand. "Go ahead," she urged him. "Business always comes first. I'm not going anywhere."

"Thank you," Turner breathed as he dashed back out into the gallery.

Which left Theodosia face-to-face with her oil painting. Then she stretched her arms wide and picked it up. She turned it this way and that, wondering how it would look over her fireplace or in her dining room.

Probably pretty good, she decided. *Correction, probably pretty great.*

She carried the painting over to a nearby desk, rested it against a stack of books, and turned on a tensor lamp.

Even better. Now the colors fairly glowed, as if they had been infused from within.

"I see you found some better light," said Turner's voice right behind her.

"I want it," said Theodosia, suddenly making up her mind.

"I thought it had your name written on it," said Turner. "I mean besides the artist's signature."

"But could I . . . I have to move a little money around."

"No problem," said Turner. "I'll keep it in storage if you want and you can pay me whenever. Or you can take it now and pay me over time. I know you're good for it." He grinned. "Better yet, I know where you live."

"It's no problem," said Theodosia. "I have the money." She was a cash-and-carry girl and prided herself on it. She liked to pay bills promptly and didn't believe in maxing out her Visa card. In fact, she hardly ever used it. Some people believed in building a nest egg; others blithely put their lattes on a credit card. She was firmly in the nest egg camp.

Turner took the painting from her. "I'm glad this one's going to a good home." He carried it over to a cubbyhole that was labeled SOLD and stuck it in there. "There. All safe and sound."

"I was wondering," said Theodosia, "do you have any of

Drew Knight's work on display? Or is there something back here that I could look at?"

Turner's face lit up. "Yes, I should have something." He opened the drawer in a large metal flat file and absently shuffled through a stack of prints and serigraphs. "Hmm . . . not here." He looked thoughtful. "Maybe back in my office?" he said, half to himself.

He turned and disappeared into a small, crowded office. Theodosia followed on his heels.

"I'm sorry things are so messy in here," said Turner as he continued to hunt for the prints.

"You should see my office," said Theodosia. "This looks good by comparison."

"Here they are." He pulled out a small landscape sketch and handed it to her. "This is one of Drew's more recent pieces."

Theodosia studied the sketch. It had been done in pen and ink and depicted the familiar hip-roofed barn at Knighthall Vineyard. In the background were undulating rows of grapevines. The sketch felt as if it had been lovingly rendered by the artist's keen eye. "This is very good."

"Isn't it?"

"I think Drew might have had a future as an illustrator," said Theodosia. She'd certainly worked with graphic artists and illustrators who were less talented.

"I've got another half-dozen landscape sketches that are similar to this," said Turner. "And a couple of his watercolors, too." He took the sketch back from Theodosia, made a motion to slide it back in the drawer, and moved a couple of other prints out of the way.

As Turner rearranged his drawer of matted sketches and prints, Theodosia's eyes roved his office and landed on two bottles of wine that were displayed prominently on his desk. A bottle of Château Margaux and a bottle of Château Latour. She pointed to them. "I had no idea you were such a wine connoisseur. Those are very fine wines." She knew each bottle sold for well over one hundred dollars. And that was for a recent vintage. Add on a few years and the decimal point slid dramatically sideways.

Turner glanced up, looking a little confused. "What?" Then he saw what she was referring to. "Oh those." He chuckled slightly. "I must confess, I really do adore a fine wine. Though my pocketbook groans at the thought of buying them."

"But you shelled out a fair amount of money for those two bottles," Theodosia said, grinning.

"Unfortunately," said Turner, "I won't get a chance to indulge. I purchased those two bottles with the express intent of donating them to the Art Crawl Ball's silent auction." He wiggled his eyebrows comically and said in a slightly theatrical voice, "Donated by the very upscale Turner Art Gallery. Have to keep up appearances, don't you know?"

"Which is terrific for the Art Crawl," said Theodosia. "But too bad for you."

A few minutes later, back on the crowded street, Theodosia was talking enthusiastically to Max about her painting.

"I think you're smart," said Max. "A good piece of art always appreciates. The stock market goes up and down, real estate can get sliced and diced, but art always holds its value."

"Always?" said Theodosia.

"Well . . . okay. I suppose a few things have gone sideways in recent years—maybe Japanese prints and English porcelains—but for the most part, art is usually a savvy investment."

"But I'm buying the painting because I really like it," she told him. "Not because I want to sell it in ten years or donate it to a museum and take a big tax deduction."

"If you're going to go the museum route," said Max, "don't wait too long. The feds might close that loophole any day now."

"No, it's definitely meant to hang in my dining room," said Theodosia.

"I just had a brainstorm." Max pointed toward a big white food truck with SIR SEAFOOD written on the side and colorful, loopy artwork that featured smiling, dancing fish. "How about a cup of chowder to top off the evening?"

But Theodosia had just seen someone else she thought she recognized. He had been a blur in the crowd, a fleeting image of a white jacket and a familiar profile. She tried to scroll back through recent memories, trying to figure out what had suddenly pinged an alert inside her brain.

Then she remembered.

Was it the Japanese man, Mr. Tanaka?

Was he still in Charleston? Yes, she was pretty sure that Jordan had told her he was. So what was he doing here? Enjoying the Art Crawl? Hanging out with Pandora?

Or spying on me?

No, she told herself. That couldn't be it, could it? Because that would just be way too weird. In fact, that would be terrifying.

15

❧

Theodosia struck a match and lit the last of the tiny votive candles that sat in the center of their just-set tables. White linen tablecloths gleamed, glasses sparkled, and the pale-pink-and-green Limoges Florale china they'd set out this morning lent an extra air of elegance.

"This is the time I like best," said Drayton. He stood ramrod-straight, like a fencing instructor, gazing out over the tables. "When everything is lovely and fresh and set for the day."

"And then our customers come rushing in and ruin it all?" said Theodosia. She hoped that wasn't where Drayton was heading with his statement.

"No no," said Drayton. "Not at all. It's just that in the morning, before we open our doors, the tea shop seems to be filled with such promise. You know that when our guests arrive, feeling a little stressed or tightly wound, all the care we've taken in setting up will help them relax and take a good deep breath."

STEEPED IN EVIL   157

"And don't forget the aromatherapy factor," said Theodosia. She knew that the very act of inhaling tea—the essence of a lemony gunpowder green tea, earthy golden Yunnan, or malty Assam—helped people to pause, unwind, and de-stress.

"We create a refuge of sorts," Drayton agreed. "An *intermezzo* from the pressures of everyday life."

"Hey, you guys!" called Haley. "How come you're just standing around when there's so much work to be done?"

Drayton turned to look at her. "Is there?"

Haley seemed to back off a little. "Well . . . yeah. I think so. I mean, don't you have tea to brew or something like that?"

"You realize," said Drayton, "we're not all Type A's like you are."

"Me a Type A?" said Haley, making a face. "You're kidding, right?" She glanced toward Theodosia. "He's kidding, right?"

"I'm sure he is," Theodosia said blandly.

"Well, good," said Haley, "because I stopped at the flower market this morning and I've got a bunch of irises that need to be arranged in vases. And I was thinking we should use those blue-and-white Chinese-looking ones."

"Yes, Haley," said Drayton, a barely suppressed grin on his face.

"Oh, and besides the candied fruit scones and poppy seed bread, I decided to bake a triple batch of white chocolate chip muffins." Haley shrugged. "We've been crazy busy with takeout all this week—a little surprising, but a good thing, too—so it couldn't hurt to have extra baked goods hanging around."

"Couldn't hurt," agreed Theodosia.

Just then the back door opened and a voice called out, "It's me! I'm here!"

"There's Miss Dimple," said Haley. "Gotta dash. I want

her to lend a hand whipping up some frosting while I work on my chicken soup. Hey, guys, don't forget about those flowers now." And with that, she was gone.

Midmorning found Theodosia in her office, once again going over the guest list that Jordan Knight had given Drayton.

"Knock knock," said Drayton.

"Come on in," said Theodosia.

"I brought you a cup of tea."

Theodosia leaned back in her chair and smiled. "Fantastic. I could use a pick-me-up."

"It's that Formosan oolong that you like." He set down a small tray that held a single small teapot and a cup and saucer. "Better allow it to steep for another minute to bring out that nice bold taste. Oh, and I have something to show you." He pulled what looked like a roll of dark blue flannel from his jacket pocket and slowly unwound it.

"What have you got there?" Theodosia asked.

"A set of strawberry forks," said Drayton. He held them up to show her a neat row of six small forks, tucked into a roll of tarnish-proof cloth.

"Wow," said Theodosia.

"Victorian in design," said Drayton, "though it's more likely that this particular set is from the twenties." He laid them on her desk.

"They're gorgeous."

"Six inches in length, quite narrow and linear, and only three tines," Drayton said. He described them as if he were an announcer on *The Price Is Right,* trying to tantalize an audience with a prize offering.

"Why such long tines?" Theodosia asked, even though she pretty much knew the answer.

"Ah," said Drayton, pleased that she'd asked. "That's for the express purpose of spearing your succulent little strawberry and dipping it in cream or sugar." He smiled. "Or even a tasty chocolate sauce."

"You're quite the collector," said Theodosia. "Always on the hunt."

"Me? What about you and your constant scavenging for old hotel-era silver?"

"I do have a penchant for that stuff," Theodosia agreed. She'd just bought a vintage silver teapot that had been used in the early 1900s at the St. Francis Hotel in San Francisco. Maybe it had even gone through the earthquake.

Drayton nodded at the list she'd been going over. "So . . . does anyone pop out at you? Even though you've looked at it before?"

Theodosia shook her head. "There's nothing here. Not that I can see anyway. Nobody in particular jumps out at me, and none of the names match up with even tertiary suspects that Jordan and Pandora have mentioned."

"You know what?" said Drayton. "There's nothing anywhere. I'm starting to lose hope."

"In me?" Theodosia asked.

"No, never!" Then Drayton hastened to explain. "Theo, you've done everything humanly possible. You've turned this mess upside down and inside out and still nothing seems to shake loose."

Theodosia took a sip of tea and looked thoughtful. "I suppose there are some murders that never get solved. What do the police call them? Cold cases."

"This murder isn't cold yet," said Drayton. "It's still warm. Well, lukewarm anyway."

"You know what?" said Theodosia. "We still haven't talked to Jordan and Pandora Knight's silent partner."

"The liquor distributor," said Drayton, holding up an index finger. "You think it would be worthwhile?"

"Couldn't hurt," said Theodosia. "Nothing else has panned out so far."

"Well, let me give Jordan a call and see if we can track this fellow down. His name was Alec something?"

"Maybe Alex?"

"I think that's it," said Drayton.

"Drayton?" Miss Dimple's tentative voice suddenly called out to him.

Drayton spun on his heels, eyebrows arched. "Yes?"

Miss Dimple appeared in the doorway. "You have a visitor. Actually you both do." She smiled and stepped back. "It's Miss Josette!"

Drayton was suddenly upbeat. "Miss Josette! Come in, dear lady."

Miss Josette was an African-American woman, probably in her late seventies, but who could easily pass for early sixties. She had intelligent, almond-shaped eyes, smooth skin the color of rich mahogany, and the skillful, facile hands of an artist. She was a particular favorite of Drayton's because they both shared an interest in English poetry.

Miss Josette greeted them both, then shoved the sweetgrass basket she'd brought along with her into Drayton's hands. "That's the style you wanted, correct? A cross-handle basket with a pedestal base?"

"It is?" said Drayton. Sweetgrass baskets had become celebrated pieces of art in the low country. They were elegant and utilitarian baskets, woven from long bunches of sweetgrass, pine needles, and bulrush, then bound together by strips of native palmetto trees. The skill to weave one, and it was formidable, was usually passed down from generation to generation.

"I asked her to bring that particular basket in," said Theodosia.

"You just need the one?" said Miss Josette, turning her attention to Theodosia. "Because I've got a stack of baskets in my car if you want a few more. A couple of fruit baskets and some bread baskets, too."

"Just the one for now," said Theodosia. She gestured over her shoulder where a few sweetgrass baskets were stacked. "As you can see, we still have a good stash of your baskets. But I wanted one of your larger, handled baskets so I can assemble a special tea basket for a silent auction."

"Which silent auction is that?" asked Miss Josette.

"You know that Art Crawl that started last night?" said Theodosia.

Miss Josette nodded. "I've heard about it, sure."

"Well, there's also a fancy party on Saturday night for all the gallery owners and some of the people from the different museums," Theodosia said.

"And corporate sponsors, too," said Drayton.

"Anyway," said Theodosia, "they're asking businesses in particular to donate merchandise for a silent auction."

"To help raise money for the arts," said Drayton.

"So that's what you two are up to?" Miss Josette asked.

"Pretty much," said Theodosia.

Miss Josette let her sharp gaze wander from Theodosia to Drayton and then back to Theodosia. "Somehow I don't quite believe that. You both look a little unsettled." She moved a step closer to Drayton. "You in particular have a perplexed look on your face."

"I do?" said Drayton. Even though he tried to look impassive, he scrunched up his face.

Miss Josette studied Theodosia. "And I'm guessing that you're working on another one of your mysteries."

Drayton was flabbergasted. "How on earth did you know that?"

"My dear fellow," Miss Josette said in a patient voice, "my granny Alisa Mae was a *gris gris* lady. And I happen to be the one in the family who inherited a tiny bit of her sparkle."

"Sparkle," Drayton repeated slowly. Now he really looked puzzled.

"You know what I'm talking about," said Miss Josette. She lifted a hand halfway to her face. "The ability to see."

"See," said Drayton.

"The future," said Miss Josette. This time she almost but not quite rolled her eyes at him.

"Oh my, I am being dense," said Drayton. "See into the future? Really? You certainly never mentioned *that* particular gift before." He sounded more than a little doubtful.

But Theodosia was more than willing to jump on board. "Well, there you go," she said. "That's exactly the kind of outside help we've been looking for."

"Really?" said Drayton. He glanced at Miss Josette, who cowed him with a serious look. Then he turned his eyes to Theodosia. "I guess I'd be willing to give it a try. But does it really work?" Doubt still colored his voice.

Miss Josette continued to gaze at him with hooded eyes.

"Okay then," said Drayton, obviously unsettled. "How exactly do we tap into this rather remarkable gift of yours? Can we lay out some playing cards? Or read some tea leaves? Maybe you . . . um . . . *do* have the ability to see what we more distracted mortals can't."

"Tea leaves," said Miss Josette. "That should work just fine."

"Any particular type of tea?" asked Drayton.

"*Strong* tea," said Miss Josette.

Drayton was back a few minutes later. He had a teapot filled with Ceylon black tea along with three cups and saucers. He set the tray on Theodosia's desk and said, "Shall I do the honors?"

"Just one cup," said Miss Josette.

"That's all you need?"

"That's all *you* need," said Miss Josette.

"All right, fine," said Drayton. He picked up the floral teapot and poured a stream of golden tea into one of the teacups. "No tea strainer," he said. "Isn't that how it works? We just let the tea leaves burble and swish around in the cup?"

Miss Josette nodded. "That's right."

"Now what?" Theodosia said.

"You must drink some of the tea," Miss Josette instructed.

"Me?" said Theodosia.

Miss Josette nodded. "You're the one seeking an answer, correct?"

So Theodosia took a few sips, and then slowly drank the rest of it down to the last inch or so.

"Now we take a look," said Miss Josette. She bent over the teacup and studied it carefully as Theodosia and Drayton moved in tentatively, the better to see. "Okay," she said finally.

"Everything's going to be okay?" asked Drayton.

"Not okay," said Miss Josette.

"Then what?" Theodosia asked. "Is there trouble on the horizon?"

Miss Josette turned bright, watchful eyes on both of them and said, "You need to be very, very careful. Both of you."

"We do?" said Drayton.

"We are," said Theodosia.

Miss Josette held up an index finger. "Especially . . ." She stopped.

"What?" said Drayton.

"Especially if you set foot anywhere outside of Charleston."

Theo and Drayton exchanged hasty glances.

"Gulp," said Theodosia.

"You've been investigating something out of town?" she said. But it wasn't meant as a question.

"Yes, sort of," said Drayton. "As a matter of fact—"

"I don't mean to frighten you," Miss Josette told Theodosia. "Because you do have some powers of your own."

"I'm not sure I'm following you," said Theodosia.

Miss Josette favored her with a kind smile. "You're a bit of a *gris gris* lady yourself, Miss Theo. When you go out into the forests and swamps, you understand some of the secrets about roots and herbs and tree bark and tea."

Theodosia nodded. "Okay, I suppose I do. I know some of it anyway. Like dandelion greens and things."

"Really, Miss Josette," said Drayton, sounding a little unsettled. "This prognostication thing is a whole new side of you that we've never seen before."

Miss Josette nodded, but her concentration remained firm. "You're looking for a thief?"

"More like a killer," said Theodosia.

"A killer is a thief," said Miss Josette. "He steals life." She glanced sideways at Drayton. "Do you have a bayberry candle?"

He frowned. "We probably have one out front."

"Keep one close to you," said Miss Josette. "Remember, a bayberry candle burned to the socket, reveals the thief with wealth in his pocket."

"This is all very confusing," said Drayton.

Miss Josette smiled serenely. "All I'm really telling you is to trust your own instincts."

"Well, *that was* beyond strange," said Drayton. He was standing behind the front counter, tapping a finger on a tin of tippy Yunnan tea.

"It was different, that's for sure," said Theodosia. She'd just returned from a spin around the tea shop, where she'd poured refills for all their guests. Miss Dimple was hustling out plates of scones and tiny glass dishes mounded with Devonshire cream.

"Who knew Miss Josette could read tea leaves?" said Drayton.

"Who knew?" said Theodosia.

"I don't mean to change the subject . . ."

"Yes, you do," said Theodosia. "Miss Josette's words unnerved you because you tend to be a practical, linear thinker who relies on logic. Kind of like Mr. Spock on *Star Trek*."

Drayton pursed his lips together. "I don't believe I understand that reference at all."

"You can't fool me," she told him.

"Changing the subject," said Drayton as he dug into the front pocket of his apron and pulled out an index card, "Haley deigned to give me our luncheon menu for today."

"I guess we are changing the subject."

Drayton made a big production out of clearing his throat. "Chicken and vegetable soup, crab Rangoon with an Asian slaw, blue cheese and grape tea sandwiches, and . . ." He wrinkled his nose. "Something Haley calls her ladybug tea sandwiches?"

"With cream cheese and cherry tomatoes sliced so they look like wings," said Theodosia. "You remember, she's made them before." Haley did enjoy being fanciful and creative.

"Okay," said Drayton. "And you remember about the candied fruit scones and white chocolate chip muffins?"

"And the poppy seed bread," said Theodosia.

"Right."

Theodosia walked over to the highboy, which served as her gift shop area. She perused the shelves, thinking about which items might go into her tea basket. A couple of tins of tea were critical, of course. And so was a teapot. She had a nice stash of teapots she'd picked up at tag sales around the area, but maybe she would pop next door to the Cabbage Patch and buy a brand-new one. That might be better. Theodosia eyed the shelves again. And then, because there was an assortment of candles sitting right in front of her,

Theodosia decided to heed Miss Josette's words. So she reached out and grabbed a bayberry candle.

"Gee, that smells nice," Miss Dimple commented, once Theodosia had carried the candle up to the front counter.

"It's going to go in my tea basket," she said. "For the silent auction at the Art Crawl Ball."

"I've seen those gorgeous baskets you put together," said Miss Dimple. "A person would be lucky to get one."

"You think?" said Theodosia. "You'd bid on it?"

"Sure, I would," said Miss Dimple. "Drayton, wouldn't you?"

Drayton was busy measuring out tea. "Hmm?" he said absently. "What?"

Miss Dimple chuckled so hard that little mounds of flesh all over her small body began to tremble and shake. "Don't you just love Drayton when he pretends to be all fussy-busy? Isn't he a stitch?"

"That's our Drayton," said Theodosia. "A laugh a minute."

Then, just when the teashop was filled with luncheon customers, just as Theodosia was pouring tea for a tea group from Moncks Corner, the front door whapped open. And Pandora Knight strolled in, slick as you please, looking like the proverbial cat who swallowed the canary, with Mr. Tanaka on her arm.

16

❦

"Pandora!" Theodosia gasped. She didn't mean to gasp. She just hadn't expected the woman to stroll in unannounced like this, looking so cool and collected.

Pandora was dressed in a peach sundress, large-brimmed white hat, and bone-colored ankle boots. Tanaka was equally well dressed in what appeared to be a custom-tailored Italian suit that fit his narrow waist and torso perfectly.

Inclining her head slightly, Pandora said, "Theodosia, darling, I don't know if you've ever been formally introduced to my new business partner, Mr. Michio Tanaka." She tossed off the words *new business partner* with breezy aplomb.

Something felt amiss, but Theodosia managed a polite, "Nice to meet you," shaking hands with a smiling Mr. Tanaka. "Let me see if . . . yes, we do have a table for you." She led them to the small table by the window. When they were settled in, she said, "Can I start you off with some tea?"

"Do you have Gyokuro tea?" asked Mr. Tanaka.

"Yes, we do," said Theodosia. "We even serve a first-flush Sencha if you'd prefer."

"Even better," said Mr. Tanaka.

Theodosia hustled back to the front counter and said to Drayton, "Break out the tetsubin teapot and the ceramic cups; we have a guest from Japan."

Drayton glanced over. "I see that. Pandora and Mr. . . ."

"Tanaka," finished Theodosia.

"He was at the . . ."

"Yes, he was," said Theodosia. "And now Pandora is introducing him as her business partner."

"What!" said Drayton.

"Strange, huh? I'm going to try to get to the bottom of this." Theodosia grabbed two scones from the kitchen and quickly assembled a tea tray. Once Drayton had the Sencha brewing, she carried it all to their table.

Pandora and Mr. Tanaka were whispering excitedly to each other. But when they saw Theodosia approach, they fell completely silent.

"It looks like the two of you are busy doing business," Theodosia observed. Though she had no idea what could be so private. After all, they'd come waltzing in, blithely announcing their partnership to everyone who was in earshot.

"Are we ever," said Pandora, a look of triumph lighting her face. "I'm happy to report that Mr. Tanaka and I have just arrived at a landmark agreement. His company, Higashi Golden Brands, is going to distribute Knighthall Vineyards' red wine."

"That's wonderful," said Theodosia.

"Cases and cases of red wine!" Pandora enthused. "And basically, it's an exclusive contract!"

Theodosia placed their tea and scones on the table. "*All*

your red wine?" That seemed a little strange to her. "As in every single bottle?"

"That's right," said Pandora.

"Wow," said Theodosia. "That really is an exclusive." She thought it a bit strange to distribute all their wine in a single market. Besides, it must cost an arm and a leg to ship wine to Japan. And what kind of condition would the wine be in after such a long and bumpy journey?

"I take it red wine is the preferred wine in Japan?" Theodosia said.

Pandora giggled. "If it isn't now, it will be soon."

"Red wine is *extremely* popular," intoned Mr. Tanaka. "In fact, it's a close second to traditional Japanese sake."

"Well, good luck to both of you," said Theodosia. "I'm glad you worked out such a sweet deal." As she hurried back to the counter, she was wondering why Tanaka was so willing to strike up an exclusive deal with a mid-tier South Carolina winery that wasn't particularly profitable.

"What's a sweet deal?" Drayton asked her. "I couldn't help but overhear a snippet of your conversation."

"Pandora's just negotiated a major contract," Theodosia told him. "Mr. Tanaka is going to distribute Knighthall's wine in Japan. And apparently it's going to be *red* wine."

Drayton looked puzzled. "Why just red when Jordan's passion has been white wine? And what's going to happen to the distribution deals that Jordan set up locally? With the various inns and restaurants and liquor stores?"

"I have no idea," said Theodosia. "Maybe they'll be declared null and void now that Knighthall is putting all its efforts into shipping their wine to Japan."

"Still . . . that seems awfully strange. After all the work Jordan put in. And why wine from South Carolina? It's not like we're on a par with Napa or Sonoma."

Theodosia shrugged. "At least they negotiated a successful contract with a willing distributor. That's a lot more than Knighthall had before. You said it yourself . . . well, Jordan implied it, too . . . they were struggling to stay afloat."

"Yes, I suppose you're right," said Drayton. "But it still seems awfully unfair. As if Jordan is taking a backseat in all of this."

"Maybe he's not the savvy businessman you thought he was," said Theodosia.

Drayton nodded slowly. "I suppose that's possible."

"Maybe he's good when it comes to software, but not so good at running a winery."

"Excuse me," said Miss Dimple. "I don't mean to interrupt you two dears, but do we serve Moroccan mint tea? The ladies at table three are asking for it."

"We certainly do," said Drayton, reaching for a tin. "Shall I brew a pot?"

"Please," said Miss Dimple. She nudged Theodosia with a chubby elbow. "That fellow at table six? The lovely Japanese man?"

"Yes?" Theodosia said.

"He's so formal and polite," said Miss Dimple. "I dropped a bowl of lemon curd at his table and he made a kind of bowing gesture. I guess that's what they do in Japan, huh?"

"I guess so," said Theodosia.

"I'll have your Moroccan mint tea in two shakes," said Drayton. "But in the meantime, can you deliver this pot of honey hibiscus to table two?"

"Of course," said Miss Dimple.

"Drayton," said Theodosia. She was leaning with her elbows on the counter, mulling things over. "Do you still want to go to Oak Hill Winery tonight? To their wine tasting?"

"You know, I really do." He gave a rueful smile. "I'm thinking maybe I can learn a thing or two from all these tough businesswomen who run wineries." He gave her a slow wink. "And tea shops."

Some thirty minutes later, Theodosia was just emerging from the kitchen when she saw Pandora shaking hands with Mr. Tanaka and bidding him good-bye.

Then Pandora spun around, saw Theodosia, and held up an index finger in a slightly imperious gesture. "May I have a word with you?" she asked.

"Certainly," said Theodosia.

Pandora smiled. "In private?"

Wondering what this was all about, Theodosia said, "Why don't you come on back to my office." She led Pandora past the kitchen and into her little cubbyhole. "As long as you don't mind the mess."

"Not a bit," said Pandora. "You should see my office; it looks like some kind of bizarre sinkhole. Where all the junk just kind of swirls around!"

Theodosia seated herself at her desk and let Pandora take the overstuffed upholstered chair that faced it. The tuffet, as they always referred to it.

"What's up?" Theodosia asked. Did Pandora suddenly have a lead on someone? Or was this going to be another trumped-up accusation? Or maybe this was a discussion about her business deal?

Turned out Theodosia was wrong on all counts.

Pandora licked her lips and started in. "I know Jordan was the one who asked you to get involved in this whole sorry mess, and I truly thank you for everything you've done."

"You're welcome," said Theodosia. "But I don't think I've done very much in the way of solving this case."

"Oh, you have," said Pandora. "You're too modest. You've done way more than you think you have."

Theodosia leaned forward. She knew there had to be a point to all of Pandora's platitudes.

"But I think you've done about as much as you can," said Pandora. She cocked her head to one side and offered up a rueful smile. "I think . . . well, I think we should just let Sheriff Anson take it from here on."

"Seriously?" said Theodosia. She almost didn't believe her ears. "Even though you've said repeatedly that you didn't have any faith in him?" This was shocking! A complete about-face!

"I suppose I've changed my mind," said Pandora. Now she blinked rapidly and seemed to conjure up a wistful look. "Or maybe I've just accepted that Drew's murder will never be solved." She nodded, as if she liked her answer. "Yes, you could say I've come to terms with it."

But I haven't. And I doubt that Jordan has, either.

"Let me get this straight," said Theodosia. "You're asking me to back off from any sort of investigation, is that correct?"

Pandora nodded. "Yes, I guess that is what I'm saying. But Theodosia, I'll be forever in your debt. And so will Jordan."

"Sure," said Theodosia, trying not to grit her teeth. "No problem."

"Guess what?" Theodosia said to Drayton.

"Now what?" said Drayton. He was fussing at the counter, mixing a pitcher of coconut iced tea for a group of women who'd driven in from the Isle of Palms for afternoon tea and treats. "Do you think Haley has any of those candied fruit scones left?"

"I'm sure she does. But listen, I've got news. Pandora news."

He looked up. Now she had his attention. "What's going on?"

"I've basically been relieved of any and all investigatory duties."

Drayton carefully poured steaming hot water into a blue-and-white teapot, and then said, "No kidding. Really?"

"Really."

He frowned. "That's very strange. I wonder if Jordan feels the same way."

"Pandora made it sound like he did," said Theodosia. "Like it was a joint decision."

"Do you think it was? A joint decision, I mean?"

"Probably not."

Drayton fussed with the teapot, and then said, "Maybe, in the long run, this will turn out to be a good decision. The investigation wasn't going all that well anyway."

"No, it really wasn't," Theodosia admitted. "We did kind of decide that earlier today."

"Then it was nice of Pandora to come and tell you herself. Instead of just sending you an e-mail or sticking a Post-it note on the door."

"Then why do I feel like I've just been scraped off the soles of her shoes?"

"Do you?" said Drayton.

"Kind of . . . yes, I guess I do."

"Maybe Pandora is just sick and tired of the whole thing," said Drayton. "The investigation, the wrangling with Jordan . . . maybe she just wants out."

"Oh, I think Pandora is definitely sick of the whole thing," said Theodosia. "Especially since there was no love lost between her and Drew."

"But Pandora didn't kill him," said Drayton. "She'd never do that. She's a little strange, but violence just isn't part of her nature."

Theodosia was about to say, *But avarice is,* then changed her mind. Instead she said, "No, I'm pretty sure she wasn't involved. Pandora's hot button seems to be money."

"That's what it sounds like," said Drayton. "Even though she wasn't able to persuade Jordan to sell the winery to Tanaka outright, she still negotiated a deal to distribute their wine in Japan."

"So she really is controlling things," said Theodosia. "Including shutting down the investigation."

"Well," said Drayton, "it's not completely shut down. Sheriff Anson is still pursuing things on his end, right?"

"I guess so," said Theodosia. "I sincerely hope so."

"Do you think I should still call Jordan and ask him about the silent partner?"

"I think you should," said Theodosia. "And I'm going to pursue another angle, too."

"Which is?"

Theodosia hesitated. "I'll let you know."

Once Theodosia got her courage up, the rest was easy. She dialed the number for Jack Alston at Charleston's local ATF office and waited while he came on the line. Alston had been involved in a cigar-smuggling case that Theodosia had been dragged into a couple of months ago. He was smart, decisive, and looked like Central Casting's idea of an FBI agent. But Alston was ATF all the way. And with his piercing blue eyes, short, almost brush-cut gray hair, and high cheekbones, Theodosia had found the man to be devastatingly handsome. And there had been that little vibe of . . . what would you call it? Interest or tension between them.

"Well, well," said Alston in a low, baritone voice, "I was wondering if I'd ever hear from you again."

Theodosia had been wondering the same thing. Alston

had been friendly, verging on flirtatious, the last time they'd seen each other. She'd had the distinct feeling he might be calling her for a date. No call had been forthcoming. Oh well, she probably would have turned him down anyway. Things were pretty serious with Max.

"What can I do for you?" Alston asked. "Point you toward a hijacked semitrailer filled with Cuban cigars and French brandy?"

"How about wine?" said Theodosia.

"Hijacked wine," said Alston. "We don't see that too often. It would have to be very good wine."

"This isn't," said Theodosia. She paused, trying to collect her thoughts, feeling a little nervous about what she was asking. "Have you heard anything about a murder that took place at Knighthall Winery just outside of Charleston?"

"No, should I have?"

"Probably not. But I was there when it happened and kind of got dragged into the whole sorry mess."

"Wait a minute," said Alston, "I'm looking it up right now on my computer. Running a quick search."

Theodosia heard the tip-tap of keys, and then Alston said, "Yup, here it is. Drew . . ." He mumbled a few words. "Son of a. . . Holy Shih Tzu, lady! You were there?"

"Yes, unfortunately. It was kind of a fancy party for their big barrel tasting."

"And now they've got you over a barrel?"

Theodosia hesitated.

"Sorry," said Alston. "Bad pun. So what can I do for you?"

"That's the weird thing," said Theodosia. "I'm not really sure. Murder was committed, there are no suspects . . . but I feel like something strange is going on."

"Strange how?"

Theodosia breathed a huge sigh of relief. He seemed to be taking her seriously.

"Maybe because Knighthall just signed an exclusive

contract with a Japanese distributor to sell their wine overseas," she said.

"Nothing strange about that," said Alston. "Happens all the time."

"I suppose."

"Look, would you like me to dig into this a little further? If I can, that is. I'm not promising anything."

"Would you really?" said Theodosia.

"Hey, I just offered, didn't I?"

"Thank you," said Theodosia. "I really appreciate it."

"No problem, pretty lady. You can pay me back later," Alston said with a wicked cackle.

Uh-oh.

"So Knighthall Winery signed a distribution deal with who?" asked Alston.

"Higashi Golden Brands in Japan."

"Got it. Okay. I'll do some checking and get back to you."

"That's it?" said Theodosia.

"Sure," said Alston. "Unless you'd like to——"

"I appreciate this, I really do," Theodosia cut in hastily.

"I've got your business phone, but maybe you'd better give me your cell phone number, too. Us federal agents like to keep on top of things."

Theodosia gave him the number.

"Thanks," she said.

"I'll be in touch," said Alston.

That's what I'm afraid of.

Drayton was suddenly standing in front of her. "Earth to Theodosia," he said. "I've got that information you wanted."

"The liquor distributor . . . the silent partner?"

"That's right." Drayton set a slip of paper down on her desk. "Alex Burgoyne. And a meeting's already been set up."

"For . . ."

"Today," said Drayton. "At two thirty."

Theodosia glanced at her watch. "That's, like, in twenty minutes."

"That's right," said Drayton. "We work fast around here."

"I should say."

17

❦

Theodosia headed east on Broad Street and found that traffic was light even for midafternoon. Turning left on East Bay Street, she stole a glance to her right and enjoyed a gorgeous view of Waterfront Park and Charleston Harbor. Several sailboats and catamarans sliced briskly through the smooth water, taking full advantage of favorable boating conditions. Just past the farthest sailboat, Theodosia could make out the white double-decked Fort Sumter Ferry, which was undoubtedly heading back to Sullivan Island with a full cargo of tourists.

The day was a picture-perfect example of why residents and tourists alike dearly loved Charleston. With a soft, salty breeze gusting in off the harbor, helping to nicely cool down afternoon temperatures, the cloudless azure sky mimicked the water of a tropical bay, and the city fairly shimmered in the sunlight.

Despite the day's temperate perfection, Theodosia was troubled. She'd tried in vain for the last hour to reach Jordan Knight. Was he in despair over the Japanese distribution deal? Satisfied with it? Or resigned to it?

Theodosia also wondered if Jordan had blithely signed off on Pandora's decision to remove her from the investigation. While she and Jordan Knight were far from friends, she still felt a strong affinity for the man—mostly because of Jordan's close friendship with Drayton. Drayton was one of a handful of people that she herself could count on no matter what. When push came to shove, she could always trust Drayton.

Theodosia pulled to a stop across the street from a large, cement block building with a sign out front that read, PALMETTO LIQUOR DISTRIBUTING, INC. Trucks were backing up to three large loading docks on one side of the building, and men in overalls were wandering around with clipboards. Obviously, this was ground zero for the liquor distribution business as well as the home office of Alex Burgoyne, Jordan and Pandora Knight's silent partner.

Theodosia wondered just how silent Burgoyne had been when he found out that the Knights—most likely Pandora now acting as major shareholder—had negotiated a deal to sell their wine exclusively to Tanaka and his overseas conglomerate. Did he even know?

Theodosia figured Burgoyne had to be aware of the sale. Despite having only a minority share in the winery, he would most likely have to sign off on any major business decision.

Stopping at the security desk just inside the building, Theodosia gave her name to the gargantuan guard sitting behind the desk. The man nodded, leaned forward, and laboriously hand-printed a temporary stick-on badge for her. Then he handed her the badge and grunted, "Elevator is that way."

Stepping off the elevator on the second floor, Theodosia was greeted by a no-nonsense hallway. She followed a strip of green indoor-outdoor carpet into an office where a thin blonde sat smiling behind a glass-and-brass reception desk.

"Good afternoon," the blonde said. Her cheeriness seemed like a ploy to compensate for the gruffness shown by the no-necked behemoth security guard one floor below.

"Good afternoon," Theodosia replied. "I have a two-thirty appointment with Mr. Burgoyne . . . I'm Theodosia Browning."

"Of course, Ms. Browning. Mr. Burgoyne is expecting you. He's on the phone right now, but I'll let him know that you're here. Please have a seat and help yourself to some coffee. Or if you'd like something stronger to drink . . ."

Theodosia waved a hand as she walked to a black leather sofa and sat down. She sighed and turned her gaze toward a large flat-screen television on the opposite wall. The volume was turned off, but on the screen Rachel Ray was organizing a contest between two audience members to see who could frost a birthday cake the fastest. Theodosia decided that if Haley were part of the contest, it would be no contest.

Just as the contestants were panicking and frosting was spattering everywhere, the blonde behind the desk called out, "Ms. Browning?"

Theodosia looked over.

"Mr. Burgoyne can see you now," said the receptionist. She burst up from her desk with an explosion of smiling energy and pushed open a heavy oak door. "Ya'll have a good meeting!" she said.

Theodosia wasn't sure if this was going to be a good meeting or not, but she'd take all the good wishes she could get. Burgoyne was a wild card and she knew this little confab could go either way. He could shed a little light or he could clam up completely.

The door closed behind her and Theodosia found herself in Burgoyne's expansive office, where a mammoth teak desk dominated most of the space. It was set against a floor-to-ceiling window that looked out over a parcel of green space. Beyond was a labyrinth of streets that led to the harbor.

Theodosia had expected wood panel walls, lots of liquor bottles, and maybe the trophy heads of a few dead animals. But as Burgoyne smiled at her from across his desk, she was pleasantly surprised. He looked positively welcoming, and the walls on either side of her were hung with dozens of pieces of original artwork.

"I see you noticed my artwork," Alex Burgoyne's deep voice intoned. He sounded pleased.

"Looks like you've got your own gallery here," said Theodosia.

Burgoyne nodded. He was dressed casually in a red-checked shirt and faded blue jeans. His dark hair curled softly over his forehead and he appeared to be about fifty years old. He was also in excellent shape, with the kind of narrow waist and broad shoulders that announced he was an exercise devotee.

Theodosia smiled and extended her hand. "I'm Theodosia. It's nice to finally meet you."

Burgoyne stood up and shook her hand with a firm dry grasp, the grip of a man well practiced in the art of shaking hands.

"I'll bet you were expecting a full bar and disco," Burgoyne teased. "Instead of contemporary art."

Theodosia laughed in spite of herself. Burgoyne was a true salesman; he was adept at getting people to like him and feel comfortable around him.

"I have to admit if I'd seen a poster for *Saturday Night Fever,* I wouldn't have been too surprised," said Theodosia.

Burgoyne laughed, a genuine, good-natured chuckle. "Please take a look," he said, obviously eager for her to view his artworks. He struck Theodosia as a man happy to show off his pride and joy, a kid with a shiny new toy. "All my art was done by local artists. You see . . . Roger Tremaine . . . Jacques Brissard . . ."

"Very nice," said Theodosia, appropriately impressed.

"Now you may recognize this particular artist," Burgoyne said, indicating a pencil drawing at the far end of the line of framed art.

An exquisite pastel drawing depicted Pineapple Fountain at nearby Waterfront Park. Water dripped from the two fluted sides of the fountain into the pool below, and two children—a boy and a girl—would be forever young as they splashed and played in the pool of water, their watchful mother resting just to their right on the marble ledge fronting the half-circle hedge. It was evocative and beautiful. The signature at the bottom was that of Drew Knight.

"Beautiful," Theodosia whispered. She could see why Burgoyne had it in a place of honor near his desk, presumably where he could gaze at it as he worked.

"Yes, it is. Drew was quite a talent, which is why his senseless death was even more of a tragedy." Burgoyne paused. "I'm guessing that's why you wanted to talk to me? Jordan mentioned you might be stopping by to ask a few questions."

"That's right," Theodosia replied. She also wondered if he knew she'd been fired by Pandora. But if he did, he wasn't giving any indication.

"Well, as my father used to say, let's get to it."

More of that sales pitch. Theodosia wondered if his folksy demeanor was an act or if he really did quote his daddy, Mark Twain, and Foghorn Leghorn as evidence of his Southern gentility.

Burgoyne escorted her to a dark brown leather chair, then walked around to his desk chair and sat down. He steepled his fingers together and leaned back to await her questioning.

"As you already know," said Theodosia, "I've been doing

some checking around on behalf of Jordan and Pandora. They aren't overly satisfied with how the formal investigation is proceeding so far, and I agreed to try to glean some additional information into the circumstances surrounding Drew's death."

Burgoyne nodded silently.

"May I ask . . . how well did you know Drew?"

"I really didn't know him personally," Burgoyne began. "I saw him around the winery from time to time. Bought a few of his pieces of art, as you can see. He always seemed cordial enough . . . and maybe a little distracted."

"Did you ever see him around the winery with anyone? Friends? Acquaintances?"

"Well, you probably know about Tanya. I mean everyone knows about Tanya. She's kind of hard to miss." Burgoyne laughed. "I guess other than her. No. I never noticed him with anyone else. But we didn't travel in the same circles, either."

"Ever have any conversations with Jordan about Drew being in trouble? Or having difficulty with someone?" Theodosia was getting the feeling that Burgoyne didn't know all that much. There didn't appear to be any dishonesty; he simply wasn't very plugged in.

"I don't like to speak ill of the dead, but . . ." Burgoyne paused. "Well, you knew he was a doper, right?"

"Yes. I'd heard Drew had some problems with drugs."

"I don't know what he was on, but sometimes when I ran into him, it was like he wasn't really there—you know? Jordan never said much about it, but I could tell the issue was wearing on him. He developed a lot of gray hair these last two years, and not all because the winery wasn't doing well."

"There could be lots of reasons for that," Theodosia responded.

"Yes, marriage on the rocks . . . failing winery . . . cracked-out kid. I'm amazed the guy could pull himself out of bed in the morning."

"You knew about the Knights' marital problems?" Theodosia asked.

"It was hard to miss," said Burgoyne. "I finally cornered Jordan about it one day, and he told me that they were getting a divorce. No surprise there. Pandora was never around, and when she was, they barely spoke to each other."

"How do you feel about the deal Pandora just brokered with Higashi Golden Brands?" Theodosia asked. "That can't be good news to you, can it? I mean . . . now you won't even have distribution rights to your own wine."

Burgoyne looked thoughtful. "Yeah, but as a partner . . . heck, even as a minority partner, I'm still going to make a fair amount of money. Maybe even more than if we finally made it big selling domestically. Either way, at least it's stable money for a while. Knighthall was becoming a money pit. Every few months I had to drop a little more into that place to help keep it afloat. Jordan kept saying 'Just wait until we release Knight Music,' but now that the wine is close to distribution, things haven't really changed." He shrugged. "One wine can't make that much of a difference anyway."

"Still," said Theodosia, "is it really good business to put all your proverbial eggs in one basket? It seems like an odd marriage—Japan and South Carolina wine? Why Japan? And from Tanaka's standpoint, why Knighthall wine?"

"Interesting that you should ask," Burgoyne replied as he reached into his top drawer and removed the most recent issue of *Wine World* magazine. Burgoyne licked the tip of his index finger and paged through the magazine, pausing once before continuing to the article he was looking for. "Now check this out. This magazine and the author—Mr. Mark Pendleton, a guy who really understands the wine business—says that the Japanese market is, quote, 'ripe for the American wine business. By the year 2020, Japan will be the world's third largest importer of international wine,' unquote." He grinned. "Now, if we can get in on the ground floor of something like that, we can make a killing."

"Your business decision is based on a magazine article?" Theodosia asked.

"Well, I've been in the wine and spirit business for a long time and seen a lot of changes. And one thing I've learned is that it's always better to be the porpoise out on the bow of a big ship rather than a small fish swimming frantically to catch up."

"I hear you," said Theodosia.

"And Pandora has done her research," Burgoyne continued. "The thing is . . . Tanaka is guaranteeing more revenue over the next five years than we could have ever made if Knighthall took off big time in the States."

"That does sound impressive," said Theodosia. She thought about a phrase she'd once heard on one of her favorite police procedural shows. It was, *Follow the money*. She wondered if Pandora and Burgoyne were following the money. Or were the Japanese the ones who were doing so?

And how did any of that relate to Drew's murder? In this case, was *Follow the drugs* a far better maxim? Is that where the real story was? Theodosia made a mental note to try to contact Tanya again. Maybe there was more information to be had from her. She also needed to get Carl Van Deusen alone. Maybe then he could answer her questions honestly. Other than that, she had nothing. Maybe this conversation with Burgoyne really was a dead end. It had initially felt productive but now she wasn't so sure.

"Thank you for your time." Theodosia stood up abruptly and reached out to shake Burgoyne's hand for a second time. "I really appreciate it."

"No problem," Burgoyne said as she turned and started for the door. "Happy to help—if I really did."

Then Theodosia saw them, on the wall opposite Drew's artwork, propped up in the corner. Golf clubs.

"Mr. Burgoyne, do you play golf?" Theodosia turned to ask.

Burgoyne bobbed his head. "I'm certainly not very good, but I have to admit—I find supreme pleasure in chasing a little white ball around on weekends."

"May I ask where you play?" said Theodosia. Except, deep down, she knew the answer before he said it.

Burgoyne gave her a benevolent smile. "I just got a membership at Plantation Wilds."

Theodosia called Tanya and left a message, asking her to return the call. She was pretty sure the model would ignore her. But no matter. She'd try again later. And keep trying for as long as it took.

Carl Van Deusen was another matter. If she stopped by Smalley's Bistro, she could probably catch him before the restaurant fired up for the evening.

She checked her watch and decided now was as good a time as any. It was past four o'clock, and if she took the long way down the harbor, she could pretend that Smalley's was on her way home. It was such a beautiful day, the drive would be worth the effort.

Turning right onto Concord, Theodosia could see that the Fort Sumter Ferry was returning to its launch just up from the Maritime Center. A blaring foghorn announced the boat's arrival into port.

As she turned onto Calhoun Street, she passed by the Charleston County Library with its impressive front of white pillars. The library was an excellent example of the Greek Revival style so prevalent in Charleston. Just past the library, Theodosia turned onto Anson Street and idly wondered if Sheriff Anson might be a descendant of the street's namesake. What, she wondered, did Sheriff Anson think of Jordan and Pandora Knight's contract with Tanaka? Did he even know about it?

Traffic was a series of stops and starts, so she didn't arrive at Smalley's until almost five. Evidently the dinner rush hadn't started yet because only a handful of cars shared space in the bistro's parking lot.

Removing her sunglasses, Theodosia entered Smalley's Bistro. She was instantly bombarded with the wonderful aromas of freshly baked dill bread, corn muffins, and grilled fish. Her stomach growled in anticipation, but she ignored it. She had business here.

The maître d', her nemesis from a few days earlier, was standing at the copper-plated host stand leading to the dining room. He was talking intently into the ear of one of the female servers. The server was listening, but seemed more than a little anxious to get away from a man who stood just a little too close for professional conversation.

Theodosia stood patiently a few feet in front of the pair, waiting to catch their attention.

The server finally nodded her assent and quickly made her getaway into the dining room. The maître d', whose name Theodosia remembered as Philip Rusk, made a couple of notes in a notebook. Then he lifted his eyes and gave her a radiant smile. "Good evening," he purred. "Welcome to Smalley's. Do you have a reservation?"

"No," Theodosia admitted. "I'm not here for dinner. I'd like to speak with one of your employees."

Instantly, the smooth talk was over and Rusk quickly discarded his smile and all manner of decorum. He pulled himself up to his full height, probably a little over six feet, and stared down his nose at Theodosia. His diction became clipped as he said, "We are just about ready to welcome our dinner guests. I'm afraid we do not have time for anyone to entertain idle chitchat with our staff."

Theodosia groaned inwardly. This guy was beyond rude. He was just plain nasty.

"You don't even know who I want to speak to," Theodosia replied, her anger barely in check. She could feel her face flush as she fought to control her temper.

"It doesn't matter," said Rusk. "Please contact our employee when he or she is not at work."

"But you're not even busy at the moment," Theodosia began.

Rusk sighed deeply and a little lightning bolt of a blood vessel began to pulse in his forehead.

"Before we reach an impasse here," said Theodosia, "maybe you could tell me if Carl Van Deusen is working tonight?"

Rusk studied her and rocked back on his heels. "Is that who you wish to speak with?" His eyes narrowed as he stared at her. "You realize Mr. Van Deusen is a suspect in a murder case? The police have already been here asking questions."

"He's actually a witness, not a suspect," Theodosia replied. "Really, I just want to talk to him. A couple of minutes—what can it hurt?"

"You want to ask him some questions, too?" said Rusk. "About the investigation?"

"I . . . yes, I do," said Theodosia.

Rusk smirked. "And just who do you think you are— Angela Lansbury?"

"Look," said Theodosia. "I'd love to hang around here and trade witty repartees with you. But all I want to know is—is Van Deusen here?"

"No," said Rusk. "No, he is not."

18

❧

The party at Oak Hill Winery wasn't as elegant as the one orchestrated at Knighthall Winery, but it made up for it with casual charm. Dozens of picnic tables were arranged on the grassy lawn that surrounded the winery's production center. Inside a large open-sided shelter, wide planks had been laid across oak barrels to serve as a rustic, temporary bar.

And what a bar it was! Oak Hill Winery had seemingly turned out ten different wines—five red, four white, and one sparkling—and they were all lined up and available for tasting tonight. And if that wasn't enough, two men in aprons and tall white chef's hats were manning an enormous outdoor grill, where chicken, ribs, and miniature shish-kabobs sizzled and snapped over open flames.

The first thing Drayton said, when he saw the guests, grill, picnic tables, and country-western band, was, "I think I'm overdressed."

"Nonsense," said Theodosia. She patted his arm. "You

look perfectly fine." Drayton was, of course, wearing a beige linen jacket, bow tie, and tan slacks.

"Do you think I should ditch the tie?"

"I think you should stop worrying so much," said Theodosia as she tugged at his elbow and pulled him into the fray. They wove their way through a group of energetic dancers and headed for the wine bar.

Two glasses of wine and he'll relax. Well, maybe three.

"What would you like to taste first?" asked the bartender. He had curly dark hair and his face was flushed pink. Probably from imbibing in his own offerings.

"How about we start with the white wine?" Drayton suggested.

"Fine with me," said Theodosia.

"This is our White Shadow," said the bartender, holding up a bottle. "Crisp and light with a hint of apple and citrus." He poured out two small servings with a flourish. "I think you're going to like it."

Theodosia and Drayton both sipped gingerly.

"I do like it," said Theodosia.

"Very refreshing," Drayton pronounced as he swirled his glass to oxygenate the wine even more.

"A full pour then?" said the bartender.

"Please," said Drayton.

They sipped their wine as they strolled the grounds. Colored lights twinkled in stands of oak and palmettos. Small fire pits had been set up with three or four chairs snugged around each one, perfect for conversation. The mood of the party was languid and casual. People laughed, smoke wafted enticingly, a few young women strolled barefoot, and a tricolor collie dog wandered the grounds.

After they'd sampled their wine and nibbled a steak and onion shish-kabob, Drayton was all set to head back to the bar and sample one of Oak Hill's red wines.

"Red wines are really my favorite," he confided to Theodosia as they sauntered along. "I consider white wines more of . . . an appetizer."

"Did you know that there is actually wine-flavored tea?"

"Now that sounds a little too strange," said Drayton.

"But it's true," said Theodosia. "Crispin's Tea makes one. And there are all sorts of recipes for wine-flavored tea popping up on the Internet."

"Just please don't serve it to me. I prefer to keep my tea and wine worlds quite separate."

But just as they set out for the bar, who should they run into but Tom Grady!

"Mr. Grady!" said Theodosia. She was surprised to see him here but knew she shouldn't be. Hadn't Grady made mention of the fact that he might be looking for another job? Sure he had. Of course he had. Now she also knew for sure how Georgette Kroft had known she was looking into things. Grady had simply told her.

Theodosia made hasty introductions.

"Ah," said Drayton. "You're not about to jump ship, are you?" He was making a joke, but his words seemed to make Grady more than a little uncomfortable.

"It's a small world," said Grady. "The winery world is anyway. There aren't that many around here."

"I understand there are a couple more wineries just north of here," said Theodosia. She was trying to be polite and maybe drag a few tidbits of information out of this fairly reticent man. Because, face it, she was curious and a little suspicious of Grady. Was he thinking of accepting a job at Oak Hill, or was he running away from his job at Knighthall?

"Ayuh," said Grady. "There are a couple more wineries in the area. Maybe you've heard of Spring Grove Winery and Chesterfield Cellars?"

"How are they doing?" Theodosia asked. She thought about Timothy Neville's dire remark that barely half of the upstart wineries had managed to survive.

Grady held out his hand and made a seesawing motion. Obviously, he knew the score, too.

"But Georgette seems to be doing fine," said Theodosia. "Better than fine. She confided to me that she has distribution in several states."

"That's true," said Grady. "She's doing well and has developed a real cult following for her sparkling wines."

Drayton was watching Grady intently. "So are you simply checking out the competition? Or are you getting ready to jump ship?"

Grady cast his eyes downward and did everything but dig his toe into the sand. Finally he said, "Yeah, I guess you could say I've been in talks with Georgette about coming on board here as her manager."

"What about Knighthall Winery?" asked Drayton.

"It's getting awfully depressing over there," said Grady. "Jordan just hasn't been the same for the last half a year. And now with Drew . . . well, it feels like everyone's just thrown in the towel."

"You realize," said Drayton, "it takes time to build a business."

"Five years is a long time," said Grady. "Long enough for me anyway. Knight Music was the light at the end of the tunnel, but now it's just not going to happen."

Theodosia's brows pinched together. "It seems to me that everything is beginning to turn around for them. Pandora just cinched a huge distribution deal in Japan. Maybe that's all it takes for Knighthall to really make a go of things."

"I'm happy for Pandora," said Grady. "But all she ever talks about is turning out red wine. She doesn't need me for that. All along, Mr. Knight and I had our heart set on doing a white Bordeaux and even some sparkling wines." He hesitated. "But Pandora is just obsessed with this whole Japan deal. And Pandora always seems to get her way."

"I'd have to agree," said Drayton. "She's a very forceful woman."

"But the thing with Drew . . ." Grady shook his head sadly. "That just tore the heart out of things. For me and for Jordan." And with barely a nod good-bye, he walked away.

"That's one way to add a downer note to the evening," said Theodosia as she watched him go.

"But he's right," said Drayton. "Even we've let up on our investigation somewhat. We're sad about Drew's death, but feel like we should probably move on." Now he seemed thoughtful and a little morose, too. "Though it's still tragic that his murder remains unsolved."

"I hear you," said Theodosia. "But . . . what are you saying exactly? That we should respect Pandora's wishes to no longer be involved?"

"I'm not sure what I'm saying," said Drayton.

"You know," said Theodosia, "Grady could be lying."

"About . . ."

"About everything. Grady could be lying to ease his way out of Knighthall Winery. Or for all we know, he could be the killer. Who knows what went on between him and Drew Knight?"

"This is all very confusing," said Drayton.

Theodosia wandered over to one of the fire pits while Drayton went to fetch glasses of red wine for them. All around her, young people laughed and joked, kissed and danced, while she mulled things over. She knew Drayton was ambivalent about their continuing investigation, and part of her also wanted to walk away from it. Just . . . let it go. At the same time, that little voice deep down inside of her scolded at her, telling her she should not walk away. Because she'd never walked away from any challenge in her life! So why start now?

When Drayton returned, he presented a glass of red wine to Theodosia and said, "This is their Palmetto Passion. Supposed to be a mix of five different grapes."

Theodosia took a sip. "It's good. There's kind of a plum and cherry taste."

"Do you think it's as good as the red wine we tasted at Knighthall Winery?"

"It's awfully close," said Theodosia.

"Excuse me," said a voice at her elbow. "May I offer you a piece of bruschetta?"

Theodosia turned as the waiter held out his tray and hastily continued his pitch.

"We have fig with goat cheese bruschetta and pesto with plum tomatoes."

Theodosia stared at the waiter until recognition finally dawned. "Carl?" she said slowly. Then with more urgency. "Carl Van Deusen?" She'd just been looking for him!

Van Deusen's dark eyes bore into her for a few seconds, then he, too, blinked with recognition and said, "You almost got me fired from Smalley's, you know!"

"I'm sorry," said Theodosia. "I didn't mean to cause you any trouble."

Van Deusen seemed to soften a bit. "Aw, that manager you had the run-in with is a real jerk. Hardly anybody gets along with him."

Theodosia and Drayton each took a piece of bruschetta as Theodosia made hasty introductions.

"You know," said Theodosia, "you never did tell me about your relationship with Drew."

"There's not that much to tell," said Van Deusen.

"But you and Drew were friends. You attended his funeral."

Van Deusen nodded. "Drew and I were buddies, yeah."

"What kind of buddies?" said Theodosia. *Drinking buddies? Drugging buddies?*

"Just . . . buddies," said Van Deusen. "Friends."

"Good friends?" said Drayton.

Van Deusen took a step backward and clenched his jaw. "Hey, what is this? An episode of *Law & Order*?"

"Very funny," said Theodosia.

"Look," said Van Deusen. "We were friends; we helped each other out. Drew even gave me his car to drive."

"When did he do that?" asked Theodosia. *Is that the answer to the missing Porsche?*

Van Deusen stared at her. "I don't remember."

"Could it have been last Sunday?" she asked.

He shrugged. "I don't know . . . maybe."

"Does anybody else know about this? Did you talk to Sheriff Anson about this?" Theodosia asked.

Van Deusen saw the look on her face and went into full protest mode. "Look, lady, I didn't touch a hair on Drew's head! I just told you, he was my friend!"

"Then who do you think killed him?" asked Drayton.

Van Deusen thumped a hand hard against his chest. "That's what *I'd* like to know!"

"Excuse me." Georgette Kroft, wearing a red-and-black Burberry dress and matching sandals that would have been better suited for a teenage girl, was suddenly staring at them. "Aren't you supposed to be circulating with that tray of hors d'oeuvres?" she asked Van Deusen. She wrinkled her nose. "Yes, I definitely think you are."

Van Deusen eased away. "Sorry, ma'am."

"And don't call me ma'am," she snorted. "I don't look *that* old!"

"Yes, ma'am," said Van Deusen. And this time he bolted.

"Theodosia," said Georgette, grinning broadly now. "Thank you for coming." Her eyes flicked toward Drayton. "And this must be the infamous Drayton?"

"Thank you for your kind invitation," said Drayton. "This is a lovely affair."

"Yes, isn't it just?" said Georgette. Her eyes flicked back to Theodosia. "You know, dear, we really must talk about our collaboration."

"You've said that before," said Theodosia. "About a joint tea and wine tasting?"

"Now that sounds interesting," said Drayton.

"Doesn't it?" said Georgette. "I do believe your tea shop and my winery cater to the same sort of crowd. Which is why I think a joint tasting event would be spectacular."

"Perhaps it could be done to benefit a particular charity," said Drayton. "Say the Heritage Society or the Opera Society."

"Or it could also be done for profit," said Georgette.

"There's that, too," agreed Drayton, barely suppressing a smile.

"Anyway," said Georgette, "I want the two of you to think about it. And after you taste my special surprise wine in a few minutes, you might be even more excited about the concept."

"Okay," said Theodosia.

"Oh," said Georgette. She had turned away from them and now she looked back at them. "Are the two of you still scrambling after clues in the death of that young man?"

"I wouldn't exactly call it scrambling," said Theodosia. "Why, do you have something you want to share with us?"

"Not exactly," said Georgette. "But I do have a suspect in mind."

Theodosia frowned. "And that would be . . ."

Georgette held up a finger. "All in good time."

19

❧

"*What on earth* was that woman babbling about?" said Drayton as he watched Georgette push her way through the crowd. "Do you really think she knows something?"

"It's more likely she suspects someone," said Theodosia. "But then again, don't we all harbor our own suspicions?"

"I suppose so," said Drayton.

Feeling a little unsettled by Georgette's words, Theodosia took another sip of wine and glanced around. That was when she spotted a strange-looking man slinking through the crowd.

"Oh my," said Drayton. He'd spotted him, too.

"What?"

"Flagg," said Drayton. "You know, the writer?"

Dressed in a pair of too-tight khaki slacks and a red polo shirt, Harvey Flagg moved through the crowd like a nasty virus on a crowded cruise ship. He was back-slapping and high-fiving any number of people who could easily serve as fodder for the next juicy story in Bill Glass's *Shooting Star.*

When Flagg noticed Theodosia and Drayton watching him, he casually sauntered over to them.

"Hey, Drayton," Flagg said in an annoying bray. "Sorry I didn't make it to your lunch thing the other day."

"Don't be," said Drayton. "Our idea of publicity doesn't include one of your nasty little stories filled with gossip and innuendo."

"Or one of your photographs of someone in an unflattering pose," Theodosia added.

Flagg smiled crookedly at Theodosia. "You must be Theodosia." Though he was short and overweight, he had a narrow, pinched face and one eye that never seemed to focus completely.

"Run along," said Drayton. "We're not interested in your brand of gossip."

Flagg reared back as if highly offended. "Don't get all holier than thou on me, folks. There's a good reason gossip rags outsell old school magazines like *Newsweek* and *Time*. Readers want dirt. In fact, they crave it. Who doesn't want to know what celeb's got a coke problem, or who just got kicked off a movie set." He winked. "Even locally, our audience is dying to know who's coveting whose neighbor. Or which fat cat's fancy house just slid into foreclosure!"

"If you were looking for a salacious story," said Theodosia, "it's too bad you missed the barrel tasting at Knighthall last Saturday."

Flagg suddenly looked as if he'd been kicked in the stomach.

"That's right," Drayton echoed. "You missed a heck of a scoop."

"Couldn't you smell the blood in the air?" said Theodosia. "Or have we all been giving you just way too much credit?"

Flagg's mouth pulled into a wolfish snarl and his eyes blazed. "I'll have you know I *am* writing a story about that! In fact, I'm talking to a few people who seem to be flying way, way under the radar. You just wait and see." He glanced around quickly, then added in a slight wheedling tone, "You know, if you've got a couple of minutes right now, I wouldn't mind interviewing the both of you. I hear you're thick as thieves with Jordan Knight."

"Doubtful," said Theodosia, turning away from him.

Drayton flapped a hand. "Run along, we're simply not interested."

Flagg was about to say something else when a loud blast of static pierced the air. Theodosia glanced around and saw Georgette Kroft, microphone in hand, standing atop a make-shift stage. She was smiling like she was about to announce the new Miss America.

"May I have your attention in three?" Georgette boomed. The crowd quieted a little. "May I have your attention in two?" The crowd was nearly silent except for a few giggles. "May I have your attention in one?" she asked. Now the crowd was silent.

"Here we go," Drayton whispered to Theodosia.

"Friends," Georgette began. "Thank you all for coming tonight. Oak Hill Winery is supremely honored to host so many local dignitaries. I'd love to name names, but I'm sure I'd miss someone."

The crowd laughed on cue.

"We are also incredibly pleased to share our exquisite new Syrah with you tonight," Georgette continued. "No, you haven't had the pleasure of tasting it yet, but in a matter of moments you'll get your chance. Waiters will be coming through the crowd to offer you a taste of our new Palmetto Prestige Syrah."

As she said the name, a cadre of waiters appeared in two lines from each side of the stage. Then they moved into the crowd, their trays rattling with wineglasses. Immediately, a waiter with a long dark ponytail stopped in front of Theodosia and Drayton and offered them a glass.

"Thank you," said Theodosia as they both accepted wineglasses filled with the Prestige Syrah. She saw that the wine was reddish-orange, almost copper in color, seeming to defy the notion of what was a traditional Syrah.

"Friends," Georgette boomed again, "you don't need to get your eyes checked. This is most definitely a Syrah, but it's our own unique spin on what we're calling a white Syrah. Palmetto Prestige is made from a combination of home-grown Sangiovese grapes and special Cannaiolo grapes that were imported direct from Italy."

"Different," muttered Drayton.

"When I barrel tested this wine," said Georgette, "I picked up some lovely hints of cinnamon and pomegranate. And I can't wait to hear *your* learned opinions. So please . . . raise your glasses and enjoy!"

Theodosia sipped gently. While she couldn't quite place the pomegranate, she did detect a wonderful, creamy nectarine flavor. "It's awfully good," she told Drayton.

"Unusual," said Drayton. "But you're right, it's really quite good."

An hour later, after a few friends were greeted, more wine was imbibed, and some honey-barbecued ribs consumed, Theodosia and Drayton headed for the parking lot.

"All in all an enjoyable evening," said Drayton as they strolled through a garden gate beneath a wooden trellis that hung heavy with swirls of purple Clematis.

"It was nice," said Theodosia.

The gravel parking lot, just a few steps ahead of them, was now practically half empty. The evening had drawn to a close, people had left. Still there were a heroic number of Lexus, Audi, and Mercedes automobiles left in the lot.

"Take a look at all the high-end cars," said Theodosia. "Georgette surely knows the right people to invite."

"Maybe even more than Jordan did," said Drayton. "Besides, people who drive luxury cars are not exactly the type who buy three-dollar wine at Trader Joe's."

"Maybe that's the key to Georgette's success," said Theodosia. "Knowing the right people."

"I suppose it never hurts," said Drayton.

"Or maybe she prices her wine higher," said Theodosia.

As they climbed into the Jeep, Theodosia wished that Max had been able to join them. Oh well, some other time. This week he had his hands full with the Paint and Palette Art Crawl and, of course, the Art Crawl Ball. And from all indications, the Art Crawl had been wildly successful thus far.

Off to her left, an engine roared to life, throaty and rumbling, breaking up the subtle night music of the crickets and tree frogs. A loud voice shouted out as the engine revved louder. Then tires spun wildly in the gravel and Theodosia heard little bits of gravel tick-ticking and pelting against the nearby cars, like a hail of buckshot.

Suddenly, a red sports car burst past her, swerving madly as its tires struggled for purchase in the loose gravel. More cars were pelted with gravel and a tiny rock pinged off her own windshield.

"Silly hot dogger," Drayton muttered.

But Theodosia had caught sight of the car just as it shot off into the darkness. It was a red Porsche! Just like Drew Knight's car!

"Did you see that?" she asked. "The car!"

"Yes," said Drayton. "A crazy person who probably drank too much wine. It's a pity we didn't catch his license plate number."

"That was a Porsche!" said Theodosia.

Drayton gazed at her as they pulled away. "Yes?"

"Drew Knight's Porsche went missing. Remember? And Carl Van Deusen just mentioned that Drew had loaned him his car?"

"Good heavens, you don't think . . ."

"I don't know what to think." Theodosia clutched the steering wheel as she rolled out of the parking lot and headed down the ribbon of road in the darkness. She thought about what Janet at Virtuoso Staffing had told her about Carl Van Deusen—that he'd been acting strangely that night at Knighthall. Was Van Deusen a drug user, too? Could he offer some insight into a possible drug deal that Drew had been involved in? Did he know who Drew's dealer was? And could this drug dealer be the actual killer?

Theodosia decided she definitely needed to have a one-on-one with Carl Van Deusen. And pretty darned soon.

"Dark out here," murmured Drayton. He'd been sitting quietly in the passenger seat not making a peep. "And getting foggy. Makes it difficult to see the road in spots."

"It is getting tricky," said Theodosia. All around them the dark crept closer and closer, barely kept at bay by her halogen high beams. This was an area that had once been inhabited by rice plantations, back when Carolina gold had been the premier cash crop. So there were still plenty of old dams, swamps, hills, and twisting roads to be had.

Theodosia tried to focus on her driving, not on problem solving. But as she climbed a slight rise, she caught sight of two bright lights coming up fast behind her. They crested a hill behind her, and then disappeared from view in her rearview mirror. Thirty seconds later, they were right behind her again. This time a little closer. She checked her speed and saw the needle hovering at sixty. Which meant the speed demon car behind her was flying along at perhaps seventy or eighty miles an hour.

"What's wrong?" Drayton asked, sensing something was amiss.

"Just a crazy driver behind me. A speed demon."

"There's somebody ahead of you, too," he said.

"I think it's that Porsche that blew out of the parking lot just ahead of us. Maybe . . . Van Deusen."

"Maybe," said Drayton. He turned his head. "That car behind you is coming up awfully fast."

"I see that," said Theodosia as her heart skipped a little beat. Her instinct told her that the speed demon behind her wasn't an intentional threat. Still, moving at such a super high speed, he was a hazard to anyone sharing this deserted stretch of road.

"Goodness!" said Drayton, still glancing back over his shoulder. "Now he's almost on top of us!"

Theodosia didn't need an announcement from Drayton to tell her that. The speed demon was a mere fifty yards behind her and closing at a very rapid rate.

"I think he's going to pass us," said Theodosia. They were approaching a fairly steep hill and the solid yellow lines clearly marked a no-passing zone.

That didn't stop the speed demon car as it whipped past them, its overtaxed engine whining loudly.

"Whoa!" said Drayton, gripping instinctively for a door handle.

"It's okay," said Theodosia as they topped the hill. "He's gone. He's way past us now." Theodosia tapped her brakes as they rolled down a gentle hill and boggy swampland stretched out on either side of them. "Gonna bug somebody else."

"Look!" said Drayton, pointing at the curving road ahead. "There he is. Gracious . . . I think he's going to pass that other car, too!"

"Pass that Porsche," said Theodosia, peering ahead. "Yeah, looks like it."

But just as Theodosia's nemesis rolled up alongside the Porsche, he jerked hard to the right and swerved directly into the Porsche, hitting it and sending it careening wildly.

"Speed demon hit that car!" Theodosia yelped. She could barely believe her eyes!

There was a mad flashing of taillights and then a horrendous squealing of tires.

"Did you see that?" Theodosia cried. "Swerved right into him!"

The car that had been hit was fishtailing wildly, its rear end shaking like crazy as it struggled to hold the road. It seemed to hover for a moment, trying hard to regain traction, then it bounced up and seemed to lift right off the ground.

Theodosia and Drayton watched helplessly as the stricken car torqued and spun sideways in the air. Then it flew off the right side of the road and tumbled, end over end, down a steep embankment.

Meanwhile, the speed demon had disappeared down the road.

"Dear lord!" Drayton shouted. "That car was run completely off the road! Right into the swamp, I think."

Theodosia jammed her foot down on the accelerator and roared toward the scene of the accident. *Someone could be hurt. Someone had to be hurt!*

"Mercy me!" Drayton cried. "I do believe we just witnessed a hit-and-run!"

20

❧

Theodosia raced down the highway, desperate to reach the hapless car that had been sideswiped and run into the swamp. Drayton was chattering away in the seat next to her, but she was barely paying attention to him. She was totally focused on reaching the scene of the accident as fast as humanly possible.

She wondered if the driver was dead, immobilized, or struggling to get out before his car was swallowed up by the dank water. Could it be Van Deusen who'd been driving that car? And if so, were there any passengers?

Ten seconds later Theodosia rocked to a stop. Skid marks on the pavement told part of the story of the collision, but there was no sign of the car that had been hit. It had vanished like a specter in a fevered dream.

"Where's the car?" Drayton screamed. "The one that got hit and bounced all over the place?"

Theodosia flipped her hazard lights on and flung open

her door. "It's in the water," she said. "I'm pretty sure it landed in the swamp."

"So . . . what are we going to do?" cried Drayton. He stared at her in horror. "Oh no, you're not going in after it, are you?"

"Do you see anybody else around here?" asked Theodosia. She paused long enough to rummage in her handbag. "Here." She grabbed her cell phone and pitched it to Drayton. "Get busy and call Sheriff Anson."

Drayton fumbled the phone in sudden panic. "I don't know how! I don't know the number."

"Just hit 911."

"Oh."

"And tell 'em to send help! Lots of help! And an ambulance!"

Theodosia didn't stick around to see if Drayton could manage. There simply wasn't a moment to waste. She jumped from her car and stumbled down the slippery bank. Standing in a sea of reeds, up to her ankles in mud, she gazed out across the dark swamp and quickly located the car. It was some fifteen feet out, sitting low in the water. She couldn't see any lights or movement, but she was fairly sure it was the red Porsche that she'd seen earlier.

Had Carl Van Deusen been driving it? She was about to find out! If only she could . . .

Above the swamp racket of frogs and crickets, there rose a terrible sucking, gurgling sound. As Theodosia scanned the boggy landscape again, she was stunned to see that the car was starting to settle.

Oh no!

Stepping into the water, thinking she might call out to the driver, Theodosia immediately sank to her waist in dark and brackish water. And as awful as that was, the cold was even worse. It chilled her to the bone, causing her breath to come out in ragged gasps. Because despite the omnipresent Carolina heat, the icy aquifers deep below these swamps kept them glacially cold all year round.

Theodosia took a single step forward as the cold water began to insidiously suck at her energy. She felt her muscles contract and tighten in protest.

"Hello!" she cried out. "Is anyone there? Can you hear me?"

There was no answer, save the sound of a soft wind easing its way through the cattails and rushes.

"Carl?" she called again. "Try to hang on! We've called for help!"

She was about to turn back, to make sure that Drayton had called for a rescue squad, when the strange burbling sound erupted again. She peered through the dark and saw the car beginning to go nose down.

Oh no! Now what do I do? What if it slides all the way under the water? Then . . .

Theodosia took about one second to make up her mind, and then plunged headfirst into the water. Summers spent at Folly Beach had made her a strong swimmer and honed her freestyle crawl. She pulled hard and straight as her arms flew through the air then dug deep into the brackish water. Her legs moved rhythmically in a hard flutter kick. She swam as hard and fast as she could until she reached a tangled mass of roots and cattails that blocked her route to the half-submerged car. Gathering all her strength, she pulled herself over the top of the brush and then slid down the other side. From now on, she would have to walk or crawl.

The mucky bottom sucked off both her shoes as she struggled to find some sort of foothold below the water. A root, a submerged tree stump, anything to help propel her forward. Green duckweed clung to her clothing and the water reeked of rotten eggs. And every step, every few inches forward through the swamp, sapped more and more of her energy.

She caught her foot on a hidden root and pitched forward, catching herself on the upright trunk of a half-rotted cypress. She tried very hard not to think about alligators or snakes or anything else that could be lurking in this dark water.

But she knew how alone she was out here.

Drayton was back on the bank, of course, but he was so far away he'd never reach her in time if she foundered and went under. And did he even have the strength to save her? To swim out here? Probably not.

That thought triggered another jolt of fear inside her.

No, I can't think that way! I can't let the fear take over!

Theodosia ground her teeth together and fought hard to fight her rising tide of panic.

I can do this! I have to do this! There's nobody else.

A few more stumbled steps and half-swimming strokes brought her eye to eye with the half-submerged car. She rapped her knuckles against the driver's side window and peered in.

She was pretty sure it was Carl Van Deusen who was sitting in the driver's seat. But he was slumped over the steering wheel like a rag doll—not moving or twitching a single muscle.

Knocked out cold? Has to be.

Theodosia batted her fists against the window, trying to rouse him. But Van Deusen remained unmoving and unhearing, collapsed over the wheel.

"Carl!" she shouted. "Carl!"

There was no response. More bubbles broke the surface as the nose of the car dipped farther and farther down. Now the water level was right at the bottom of the driver's side window. It would only be a matter of minutes before the dank water seeped inside, flooding the car and drowning poor Van Deusen.

"Carl!" Theodosia called out. "Wake up! Try to wake up, Carl! We have to get you out of there! This car's going to sink!"

She pawed at the side of the car, fighting to find the door handle, which was well below the water line. Her fingers flailed at the side of the door helplessly.

Where is it? I can't . . . ah, here it is.

But the minute her fingers touched the door handle, the entire vehicle seemed to shift again and settle dangerously lower into the murky water.

Theodosia flipped up the handle and fought to wrench the door open against the press of water. No luck. It wouldn't budge!

She placed one foot against the side of the car, grasped the handle again, and put her full weight behind it. "Come on!" she groaned as she pulled on the door, feeling the strain between her shoulder blades.

With agonizing slowness, the door began to creak open. Theodosia grasped the door handle with both hands and gave a final heave. The door released suddenly and she splashed backward into the water. The world went silent and dark as she sank below the surface. Thrashing around, feeling frightened and helpless, her lungs starting to burn, she struggled to right herself. Then her head popped above the surface of the water and she breathed in blessed air.

Without a moment's hesitation, she was back at the car, crawling halfway inside.

"Carl, come on!" She tugged at his shoulder, trying to rouse him. "We have to get you out of here!"

But all Theodosia's pushing and wrenching was upsetting the exquisite balance of the car. The continuous, ominous bubbling sound meant the car continued to settle even lower!

She'd heard horror stories about quagmires like this that had no bottom, or were composed only of mushy mud or quicksand. She'd heard tales about how people and animals had fallen in, foundered, and been sucked down to their deaths.

She knew she had to pull him out—now!

Theodosia grabbed his collar and tried to pull him, but he was stuck tight.

"Come on!" she yelled again, and now it felt like the car was free-floating, bobbing like a cork. How long would it stay just barely above the surface?

She reached a hand down and cupped Van Deusen's chin. If she could just keep his head above the water. Then she could at least save him from drowning!

"Theodosia!" came Drayton's voice, calling from the road. It sounded faint and filled with worry.

"I'm here!" she called back. "I'm okay!"

"How's the boy?" called Drayton.

Theodosia looked at Carl. His face was pale, his lips were practically blue, and he was barely breathing. "Not good," she called back as she gave a mighty shiver. "Not good at all."

It felt like an eternity, but was probably only five or six minutes before sirens erupted down the road.

"Someone's coming," Theodosia whispered to herself. She was cold and exhausted. It was taking her full concentration to keep her shaking hand from letting Carl's head drop down into the icy water.

She couldn't hear any voices or much of anything else beyond the blood hammering in her head. Her heartbeat felt like it had slowed to a crawl and she felt herself growing drowsy. Somehow, in her subconscious mind, she knew she might be descending into hypothermia. But she couldn't do anything about it.

So tired . . .

A loud splashing suddenly sounded in her ears.

What?

Something pinged inside her brain. *Help?*

"Help!" she called out, suddenly rousing herself. "We're over here!"

There was more splashing and then a man's voice called out, "We're coming, almost there." His words floated toward her, sounding calm and reassuring.

Another loud splash sounded behind her. Now something was coming up under the water for her.

What is it?

Theodosia felt a large object bump heavily against her legs. Then something black and shiny erupted from the water. Suddenly, two divers in wet suits were staring at her, concern etched on both their faces. One grabbed her under the arms and gently pulled her out of the car. A second one slithered in and grabbed Carl.

Gratefully, Theodosia allowed herself to be towed back to shore.

Theodosia accepted a blanket that was put around her shoulders by a kindly EMT, but she refused any other medical treatment.

"Are you sure?" said Drayton. He was anxious beyond belief.

"Really," she said, "I'm just a little damp."

"You were soaked and shivering like crazy when they brought you out."

"Yes, and now I'm starting to warm up."

She and Drayton were huddled next to her Jeep, sipping hot coffee and watching in amazement at the circus that was going on around them. Van Deusen was hauled out and laid flat on a gurney. Oxygen was administered. Sheriff Anson strode back and forth, barking directions. And once a tow truck arrived, a cable was stretched out to the Porsche and attached. Then it was reeled in like a fish hooked on a Rapala.

"That baby's trashed," said Theodosia, once the Porsche was hauled back up on dry land.

"You never know," said the EMT who'd given her the blanket and cup of coffee. "Sometimes all you have to do is drain the gas tank and change the distributor cap."

"Still," said Drayton. "You wouldn't want to buy it secondhand, not knowing its history."

"It's a lemon now," said Theodosia.

Sheriff Anson moved in on the Porsche like a hunter stalking its prey, directing his deputies to conduct a complete search of the car.

"The trunk, too?" asked one of the deputies.

The sheriff nodded. "Absolutely."

The deputy grabbed a crowbar and stuck it under the edge of the trunk. Two seconds later it popped wide open.

"Now it's going to need bodywork, too," said the EMT. He seemed saddened by the Porsche's damaged condition.

"Got something here, Sheriff," said one of the deputies. He reached in with one latex-gloved hand and pulled out a pistol.

"Let me see that," said Sheriff Anson. He pulled on a pair of gloves and gingerly accepted the gun. When he checked the chamber, he nodded and said, "Yup, it's loaded." He rocked the mechanism back and released the bullet from the chamber before removing the clip. Turning it over in his hands, he said, "Same caliber as the gun that killed Drew Knight."

"You can tell that, even though it's waterlogged?" said Theodosia.

"It looks right to me," said the sheriff. "But we'll confirm it with a ballistics test."

"So what are you saying?" asked Drayton.

"Just offhand," said Sheriff Anson, "if it's the same pistol that was used to kill Drew Knight, then it's probably the same person, too."

Theodosia was stunned. "So what was the murder all about anyway? Drugs?"

Sheriff Anson nodded. "Probably. Nine times out of ten, when you see these killings committed by younger people, it's all about drug deals."

"So where are the drugs?" asked Drayton. "Where's his . . . what would you call it? His stash?"

"Probably back at his apartment," said Sheriff Anson. "We'll send a team in there tonight—tear it completely apart."

"You know," said Theodosia, "I don't mean to throw a monkey wrench into things, but that car got run off the road by someone else."

The sheriff cocked an eye at her. "Are you sure about that?"

Theodosia nodded. "Yes. So that might complicate things."

"Maybe," Sheriff Anson said as he moved away from them. "And maybe not."

The sheriff might be able to blow off that hit-and-run, but Theodosia could not. She wondered who on earth could have come rocketing out of nowhere to run Van Deusen off the road.

Could it have been—and she knew this was a stretch—Jordan Knight or Pandora?

Had they somehow figured out—or assumed—that Van Deusen was involved in Drew's death and then decided to take matters into their own hands? To avenge Drew's death?

Theodosia wondered if that was why she'd been summarily fired earlier today. To get her off the case and out of the way? So they could do their dirty work?

"Come on," Drayton said, breaking into her reverie. "It's time to go."

"You're right," said Theodosia. "There's nothing more for us to do here."

"You've done enough," said Drayton. "Do you want me to drive?"

"No," said Theodosia. "I'm fine."

"You're not fine."

"Really I am. Besides, I just want to . . . think."

When they were a quarter mile down the road and all the flashing lights were behind them, Theodosia said to Drayton, "You know, it's possible that Van Deusen was selling drugs to Drew Knight."

"I think you might be right."

"And if Drew didn't have the money to pay for them, maybe he gave Van Deusen his car as payment?"

Drayton frowned. "And then Van Deusen turned around and killed Drew? That seems a little strange."

"I know," said Theodosia. "It kind of sounds liked Carl would have been killing the goose that laid the golden egg."

"So maybe something else was going on?"

"Is going on," said Theodosia.

Drayton sighed heavily. "This whole week has turned into one enormous disaster." He pressed his lips together tightly. "In fact, I'm expecting the Four Horsemen of the Apocalypse to show up any moment!"

21

❧

The next morning, Drayton was still in a tizzy. He knocked over a tall white taper while he was arranging one of the tables and chipped the rim of one of their Crown Ducal Chintz teacups.

"Drat!" he said, making a face. "I didn't mean to do that!"

Theodosia hurried across the empty tea shop to examine the minute chip. "It's not bad," she said, turning the cup over in her hands. "It's fixable anyway. With a little polymer clay and a dab of ceramic paint, it'll be as good as new."

"But it's a chip and it's due to my carelessness," said Drayton.

"Accidents happen."

"But rarely to *me*," said Drayton.

It was Friday morning and the atmosphere seemed to be filled with a low-level tension. Drayton was still acutely wound up over last night's car chase and crash in the swamp. Haley had been stunned by their retelling of the accident and Van Deusen's near-drowning. And Theodosia was feeling tired and generally on edge.

She wasn't exactly sure why. Because the events of the previous night should have yielded a certain degree of satisfaction. Not that Van Deusen had been harmed in any way, but that he'd been apprehended and his involvement in Drew's murder pretty much confirmed by the pistol stashed in his car. In fact, Sheriff Anson had given the impression that Drew's murder had been solved. So case closed.

On the other hand, this all seemed a little too tidy for Theodosia. Particularly that pistol tucked into the trunk of the Porsche.

Had Van Deusen murdered Drew and then stolen his car? If that was all true, was he stupid enough to leave the incriminating murder weapon in the trunk?

Theodosia let this thought percolate through her brain as she straightened a grapevine wreath on the wall. She knew there were inept bank robbers who dropped their wallets during the course of a robbery, stickup artists who smiled blandly at security cameras, and all sorts of other stupid criminal pet tricks that had been captured on tape. Heck, you could probably go to YouTube and laugh yourself silly over the footage.

And then there were the circumstances surrounding last night's accident. Another car had forced Van Deusen off the road.

So . . . the question remained. Had Van Deusen murdered Drew Knight? And if so, what was his motive?

Sheriff Anson had thought drugs, and that same idea danced around in her own mind, too. So maybe the next thing to do would be—

"Hey!" said Haley. She walked out into the still-empty tea shop, holding up the *Post and Courier,* a big smile on her face. "You guys made the paper!"

"Oh no," said Dayton. He touched a finger to his bow tie and patted it, as if needing reassurance.

Haley peered across the top of the newspaper. "Well, not you specifically. Just some of the details concerning last night's big chase. There's a kind of sidebar here about it."

"But Theodosia and I aren't mentioned?" said Drayton.

"Let me put it this way," said Haley as she continued reading. "You're mentioned but not named. "Ho! They made it sound like one of those *Fast and Furious* movies!"

"Let me see that," said Drayton. He grabbed the paper out of Haley's hands and scanned the article. When he finished reading, he was visibly relieved. "Praise all. We're mentioned only as 'two passersby who assisted the injured Van Deusen.'"

"That's good," said Theodosia. "That we're not mentioned by name, I mean."

"I don't know," said Haley, tilting her head and giving them a puckered smile. "I kind of like it when you guys score a little ink."

They threw open their front door then and welcomed their morning guests. Fridays always brought a big influx of weekend tourists, and today was no exception. Theodosia was always mindful about distributing Indigo Tea Shop postcards to the many B and B's throughout the historic district. That little bit of easy advertising always seemed to pay off. And she tried to do as many favors as possible to reciprocate. She catered B and B events, provided scones and muffins for their breakfast baskets, and passed out their business cards and postcards as well. A good *quid pro quo* for a cadre of small business owners.

Haley's Almond Joy scones were the sleeper hit of the morning, followed closely by her banana bread. Of course,

Drayton's private label Apple Dandy tea, a blend of black Ceylonese tea, cinnamon, hibiscus, and dried apples, also proved to be popular. He'd originally intended the tea to be a holiday offering, but customers loved it so much that now they served it year round.

By eleven o'clock, every table was occupied and all the guests were seemingly content. Which meant Theodosia had time to skip into her office and place a quick call to Sheriff Anson.

She had no trouble getting through to his office, but the good sheriff wasn't there.

"He's *supposed* to be here," his secretary told Theodosia, "but he's not." She sounded annoyed and a little bit flustered.

"Could you ask him to call me? I was . . . um . . . one of the passersby from last night. From the accident?"

"Oh sure," said the secretary.

"Can you tell me . . . is Carl Van Deusen in jail?"

"I believe he's at Mercy Medical Center, but restrained and under the watch of an armed guard. They're not taking any chances with him."

"That's good to know," said Theodosia.

The secretary politely took down her number, but Theodosia wondered if the sheriff would really get back to her. If, in his mind, this case was finally solved, then maybe he wouldn't want any further questions or entanglements.

As she was about to hurry back out to the tea shop, her cell phone rang.

"Hello?"

"Just when were you going to tell me about your romp through the swamp last night?" asked Max.

Uh-oh. "Um . . . probably tonight?"

"I've got a donor dinner tonight," said Max. "I think you know that."

"I would've called," said Theodosia. "Really I would have."

"Just what the heck did you get yourself pulled into, my dear?"

"We didn't get pulled in," said Theodosia. "Didn't you read the sidebar in this morning's paper? Drayton and I were passersby." She was liking that reference more and more. "That means we just *happened* to be there."

This time Max let loose a definitive snort.

"What were you two doing out at Oak Hill Winery anyway?" he asked.

"Tasting wine?" It was the truth, after all.

"No, I'd say you were *investigating!*" said Max. And this time he didn't hold back on his accusatory tone. "You were hot on the trail of some alleged murder suspect!"

"Who happens to be in custody right now," said Theodosia. "Even as we speak." She hesitated. "Though I seem to be the only one using a normal speaking voice. While you are—"

"Okay, okay," said Max. "Point taken." He dialed his anger back some. "So . . . they really got him? This guy Carl something . . ."

"Carl Van Deusen," said Theodosia. "Yes, they got him. He's in the hospital under armed guard."

"Well, don't you go snooping around there!" said Max.

"I wouldn't do that," said Theodosia.

"Sure you would," said Max.

Haley was hard at work in the kitchen, doing her chef-and-baker ballet, when Theodosia popped in.

"What's for lunch?" Theodosia asked. She was trying to get her head back into the game instead of worrying about Van Deusen's true role in the murder.

"You're gonna love this," said Haley. "Crabmeat casserole, baby field greens salad with my homemade Thousand

Island dressing, my special Church Street quiche, and ricotta and orange marmalade tea sandwiches."

"That all sounds wonderful."

"It is," said Haley. She quickly dipped a wooden spoon into her dressing and gave it a twirl. "Or will be soon."

Theodosia made her way into the tea room, cleared off a couple of tables, popped on fresh tablecloths, and set them up for lunch. Drayton was at the front counter, ringing up two customers while he kept an eye on two burbling tea kettles and two pots of tea that were steeping. Multitasking Drayton style.

"What's on the docket for today?" Theodosia asked him. "Teawise?"

"A Keeman, a lemon verbena, and a spiced plum tea for our luncheon crowd. But this afternoon, when I do my tea-blending class, we'll probably go a little stir-crazy."

"Ha," said Theodosia. "Good one. How many people signed up for your class?"

"An even dozen," said Drayton. "So it should be lots of fun. Not overly crowded, but enough differing tastes so we'll come up with some interesting blends."

"But probably not as delicious as your proprietary blends," said Theodosia.

"Probably not," Drayton murmured. "Then again, we all have to start somewhere."

At exactly twelve noon, Jordan and Pandora Knight rolled into the tea shop.

Theodosia saw them push through the front door and worked hard to suppress her surprise that the two of them had actually shown up here today and that they even looked happy together. Well, sort of. Then she went over to greet them.

"Jordan, Pandora . . . welcome!"

Jordan aimed a sad smile at her. "Theodosia," he said. "Hello."

"Surprised to see us?" asked Pandora.

"Well . . . yes, I am," Theodosia admitted. After the events of last night, she figured the two of them would be staking out Sheriff Anson's office, pestering him for all the sordid details.

"Oh, my goodness!" said Drayton when he caught sight of Jordan. "Give me a minute." He was busy with a customer, packing up four take-out lunches, but he clearly wanted to speak to Jordan.

"Can we talk?" Jordan said to Theodosia in a half whisper.

"Certainly," said Theodosia. "Would you like to have lunch or—"

"Lunch," Pandora said decisively. "Absolutely we could use some lunch to help fortify us."

Theodosia led them to a table over in the corner, where they could enjoy a little privacy. When they sat down, Jordan held out a hand, indicating she should sit down with them, too.

"But just for a minute," said Theodosia as she slipped into a captain's chair.

Jordan put his hands flat against the table, drew breath, and then said, "Theodosia, we can't tell you how grateful we are."

Theodosia shook her head. "I didn't—"

"Yes, you did," said Jordan. "I don't know how you did it, what magic you wrought, but you managed to solve the case. You had a direct hand in the apprehension of this horrible Carl Van Deusen fellow."

"Who wasn't really on Sheriff Anson's radar at all!" said Pandora. She was fairly quivering with outrage.

"But the two of you must have known Van Deusen somewhat," said Theodosia. "Since he was supposedly friendly with Drew."

Jordan nodded. "We'd maybe seen him around the winery once or twice, but we never thought anything about it."

"And then Van Deusen was working at your wine tasting last Sunday night," said Theodosia. "As a server."

Jordan's eyes misted over and he said, "Yes. Unfortunately."

"We don't know what happened between the two of them," said Pandora. "But the truth will eventually come out. I imagine they had some kind of terrible argument. Some kind of falling-out."

"It would have to be more than just a falling-out," said Theodosia. She was about to mention the drugs, when Jordan hastily interrupted her.

"And here I was suspicious of the people at Plantation Wilds," Jordan said, looking regretful.

Pandora touched a hand to her chest. "I feel a little silly, too. I was so sure that awful Georgette Kroft had something to do with the murder. Turns out we were both wrong!"

"In any event," said Jordan, "we are united in our gratefulness to you."

Pandora wiped at her eyes. "I think a hug is in order." She leaned over and put her arms around Theodosia, hugging her tight.

Then it was Jordan's turn. He gave her a warm hug and said, "We just want to put this nightmare behind us."

Pandora blew her nose discreetly, gave a little hiccup, and added, "And now maybe have a little lunch."

"Of course," said Theodosia. "Shall I put something together for you?"

"Why don't you surprise us," said Pandora. She was still fiddling with her hanky.

Theodosia got to her feet and said, "Give me a minute." She had more questions for them, but this was neither the time nor the place. Jordan and Pandora were finally acting civil to each other and they'd both just endured a terrible shock. So later. Later she'd delve a little deeper into what they might know about the Drew Knight–Carl Van Deusen relationship.

"And we need to thank Drayton, too," said Jordan. "What a friend—" His words were choked short by his emotions.

"Certainly," said Theodosia.

"Jordan wants to talk to you," Theodosia told Drayton. "He's pretty torn up because of Van Deusen's arrest last night, but he seems to think we're the ones who cracked the case."

"Didn't we?" said Drayton.

She shrugged. "Not really. I think we more or less just stumbled into things."

"Well, let's not go into major denial mode. If Jordan wants to be grateful and think we had a hand in solving his son's murder, let's let him have his moment."

"Fine with me," said Theodosia.

She went into the kitchen and quickly assembled a tea tray for Jordan and Pandora. Two salads, slices of quiche, a couple of tea sandwiches. As a special treat for the eyes, she grabbed a box of edible flowers from the cooler and sprinkled a few petals on the two-tiered tray. Then she carried it to the table, where Drayton was deep in conversation with Jordan and Pandora.

"They're meeting with Sheriff Anson later this afternoon," Drayton told Theodosia. "He's going to try to fit all the pieces together."

Good luck with that, Theodosia thought. But said instead, "Sounds good."

"And then we'll let you know what we know," said Jordan.

Theodosia set her tea tray down. "That would be great."

But what she was really thinking was, *Unless I get to Sheriff Anson first.*

The minute lunch was over, Theodosia hastily cleared off four tables and pushed them together so they could seat six tea-blending students at each table. Drayton, meanwhile, was measuring out some basic black and white teas into small bowls. Then he also set out bowls of lemon grass, hibiscus flowers, lemon peel, wild cherry bark, dried apple bits, and lavender.

"Do you think I have enough ingredients?" Drayton asked.

"I think so," said Theodosia. "You don't want to over-whelm their taste buds, after all."

Drayton peered at her. "Excuse me, but you're looking a tad glum for such a lovely Friday."

"Still noodling over the murder . . . the investigation."

"You know," said Drayton. "Jordan and Pandora consider you the hero of the hour—they think you solved Drew's murder!"

"It doesn't feel like I had much of a hand in it at all."

"Of course you did, dear girl," Drayton chortled. "And just wait until Detective Tidwell comes in for tea. Why, the story I'm going to tell him! The man will be pea green with envy!"

Drayton's class on microblending tea was a huge hit. His amateur tea sommeliers blended white tea with hibiscus and lavender and came up with what they called their Book Club Blend. And then they blended a rich black Ceylon tea with bits of apple, citrus, and lemon grass and dubbed it their Orchard Tea Blend.

Theodosia watched from the sidelines, but was clearly restless.

"What's wrong?" Haley asked.

Theodosia shrugged. "I don't know, I guess I'm just at sixes and sevens." She was still hoping that Sheriff Anson would call her back. And she hadn't forgotten about Jack Alston, too. She figured his investigation into Higashi Golden Brands might help shed some light on things.

"Yeah," said Haley, "you seem awfully preoccupied."

"Sorry," said Theodosia.

"Don't be. You have a right to be. It's been a pretty strange week around here."

Theodosia nodded. "Listen, do you mind if I bug out early? There's something I want to do."

"No problem with me," said Haley. "All I'm going to do is bake a couple batches of date and walnut cookies for Angie's open house tonight. You're still going to that, huh? At the Featherbed House?"

"I wouldn't miss it."

When Theodosia arrived at Virtuoso Staffing, Linda Hemmings was sitting at the front desk, signing payroll checks and stuffing them into envelopes.

When Linda looked up and saw Theodosia, she said, "See how glamorous it is to own your own business?"

"Tell me about it," said Theodosia. "I was down on my hands and knees the other day, restocking all our shelves."

"Humbling, isn't it?"

"You know," said Theodosia, "I kind of like it that way."

Linda nodded. "Keeps you grounded anyway." Then she got serious and said, "I read in this morning's *Post and Courier* about how you chased Carl Van Deusen into a swamp and cornered him single-handedly."

"It wasn't quite as dramatic as all that," said Theodosia.

"And you saved him from drowning?"

"Really, I just held his head up."

"Still," said Linda. "It sounds as if Drew Knight's murder has been solved, thanks to your quick work." When Theodosia didn't respond right away, Linda frowned and said, "I have to admit, though, I feel pretty awful about Carl. I never glimpsed that dark side of him. I guess it just goes to show that you never really know someone. You never can tell what's hidden deep down in their heart."

"Maybe so," said Theodosia.

Linda gazed at her. "Is there a problem?"

Theodosia bit her lip. "Let me ask you something. What time did your staff arrive at the winery last Sunday?"

Linda thought for a moment. "I think they had a five o'clock call. Yeah, that was it. An hour to get changed and prepped, then the event started at six. Why are you asking?"

"From what I'm hearing—and this is from several people—no one saw Drew after two o'clock."

"What does that mean?" Linda asked.

"What if Drew was already dead by the time Carl and the other waiters showed up? Could that be possible?" She knew Sheriff Anson had checked the timelines. But still . . .

Linda was suddenly excited. "It is possible! Would that mean that Carl might not be the killer?"

"Maybe," said Theodosia. "Maybe so."

Once she was back in her car, Theodosia put in another call to Sheriff Anson. And glory be, this time she was able to get through!

"Sheriff Anson? This is Theodosia Browning. Do you remember me from last night? I was the one who—"

"Yes, yes," said Anson. "I remember, I surely do. That was good work on your part. You were very brave to jump in the water and hold that boy's head up. I don't think I ever gave you the proper thanks you deserved."

"It was the least I could do," said Theodosia. "Anyone would have done the same thing." She hesitated. "I was wondering . . . when the autopsy was done on Drew Knight, did the ME know how long he'd been dead?"

"Best guess was four or five hours," said Anson.

"Does that jibe with the timeline of when Carl Van Deusen showed up at the winery?"

"It's a little off, but Van Deusen could have arrived earlier."

"I see," said Theodosia. "And . . . Van Deusen's still in the hospital? Unconscious?"

"That's right. We haven't been able to talk to him yet."

"I'm assuming the hospital has had a chance to run toxicology tests and such on him?" she asked.

"Yes," Sheriff Anson said slowly.

"I was wondering, did they find any drugs in his system?"

The sheriff hesitated for a moment, and then said, "No, they did not."

"Really," said Theodosia. For some reason, this didn't come as any big surprise to her. "But you found his stash of drugs?" she continued. "I mean, you searched his car and home and everything, right? He was dealing drugs, wasn't he?"

There was silence on the line and then Sheriff Anson said, "We haven't located any drugs yet."

"Nothing at all?" Theodosia wondered what kind of a drug dealer Van Deusen could be if he didn't have any drugs. A little prickle of anxiety rolled up her spine. "Excuse me, Sheriff, but you know that another car drove Van Deusen off the road last night, don't you? In all the confusion, I hope I made that point completely clear to you."

There was more silence on the line.

"Sheriff Anson?" said Theodosia. "Did you hear what I just said?"

"Yes," said Sheriff Anson. "I'm afraid I did."

* * *

Theodosia started her car, shifted into first, and then put it back into park. There was one more call she wanted to make. One more follow-up on a remark that had been made last night.

"Georgette?" she said, once she had Georgette Kroft on the line.

"Theodosia!" said Georgette. "I heard all about your wild rescue last night! Jumping into the swamp and such. Aren't you just the hero of the hour!"

"Not really," said Theodosia. "Georgette . . . I need to talk to you about something."

"Ooh, I'm so sorry we didn't get to chat more last night. Now, of course, I'm feeling a bit muddle-headed." She giggled. "Probably from drinking a little too much of my own wine."

Theodosia plunged ahead. "Last night you told me you had your own suspicions about who killed Drew Knight."

"I did? Yes, I suppose I did. But that's all a moot point now, isn't it? Now that Carl Van Deusen's been arrested."

"I'd still like to hear your thoughts anyway. Because I'm guessing you weren't suspicious of Van Deusen." She couldn't have been, Theodosia decided, since Van Deusen had actually been working there last night.

"Oh," said Georgette, "my guess was that awful liquor distributor."

"Alex Burgoyne?"

"Yes, the silent partner. Or quasi-partner, or whatever you want to call him."

"Tell me," said Theodosia. "Why would you suspect him?"

"Probably because he's sleazy," said Georgette. "Because he's been involved in more than a few unsavory deals."

"Is this hearsay?" Theodosia asked. "Or has he really had legal issues?"

"It's what I know!" snapped Georgette.

"And he distributes your competitor's wine," said Theodosia.

"There's that, too."

22

❧

Of all the B and B's located in the historic district, the Featherbed House was Theodosia's favorite. Not just because her friend Angie Congdon owned it, but because it personified the charm, graciousness, and gentility that was Charleston.

Tonight, lights shone brightly in the windows on all three floors and guests drifted back and forth on the ample porch that extended around three sides of the inn's main building.

Theodosia mounted the steps, crossed the porch, and pushed her way into the reception area. And was amazed at the changes the dear old place had undergone.

The walls were now painted a pale yellow, but they'd been shellacked or glazed so they fairly glistened in the light from dozens of flickering candles and the overhead Italian chandelier. A persimmon red Oriental carpet covered the polished wood floor, and wing chairs and a traditional sofa, newly covered in yellow chintz, invited guests to come sit a spell.

The geese were still there, just as Angie had promised. Needlepoint geese pillows, a hand-carved wooden goose standing guard by the fireplace, bronze goose lamps, and an entire flock of white ceramic geese.

And Angie Congdon was there, too. Standing behind the mahogany reception desk, smiling and nodding and checking in guests even as her open house party swirled about them. Theodosia stood there for a few moments, waiting. And then Angie looked up and saw her, and a big grin spilled across her face.

Angie was cute and petite with a dynamic personality. In her past life she'd been a commodity trader in Chicago. But she'd given up that crazy, stress-filled life for a slightly slower pace in Charleston. Still, Angie was the only person Theodosia knew who could prune an apple tree, set out an elegant spread of wine and cheese, fluff up six guest rooms, and then greet you with good grace and charm, all without breaking a sweat. When Angie's husband, Mark, had been murdered a few years ago, Angie had been forced to take stock of things and make a conscious decision to move the business forward. And from the looks of things, she'd certainly managed to do that.

"Theodosia!" Angie exclaimed as she rushed to greet her friend. "I'm so glad you came!"

The two women embraced and Theodosia noticed that Angie's hair color, which had been fairly dark a year or so ago, had gradually lightened over time. With help from what had to be a great colorist, she was practically strawberry blond now, which made her look years younger and more chic than ever.

"All I ever hear from Drayton," said Theodosia, "is about the fabulous changes you've been making. And that you built an addition onto the carriage house?"

"First we spruced up the reception area, parlor, and dining room," said Angie. "That turned out so well we decided to do a major overhaul on all the guest rooms. We freshened everything with paint, new coverlets and rugs, and new artwork. Then I took a careful look at my business plan and decided I was actually ahead of schedule. So I called my contractor and gave him the go-ahead to start building the addition I'd been noodling around inside my head." She grinned. "Now, six months later, it's become a reality."

"I can't wait to see it," said Theodosia.

"What are we waiting for?"

Angie grabbed Theodosia's hand and pulled her through the crowd, into the warm, steaming kitchen, and out the back door. The backyard was a veritable park, with its groupings of palm trees, flagstone patio, rose arbor, fish pond, and small greenhouse. There had been a fire, right on the heels of the death of Angie's husband, that had completely destroyed their old greenhouse. Now a new greenhouse stood in its place, a lovely circular affair with a fanciful, peaked roof. Thanks to Angie's care and hard work, it was now stocked to the rafters with orchids and bromeliads, all twining and growing in the South Carolina heat and humidity, putting out luscious blooms in her husband's memory.

"Remember how the old carriage house was?" said Angie. "With that ugly gazebo stuck up against it and the awkward cement apron?"

Theodosia remembered.

"Well, we tore all that out and built our addition," said Angie. She waved a hand to indicate the lovely Colonial-style addition with its beaded clapboard siding and high-pitched gable roof. "We added three new rooms and a big two-room suite with a hot tub." She grinned. "We call our new suite the Gosling Suite."

"You've done amazing things with this place," said Theodosia. "I'm so impressed. You should be awarded a bunch of Michelin stars or something."

"Don't I wish," said Angie. "Of course, Harold's been a huge help. And we still have Teddy Vickers as our manager."

"Teddy's always going to be here," said Theodosia. "He's practically a permanent fixture." She paused. "But Harold. That relationship is sounding a bit serious." Harold was Angie's new boyfriend of a few months.

Angie blushed. "Well, it is. Harold's charming and funny and makes me very happy. And he's extremely smart and well connected when it comes to business and finance."

"I'm not sure I even know what business your friend is in."

"Oh, Harold is a senior partner at a market research firm," said Angie. "Data Metrics. Perhaps you've heard of them?"

"I have, but the only thing I know about Data Metrics is what I've read in the business section of the newspaper. Just a capsule review and a few press releases. Since I've been out of the marketing arena, I don't keep up all that much."

Angie looked skeptical. "Are you kidding me? You're the most marketing-savvy person I know. Look at all the cutting-edge events you do for your business—your tea tastings and mystery teas and such, plus your website and T-Bath products. You're miles ahead of all your competitors and you always seem to figure out clever ways to snatch little bits of publicity. Whether it's a mention in the food and wine section of the newspaper or a guest appearance on a radio or TV show."

"Well, thanks," said Theodosia, laughing. "I guess if you ever need any advice . . ."

"I know who to ask," said Angie. She glanced toward the patio, where a group of people were sipping wine around a fire pit, and lowered her voice. "You've certainly been in the media lately."

"Oh that," said Theodosia.

"You were at Knighthall Winery when that poor boy was discovered in the dregs of that wine barrel."

"I'm afraid so."

"And then last night . . ." Angie gave a little shiver. "Theo, the whole historic district is buzzing about that."

"News travels fast," said Theodosia. "Unfortunately."

"It sounds like you were right there in the thick of things," said Angie.

"I try not to make it a habit . . ."

Angie reached out and touched her arm. "Be careful, huh? You seem to, um, get pulled into a lot of craziness."

Theodosia knew there was no sense in pretending. "I don't mean to, but I suppose I do."

"Just please take extra care," said Angie. "We wouldn't want anything to happen to you."

"I'll be careful," she said. "I'm always careful." But she knew her words sounded a little hollow.

Theodosia stayed for another fifteen minutes or so. Chatting with friends from the neighborhood, getting reintroduced to Angie's boyfriend, Harold Affolter, and making marketing small talk with him, having a quick nibble of the date and walnut cookies that Haley had baked for tonight.

But Theodosia was anxious to get home, too. It had been a long, trying day and she was tired. Wanted nothing more than to crawl between soft cotton sheets and let her dreams carry her away. So when the time seemed right, she slipped down the front walk. And in the soft darkness, with glowing street lamps illuminating her path, she headed for home.

Just as Theodosia was passing in front of the Kingstree Mansion, the house Andrew Turner was so interested in buying, she noticed a car parked in front of her house.

Now what? Theodosia wondered with a start. She suddenly remembered the speed demon from last night, the car that had come out of nowhere to drive Van Deusen off the road. Could this be him? If so, why would he be after her? Just because she'd been investigating Drew's murder?

But as Theodosia drew closer, she realized that this dark car, with its reinforced bumper and side spotlight, suddenly looked more than a little familiar.

A Crown Vic? Don't tell me . . .

Theodosia stepped out into the street and walked quietly up to the driver's side window. She bent down, peered in the open window, and found herself staring into the bright, beady eyes of Detective Burt Tidwell.

"Am I under arrest?" she asked him.

A corner of Tidwell's mouth registered the slightest of twitches. "Let's just call it house arrest for now," he said in his trademark big cat growl. Then he paused. "May I come in?"

"Of course."

Burt Tidwell was the brash and rather brilliant detective who headed the Robbery-Homicide Division of the Charleston Police Department. He was beefy and bulky and possessed a heroically oversized head with slightly protruding eyes. His personality was outsized, too, and his temperament often ranged from that of an angry grizzly bear to that of a slightly disgruntled walrus. Tonight, even though the weather was warm, Tidwell wore a slightly frayed tweed jacket with a matching vest, which stretched tightly across his bulging stomach.

Tidwell followed her into her house, stepping lightly for such a large man through her living room, dining room, and finally, into the kitchen.

Earl Grey rose from his bed to give Tidwell an inquisitive meet-and-greet sniff and then calmly retreated. He'd met this man before. No problem, no threat.

Tidwell, who barely fit between the stove and the refrigerator on the opposing wall, gave a cursory glance around and said, "Nice. Homey."

"It needs some work," said Theodosia.

"The cupboards," said Tidwell, nodding.

"Yes, they're old and tired."

"Still," said Tidwell, "you wouldn't want to compromise the character of your house." That was the thing about Tidwell. He was a brilliant cop and an all-around smart guy, too. *NCIS* meets HGTV.

Theodosia pulled a tin of Nilgiri tea down from a shelf. "Would you like a cup of tea?" she asked. Then decided something stronger might be in order. "Or perhaps a glass of wine?"

"Wine," said Tidwell. "That does seem to be the problem, doesn't it?"

Theodosia turned to stare at him. "Why exactly are you here again?" she asked. "Because this doesn't strike me as a social call. And let's face it, Detective, you're not exactly anyone's idea of a welcome wagon."

"I'm here because Drayton asked me to come and talk to you," said Tidwell. She and Drayton had befriended Tidwell over the past few years. She had gotten involved in a few of his cases—well, dragged in, actually. And Tidwell had subsequently started showing up on the doorstep of the Indigo Tea Shop. He had a nose for tea and a never-ending appetite for scones.

"Drayton called you? Really?" Theodosia didn't know if she should be thankful or a little offended.

Tidwell strolled over to the kitchen table and poked a fat finger at a pot of purple violets. "Did you grow these?"

"Yes. Well, after I brought them home from the garden store, I did."

"Gardening," said Tidwell. "Nothing like it. Thrusting your hands into the rich, dark soil. Teasing life into tiny, new buds."

"Excuse me," said Theodosia. She somehow doubted that Tidwell ever got down on his hands and knees to plant rhododendrons or pull weeds. He was merely smoke screening or pontificating or whatever. "But Drayton called you?"

"Yes, he did. In fact, your erstwhile tea blender and quasi-partner made it sound like a matter of utmost importance. Life and death." He spun and faced her. "Thus . . . here I am."

"It's nice that the two of you are so concerned about me."

Tidwell tilted his head. "Please do not take this lightly," he told her. "It seems that you have once again embroiled yourself in a rather nasty murder investigation."

Theodosia shifted from one foot to the other. "Well, I kind of noticed that."

Tidwell continued. "And I believe Mr. Conneley was hoping you might heed my sage advice."

"Which is?" said Theodosia.

"Stay out of it."

"You already said I was in it. And you do know about last night, don't you? The crash in the swamp?"

"Yes, I'm well aware of all aspects of this thing." Tidwell's eyes narrowed. "You really aren't taking my visit seriously, are you?"

"On the contrary," said Theodosia, "I'm taking it very seriously."

"You believe that the semi-incarcerated Mr. Van Deusen is not the killer everyone thinks he is." It was a statement, not a question.

"Is that what Drayton told you?" asked Theodosia.

One of Tidwell's furry eyebrows raised a half an inch. "That is what he has surmised."

Theodosia was at a loss for words. "I . . . I really don't know what to think about Van Deusen."

"Still, you have doubts about his guilt. Or his being complicit in the murder."

"Let's just say I have doubts." Theodosia opened the refrigerator and took out a bottle of Chardonnay. She pulled out the cork, grabbed two Riedel wineglasses, and poured a glass for each of them. "Here," she said, handing it to him. "Enjoy."

Tidwell accepted the glass from her. "Thank you."

"So now what?" Theodosia asked.

"I'm going to enjoy this lovely wine and then I'm going to make a note to call Sheriff Allan Anson first thing tomorrow morning. Try to see if I can get a look at his case file."

"You can do that?" said Theodosia. What she really meant was, *You'd do that for me?*

Tidwell looked into her eyes and saw their shimmer of gratitude. "Dear girl," he said. "Once I set my mind to it, I can do just about anything."

23

❦

"It's a good thing we're only open until one o'clock today," said Haley. "I can really use an afternoon off."

"I think we could all use a little time off," Theodosia responded. She was eyeing the shelves of her highboy, knowing she really did have to decide on what went into her tea basket for tonight's silent auction. The Art Crawl Ball organizers had called earlier and left a brief message for her, asking if she could please, please, please have her basket delivered to the Ballastone Hotel by early afternoon.

So . . . carrying the sweetgrass basket that Miss Josette had created for her, she shopped her own shop, making her final choices before they opened for business this Saturday morning.

Theodosia had settled on a pink-and-yellow floral teapot, brand new, from the Cabbage Patch next door. Now, as her eyes wandered across the jam-packed shelves, she picked out three tins of Cross & Cromwell Tea. Into the tea basket they went. Then she added a jar of DuBose Bees Honey, a wooden honey dipper, and two prepared scone mixes that were Haley-approved.

Her basket wasn't quite filled yet, so she chose an assortment of T-Bath products—Chamomile Calming Lotion, Feet Treat, and Verbena Hand Lotion. Oh, and she couldn't forget to include her candle. The bayberry candle that she'd grabbed earlier and set on her desk after heeding Miss Josette's warning.

It was funny, Theodosia thought, that Miss Josette's warning really had come to pass. The minute she and Drayton had wandered outside of the Charleston city limits to Oak Hill Vineyard, they *had* encountered trouble! They'd not only had a dustup with Harvey Flagg from *Shooting Star*, but they'd been pulled into the chase, rescue, and subsequent arrest of Carl Van Deusen.

And now, instead of feeling satisfied that justice had been served, Theodosia was wondering whether Van Deusen was even the killer.

Detective Tidwell had promised to look into things for her, so that was heartening. And Drayton's concern for her had been wonderful. She'd even gone so far as to thank him this morning when he'd first come hustling in. But he'd cut her off with a wave and a gruff, "No need," and gone about his business, choosing teas and fussing with tea kettles.

Haley was standing at the counter, kibbitzing with Drayton, when she carried her basket over.

"Looks like you got generous and picked out a lot of really neat stuff," said Haley.

"A lovely arrangement," observed Drayton. "I'm sure it will be much appreciated."

"It still needs a little finessing," said Theodosia. "I've got some colorful shredded paper in my office that I'll use as a base, then I'll arrange everything nice and neat, pop a sheet of clear plastic film over it, and tie it all up with a big pink ribbon."

"Zhuzh it up," said Haley. "Hey, if you want me to, I'll run your basket over to the Ballastone Hotel right after lunch. I know you're going to want to get out of here as soon as possible so you can run home and make like Cinderella!"

"Thanks, Haley. I'd appreciate that," said Theodosia.

Haley glanced at Drayton. "What about you, Drayton? Are you gonna get all gussied up for tonight, too?" Drayton and his friend Timothy Neville were escorting two women to the Art Crawl Ball. Though both women were up there in age, they were well-heeled art patrons and Timothy had twisted Drayton's arm just a bit.

"My tuxedo is brushed and my Thom McCans are shined to a high gloss," said Drayton. He cocked a wrist and glanced at his ancient Patek-Philippe watch. "The question is, are *you* ready? Since we open for business in less than five minutes."

"I'm on it," said Haley as she dashed back into her kitchen. "Not to worry."

"Are you looking forward to the big ball tonight?" Theodosia asked Drayton.

"I think I am, yes," said Drayton. "It should be a nice jolly affair. Especially with the Art Crawl still going on. All the street vendors and food trucks will make for a festive atmosphere."

"I sure hope so," said Theodosia.

The Indigo Tea Shop was swamped that morning. Customers streamed in like crazy, then a red-and-white horse-drawn jitney pulled up in front of the tea shop and let out even more customers. Those who couldn't get seated at tables seemed content to grab scones and take-out cups of tea and mill around outside in the warm sunlight.

Theodosia and Drayton worked as hard and fast as they could, but could barely keep up.

"We're so rushed, I feel like we're letting down our standards," Drayton worried.

"I feel like we're caught in the middle of a buffalo stampede," said Theodosia.

"Huh," said Drayton, smiling and betraying his first hint of humor today. "Very amusing."

Haley had come up with the perfect Saturday menu—blueberry scones, goat cheese and pimento tea sandwiches, chicken salad tea sandwiches, and something she called a walking calzone. The calzone was really a large biscuit stuffed with melted cheese, caramelized onions, and sausage slices, which could be eaten with a knife and fork or wrapped in a piece of waxed paper and eaten on the street.

"People just can't get enough of those calzones," said Drayton. "Though they're not exactly traditional tea shop fare."

"Maybe we *should* consider doing a food truck," Theodosia joked.

"Or our truck could just sell a simple cuppa and an assortment of scones to go," said Drayton.

"Call it the Scone Zone," said Theodosia.

"Or the Tea Caddy," said Drayton, his good humor fully restored.

At twelve forty-five, with scones and tea sandwiches running perilously low, Theodosia ducked into her office and placed a call to Detective Tidwell.

As luck would have it, he wasn't there.

Okay, then she would try Agent Jack Alston again. He'd promised to call her back. But so far, she hadn't heard a word.

His phone rang into oblivion, and then flipped over to voice mail.

"Hey," she said when she heard the customary annoying beep. "This is Theodosia. You were going to call me back, remember? Well . . . I was just wondering if you found out anything about that company in Japan, Higashi Golden Brands. So . . . um, thanks. And call me. Please."

She leaned back in her chair just as Drayton stuck his head in her office. "That's it, we're done," he told her.

"Done with . . . what? Customers? Serving food?"

"Both," said Drayton. "Our larder is completely depleted. We've basically run out of everything."

"Did you have to turn people away?" This was always one of Theodosia's biggest worries.

"Just two couples. Sorry, I know how much you hate to do that."

"In this case I suppose it couldn't be helped."

"Anyway," said Drayton, "the front door is locked while a few customers continue to linger. But in a few minutes I'm going to try to ease them out . . ." He saw the worried look on Theodosia's face again and said, "I know, I know, I'll be as gentle as possible."

"Thank you," said Theodosia.

As usual, Theodosia was the last one left in the tea shop. She double-checked the latch on the front door, made sure all the appliances were turned off, and then checked the kitchen for a second time. Okay. Done and done. She was looking forward to going home, sitting in the sun on her patio, and lazing away the rest of the day. Until she had to get ready for the party tonight, that was.

And just as she opened the back door, just as she cast a last glance around and was about to make her getaway . . . the phone rang.

With a small sigh, she eased herself back inside and snatched up the phone.

"Indigo Tea Shop, how may I help you?"

"Miss Browning?" The voice on the other end of the line was a scratchy whisper.

"Yes?" Theodosia said.

"Theodosia?" said the voice, so low it was barely audible.

"Yes," she said again. "This is she."

Ten seconds of dead air ensued and Theodosia was about to hang up the phone when the voice whispered, "Thank you."

Theodosia inhaled sharply. What kind of crank call was this?

"Thank you for what?"

There was a sharp cough and then the voice, sounding even more scratchy and faint, said, "For saving my life."

Theodosia's blood ran cold. "Who is this?" she demanded.

"It's me. Carl."

"Carl Van Deusen?"

"In the flesh. Or what's left of it," said Van Deusen.

"Carl," said Theodosia, suddenly at a loss for words. "What do you want?"

"Funny you should ask," said Van Deusen. "Because I really need to talk to you."

Theodosia clutched the phone tighter. "So talk."

"In person," said Van Deusen. He seemed to be fading in and out like a bad radio signal.

Theodosia was stunned. "Excuse me, but aren't you chained up somewhere under armed guard?"

"Mercy Medical Center," Van Deusen rasped. "Listen, I need to talk to you. It's extremely urgent." This time she could barely make out his words.

"I can't really . . ." She wasn't sure what to say to him. And why did he want her to come and see him? Did he want to make a confession of some sort? Was he so close to dying that he felt he had to unburden his soul to her?

There was a loud voice in the background and then Van Deusen whispered to her, "Just come."

Just as Theodosia hung up, the phone shrilled again, pretty much scaring the beejeebers out of her. Wondering if it was Van Deusen calling back, she picked it up and said in a tentative voice, "Yes?"

"Theodosia!" It was Max.

"Oh," she said. "It's you." Her heart was suddenly pounding.

"You were expecting someone else?" he said in a jesting tone.

"No, not at all." Could he tell she was up to something? *Please, no.*

"I'm just calling to give you a heads-up," said Max. "My ETA at your place is going to be about eight o'clock tonight, okay?"

"Yes," she said, feeling suddenly relieved. "Wonderful. I'll be ready."

When Theodosia pulled into the parking lot at Mercy Medical Center, her stomach was in knots. Should she be here? she wondered. Should she be doing this? Did she even dare talk to Van Deusen?

Of course, the answer to all this was a resounding no. But here she was anyway, creeping across the parking lot, walking in the front door, feeling like any moment a security guard would rush up to her and yell, "Stop!"

But they didn't.

Instead, she waited in the lobby and watched as the receptionist, a stern-looking older woman with gray hair, turned over her front desk duty to what looked like a young, fresh-faced volunteer.

Lucky, lucky, lucky, Theodosia whispered to herself as she approached the front desk.

The young volunteer looked up with an eager smile. "Help you find someone?"

"Van Deusen," said Theodosia.

The girl's eyebrows pinched together. "Could you maybe spell that, please?" she asked as she clicked a few keys on her keyboard.

"V-A-N . . ." said Theodosia.

"I got that part."

"D-E-U-S-E-N."

"Here it is," said the volunteer, peering at her screen. "Room six thirty-two."

"Thank you," said Theodosia as she skittered away quickly to avoid any questions or warnings. She found the bank of elevators, rode one up to the sixth floor, and got out. Like a little mouse checking for the big bad house cat, she peered around expectantly. The hallway was surprisingly quiet. All she saw was a cart rattling down the hall, picking up lunch trays, and a patient going for a stroll with his oxygen canister trailing behind him.

She tiptoed down the hallway, eyes forward, checking out the room numbers with her peripheral vision. Halfway between the elevator and the nurses' station, she saw a man in a blue uniform striding down the hall toward her.

Theodosia kept going, her heart suddenly beating a timpani drum solo inside her chest. *Please. Don't. Stop. Me.*

The man in the blue uniform, whom she was fairly certain was a hospital guard or policeman, stopped at the desk to chat with one of the nurses. As she passed by, she heard them giggling together over some whispered exchange. And then the nurse said in a teasing drawl, "Oh, George, what would your wife say if she knew what a flirt you were?"

Theodosia kept going until she spotted room six thirty-two. Without hesitating, she pushed open the door and slipped in.

The blinds were drawn, so the room was in semidarkness, but she could see Van Deusen lying in his hospital bed. He seemed to be sleeping. But as she moved closer to his bed, he stirred. Then he lifted his head and said, "Hello?" He sounded foggy and confused.

Theodosia moved a little closer to him. "Hello, Carl."

Van Deusen groaned and struggled to sit up. Once he managed to prop himself up on one arm, he looked at her and blinked. Then recognition dawned. "You came," he said in a thin, reedy voice. "I didn't think you would."

"Yes, I came," said Theodosia. "Because I was curious. Now please tell me what you want."

"I . . . I want you to help me."

Theodosia shook her head. "I think it's a little late for that."

"You're the only one who can!" he said urgently.

"Sorry," said Theodosia. "If you need a cup of tea, I'm your lady. If you need a lawyer . . . well, there's the phone book."

"But you're the one who's been looking into this entire mess!" Van Deusen pleaded.

"Not anymore. Now I'm out of it."

"But I'm innocent!" said Van Deusen. "I didn't murder Drew. I told you before, he was my friend!"

"Do you realize that Sheriff Anson found the gun that killed Drew in the trunk of your car? Correction, Drew's car, which you seem to have appropriated."

Van Deusen groaned and shook his head. "If a gun was there, then somebody planted it! You have to believe me!"

"Did you explain that to the sheriff?"

"I've been trying to. But nobody's listening." He fought to draw breath. "Please help me . . . right now you're all I've got!"

Theodosia wasn't sure whether to believe him or not. But somewhere, in the depths of her heart, his words touched her. She hated that this young man was chained to his hospital bed without anyone to serve as his advocate. Without anyone willing to give him the benefit of the doubt.

"I don't know," Theodosia said. "I can't promise anything. I'm still . . . oh, let's say I'm looking into a couple of things."

There was a rattle at the door.

"Jeez," said Van Deusen, looking startled. "That's the—"

Quick as a fox, Theodosia ducked behind a white screen, pulled open a door, and slid into the bathroom. She eased the door shut behind her and stood there in the stark fluorescent light, feeling a little breathless, listening to the guard's mumbled voice in the room she'd just left.

Can't go back in there. So . . . now what?

She looked at the door opposite her, pushed it open, and stepped out into the adjoining hospital room.

A man lying in bed and doing a crossword puzzle looked up at her. He had gray flyaway hair and wire-rimmed glasses perched on the end of his nose. For some reason, he reminded her of Albert Einstein.

"Everything okay in here?" Theodosia asked in a chipper-cheery voice. "You need anything?"

The man shook his head slowly. No.

"Okay then," said Theodosia. "Have a good day." She smiled brightly at him and stepped out into the hallway. And breathed a huge sigh of relief even as she wondered what her next move should be.

24

❧

Max showed up right on time to whisk her off to the Art Crawl Ball. Theodosia looked elegant and even a bit statuesque in her long black gown and strappy sandals. And she'd wound her hair up into a fun, messy topknot and secured it with a small, jeweled pin that had once belonged to her mother.

So she should have felt like she was sitting on top of the world as they cruised down Broad Street in Max's BMW.

Truth be known, she didn't.

After her impromptu meeting with Carl Van Deusen a few hours ago, Theodosia had tried to get in touch with Sheriff Anson. But he wasn't at his office. In fact, the woman who answered the phone at the Law Enforcement Center had made it quite clear that civilians simply didn't disturb duly elected sheriffs on a Saturday afternoon.

So she'd tried to get hold of Detective Tidwell. But he wasn't around, either. And Jack Alston still hadn't gotten back to her. And for all she knew, maybe he never would.

A pickle of a predicament. What to do now?

Max swung the car over to the curb and stopped at the front door of the Ballastone Hotel. A valet in a snappy red jacket quickly opened his door, while another valet rushed around to open Theodosia's door and help her out.

"Thank you," Theodosia murmured to the valet. As she turned, she saw a black Cadillac Escalade pull up right behind them and Georgette Kroft emerge from the passenger side. *No,* she told herself, *I don't want to get involved with that crazy lady tonight. Definitely not tonight.*

Then Max held out his hand to her and she was swept along into the hotel. Past a group of smiling onlookers and up a wide marble staircase.

Theodosia knew that she and Max looked like the perfect couple. Dressed impeccably in black tie, their faces shining with excitement, they appeared ready for a night of fun and dancing and silent auctions.

Yet Theodosia felt like a fraud. She knew Max would totally disapprove, would have a complete and total meltdown, if he found out she'd gone to see Van Deusen today. In fact, everybody she knew would probably disapprove—Drayton, Haley, Jordan and Pandora Knight, Tidwell, and certainly Sheriff Anson, just to name a few on a large roster of disapprovers. Earl Grey might even raise his doggy eyebrows at her.

But she'd gone and done it anyway, and now she felt like she was harboring a secret. Not quite an answer to what was going on, but perhaps a small sliver of the puzzle. Because for some crazy reason, she actually believed Carl Van Deusen. Believed that he was innocent, that he had somehow been set up.

The million-dollar question, of course, was who set him up?

For that, Theodosia had no answer.

Which was why, when Max pulled her into the Grand

Promenade Ballroom, she wore a slightly perplexed look on her face. People might have mistaken it for bemusement or even curiosity. But Theodosia was in a genuine quandary as to who might have murdered Drew Knight and foisted the blame onto Carl Van Deusen.

Would she find an answer to her dilemma here, tonight? Hardly.

Couples swirled about the dance floor as an orchestra played a sexy, romantic fox-trot. Colored spotlights formed giant globs of paint on a large palette that had been sketched in the middle of the dance floor. Oil paintings on easels and sculptures on square blocks of marble were lined up against the walls. The bar and a cocktail lounge of sorts were set up at one end of the ballroom, while long tables filled with donations for the silent auction were on the opposite side.

"What do you think?" said Max.

"This place looks absolutely magical," said Theodosia. "I think you and your crew of volunteers created the perfect gala."

Max grinned. "I think so, too."

When Max took her by the hand and led her toward the silent auction tables, Theodosia smiled and went along willingly. And promised herself that she'd make the best of it tonight. She'd set everything aside and indulge in a little fun. Correction, make that a lot of fun.

As they crossed the dance floor, Delaine and Andrew Turner swirled past them, looking radiant and dancing so closely together they looked like they'd just taken a class at Arthur Murray. And Donny Hedges from Plantation Wilds, balancing a trio of drinks, practically bumped into them. When Hedges suddenly recognized Theodosia, he grimaced and quickly darted away.

"Whoa," said Max. "What did you ever do to him?"

"Nothing really," said Theodosia.

"Who is he?"

"Just a friend of Drayton's," she said as they made their way to the silent auction tables.

There are a few things here that I want to bid on," Max was telling her.

"Which ones?" Theodosia asked, trying to shake off the encounter with Hedges and share in Max's excitement.

He grinned. "For one thing, I wouldn't mind winning your tea basket."

"Flattery will get you everywhere. But I could make one of those for you in about twenty seconds flat. So maybe pick something else."

"Okay," said Max, studying the offerings. "How about we bid on a balloon ride?" He reached for a slip of paper and read, " 'A hot air balloon ride for two floating over the picturesque countryside, complete with a bottle of champagne.' " He wiggled his eyebrows. "Ever ridden in a balloon?"

Theodosia shook her head. "Never."

"Want to?"

"Are you kidding? Sure. I think it'd be a lot of fun."

Max studied the bid sheet. "Let's see, the bidding's up to one hundred and fifty dollars. So what should I bid? Maybe one seventy-five?"

"Give it a shot," said Theodosia. "But you'll probably have to keep coming back and posting higher bids if you really want to win."

Max scrawled his bid, and then said, "Okay, now I'm going to get us a couple of drinks. What would you like?"

"Maybe a glass of white wine."

"Duly noted," said Max. "You want to wait here?"

Theodosia had just spotted Drayton and the rest of his party, seated at one of the low cocktail tables that had been arranged under a trellis of fake grapevines. "I see Drayton over there, so I'm going to stop by and say hello."

"Fine," said Max. "I'll come find you."

Theodosia pushed her way through the crowd of eager partygoers, greeting some people she knew and saying hi to a few of her Church Street neighbors.

Brooke Carter Crockett, who owned Hearts Desire, was there with her on-again, off-again boyfriend, Chad Donovan. She greeted Theodosia with a big hug.

"Where's that handsome boyfriend of yours?" Brooke asked. She looked cute in a light blue floor-length gown.

Theodosia gave a wave. "Max is over thataway, getting drinks. Did I hear that you donated some spectacular piece of jewelry to the auction?" Besides running a very successful jewelry shop, Brooke was also a skilled designer.

"Did she ever," gushed Donovan. "A necklace made out of chalcedony and sterling silver. A gorgeous piece."

"But a little heavy," Brooke confided.

"I'll have to take a look at it," said Theodosia. "I love stones with that lustrous, milky color."

"Maybe you want to bid on it," Donovan urged.

Theodosia continued on her way toward Drayton. But when she arrived at his table, she found he was sitting alone.

"Where'd everybody go?" she asked. She knew Timothy and the two Heritage Society donors had been here just minutes earlier.

"They're flitting about, being social butterflies," said Drayton. "But the real question is, where did you go?" He lowered his voice and gave her an accusatory look. "This afternoon, I mean."

"You don't want to know."

"I don't?"

"Well, maybe you do," said Theodosia. "But you probably don't want to hear about it tonight."

Drayton was suddenly all pretend innocence. "Good

heavens, Theodosia, you've pulled me into everything else that's gone on."

Theodosia grinned. "Nice try. But if you recall, it was *you* who pulled me into this mess in the first place!"

Theodosia cut across the edge of the dance floor, looking for Max. Probably, she decided, he'd run into some of his museum or gallery friends and they were chortling away about what a success they had on their hands.

As she stopped and scanned the crowd, her eyes suddenly caught sight of another familiar face.

"Tanya?" said Theodosia. Was it really Tanya Woodson, the model, strolling toward her on the arm of Duke Brothers, one of Charleston's most eligible but marriage-phobic bachelors? Yes, it was. And tonight, wonder of wonders, Tanya seemed almost eager to talk to her.

"I just heard about Carl Van Deusen," said Tanya. Her eyes were bright with excitement and she seemed a little breathless. Or maybe it was because Brothers was the heir to a Charleston banking fortune?

"He's under arrest," said Theodosia. "Sheriff Anson booked him on suspicion of murder."

Tanya made a face. "The sheriff's wrong about that one. Van Deusen's no killer."

"They found a gun in his car," Brothers offered.

"I know," Tanya said with a sharp retort. "I *do* read the newspaper, you know." Then she turned her focus back to Theodosia. "Carl was a friend of Drew's. He wasn't any kind of killer."

"You never know about people," said Brothers, pulling her away.

It was interesting, Theodosia decided, that even Tanya believed in Van Deusen's innocence. Then again, if Drew and Van Deusen had been friends, she might know him fairly well. Maybe she could even serve as a character witness if only . . .

Theodosia stopped herself. No. Not tonight. She was here to have fun and that was that.

Now if she could just find Max.

Probably, she decided, he was back at the auction table, worrying about placing a high bid on that balloon ride.

But when Theodosia returned to the table, Max wasn't in sight.

Still as she looked around, she saw that some of the other auction items were equally spectacular. Here was an antique rose gold Cartier watch donated by the Charleston auction house Hubert & Humbolt. And a week's rental on a luxury town house at Hilton Head. And an Apple iPad. And right next to it was the bottle of Château Latour that Andrew Turner had donated. She peered at the bid sheet and saw that it had already been bid up to eight hundred dollars! Wow. And here was a romantic weekend for two donated by the Lady Goodwood Inn.

Theodosia moved a couple of steps down the table, looking at the auction items, and suddenly stopped in front of her own tea basket. She gazed at it and her eyes fell on the bayberry candle. What had Miss Josette said about it? Something about revealing a thief? She couldn't quite remember her exact words.

When her cell phone tinkled from inside her beaded clutch, Theodosia hastily dug it out and answered. "Hello?" She figured it was Max, calling to try to find her. Trying to triangulate her in the crowded ballroom.

"Theodosia," came a rich, warm voice. "It's Jack Alston."

"Jack," she said, a little surprised that he'd actually called her back. She'd more or less written Jack Alston off.

"I have a little information for you about Higashi Golden Brands."

"Okay," she said.

"Basically," said Alston, "they're kind of a shady company."

This struck her as strange, since Pandora had raved about them. "How so?"

"Oh, about a year or so ago, they imported a few hundred barrels of vodka into Hong Kong. It was real rotgut stuff, aged about two days in some Bulgarian distillery. Anyway, long story short, your friends at Higashi Golden Brands bottled it up, slapped labels on it, and then sent it on to Japan, where it was distributed and sold at a rather inflated price under the name *Suntory Premium Vodka.*"

"But it wasn't premium at all," said Theodosia.

"It was like battery acid," said Alston. "And it certainly wasn't Suntory. Anyway, Suntory Group—they're a big-deal Japanese company—filed a lawsuit against them."

"What kind of suit?"

"Ah, it was basically a cease and desist. Japanese style."

Theodosia's brows knit together. "Because they appropriated their company's name."

"Well," said Alston, "that's a nice way of saying—"

"Counterfeiting," said Theodosia. She was beginning to get a low-level buzz of excitement inside her head.

"That's right," said Alston. "It's a problem that's running rampant right now. Especially in Asia. You'd be amazed at the major corporations that are getting ripped off royally. Computer companies, sporting goods companies . . ."

"And liquor companies," said Theodosia. She was suddenly staring at the bottle of Château Latour that was sitting a few feet from her.

"Lots of liquor companies," said Alston. "In fact . . ."

"Mr. Alston," said Theodosia. An idea had begun to slowly crystallize inside her brain and she was barely able to breathe. "I'm going to have to get back to you."

"Well, okay . . ." He sounded disappointed.

"I appreciate your information, really I do. But there's something I have to do . . ."

Theodosia dropped the phone into her bag and stared

fixedly at the label on the bottle of Château Latour. She studied the cross-hatched etching of the castle. And slowly, as she turned her idea over and over, an answer seemed to click into place.

Cross-hatched etchings? Weren't this remarkably similar to some of the artwork that Andrew Turner had stashed in his back room? The pieces he'd kind of covered up when he was searching for Drew's piece? The pieces he had tried to keep her from seeing?

No, she told herself, *not etchings plural. Just one little etching. That's all he would need.*

She picked up the bottle of wine and hefted it. Now her curiosity and determination burned like a white-hot flame.

Deciding to follow both her suspicions and her instincts, Theodosia carried the bottle over to Drayton. He was sitting at a table with two other Heritage Society board members, chatting amiably. When she crooked a finger at him, he promptly jumped up and came over to her.

"Tell me what you see," she said, holding out the bottle of Château Latour.

"Excuse me?" said Drayton.

"I want your opinion. Can you just . . . look at this?"

Drayton very carefully pulled his tortoiseshell half-glasses from the inside pocket of his tux and put them on. Then he accepted the bottle of wine from her and proceeded to study the label.

"Well?" she said.

Drayton gave a perfunctory smile. "This appears to be a very expensive bottle of Château Latour."

"Do you think so?" Theodosia had a fizz of excitement running through her that just wouldn't subside. "Look at the label. Does it seem a little off to you?"

"I'm not sure. Why?" He cocked his head at her. "Do you doubt its authenticity?"

"I think I do."

"Of course," said Drayton, "one really wouldn't know unless one took a taste."

"Then let's taste it," said Theodosia.

"Oh no," said Drayton. He held the bottle against his chest protectively. "There's no way I could render a learned opinion on this particular wine. While I do imbibe in fine wines occasionally, I certainly wouldn't call myself any sort of wine expert."

"Do you know someone who is?" asked Theodosia. "Do you know anyone who really knows his stuff? Someone whom you might consider a wine connoisseur?"

Drayton frowned. "Really, Theodosia, I don't know where you're going with this."

"I know you don't, and I apologize for being so abrupt. But can you please just answer the question?"

"Well, Timothy Neville certainly knows fine wines. He has a very impressive cellar filled with vintage French wines."

Theodosia looked around. "And Timothy's still here?"

"Yes, of course."

"Where is he?"

Drayton glanced around the room." He's . . . well, I just saw him a few minutes ago."

"We have to find him." Theodosia tugged at his sleeve impatiently. "Like right now."

"Why?" said Drayton. "What on earth are you up to?"

"Please just trust me on this, Drayton. I don't have time to explain."

Timothy was standing at the bar. A cocktail, an old-fashioned, rested on the bar in front of him.

"Theodosia!" Timothy enthused. "How nice to see you again. We certainly enjoyed your lovely tea the other day. I was just telling Drayton that—"

Theodosia grabbed the bottle of Château Latour out of

Drayton's hands and shoved it at Timothy. "Please, this is a Château Latour eighty-four, yes?"

Timothy blinked. "Ah . . ."

"Timothy," said Theodosia. "I'd like you to take a very careful look at this bottle of wine and tell me if you think there's anything wrong with it."

"Wrong with it," Timothy repeated. He stared at Theodosia with hooded eyes. "You think there's something wrong with it?"

"Yes, I do," said Theodosia. "But you're the expert. So I'd like to hear what you think."

Timothy shifted the bottle from one hand to the other. "Well . . ." He gave one of his trademark frowns. "For one thing, the label looks a little off."

"The label?" said Drayton. "Really?"

Timothy looked nonplussed. "She asked, Drayton, I merely answered."

"You're worried about a *label?*" said Drayton. "Really, Theo, we need to put this back immediately. It's one of the premier items in the silent auction."

Theodosia reached across the bar and grabbed a wine opener. "I've got an idea," she said. "Let's test its authenticity. Let's open this bottle of wine and have a taste."

"Theodosia!" said Drayton. "That wine doesn't belong to you. You have no right to do that!"

"Watch me!" Theodosia stabbed the corkscrew into the bottle of wine, gave it three good turns, and pulled hard. The cork came out with a resounding pop.

"What's going on here?" asked Max, suddenly coming over to join them.

"Theodosia's going to taste test this bottle of Château Latour," said Drayton rather stiffly.

"She bought it in the auction?" said Max. "Really?" He looked at her expectantly. "Don't tell me the bids have already closed?"

"No, they have not," said Drayton. "She appropriated it."

"What?" said Max as Theodosia poured out a full glass of wine for Timothy.

"Will you?" Theodosia said, focusing intently on Timothy. "Taste it, I mean?" She pushed the wineglass toward him.

Timothy shrugged. "Why not?" He picked up the glass, studied it for a moment, and took a small sip.

"Well?" said Theodosia. She was so nervous she was basically dancing on the balls of her feet. "What do you think?"

Timothy took another, longer sip, and let the wine roll around inside his mouth. Then he gazed at her impassively. "You really want my opinion?"

"Yes, of course I do!" said Theodosia.

Timothy curled his upper lip. "It's swill."

Drayton let loose a loud gasp. "What? Are you telling us this is *not* Château Latour?"

"Good heavens no," said Timothy. "Not even close."

"That's because this wine is counterfeit," said Theodosia. Now she was clutching the bottle. "Aged all of a few months at Knighthall Winery. That's why Pandora wanted to produce only red wines. That's why she struck up such a fast deal with Mr. Tanaka at Higashi Golden Brands."

Max blanched. "What are you talking about? What are you saying?"

"I'm pretty sure that Higashi Brands is planning to sell knockoff wine to the Japanese wine market!" said Theodosia.

Drayton looked utterly stunned. "Absolutely not! Jordan Knight would *never* do such a dishonest deed!" He said it with such ferocity that several people turned to stare at him.

"I doubt that Jordan knows anything about this," said Theodosia.

"Then who does?" Drayton sputtered. "Besides Pandora?"

"Andrew Turner, that's who," said Theodosia. "He has an artist—and probably a printer, too—who are creating phony labels for him." She held up the bottle for them all to see. "I think Drew somehow tumbled to Turner's scheme. And maybe even tried to stop him. And that's why Turner murdered him!"

"Turner!" Drayton cried.

"Yes, that's right," said Theodosia. "I'm absolutely positive he's the one behind this counterfeit wine scheme."

Drayton suddenly lifted his arm and pointed. "No, I mean . . . there he is!"

They all four gazed across the crowded ballroom and saw that Andrew Turner was staring at them with a watchful, suspicious expression on his face.

And then, as comprehension began to dawn, as Turner suddenly realized that he'd been made, his face darkened and his jaw tightened. He spun on his heels and, with the sprightliness of a character in a Road Runner cartoon, took off running.

"We've got to stop him!" cried Max.

"Then let's go after him!" cried Theodosia.

And from across the dance floor, as Delaine saw her date turn tail and disappear into the crowd, she called out pleadingly, "Please . . . wait!"

25

❧

Andrew Turner ducked his head and hotfooted it through the crowd like a star running back heading for the goal line.

Startled by Turner's sudden exit, Theodosia bobbled the wine bottle in her hands. It slipped from her grasp and plunged to the floor, crashing like a miniature atom bomb. Shards of glass and droplets of wine flew everywhere, causing people to turn and stare.

"I've got to—" Theodosia began.

"No, you don't!" said Max. He reached out and clutched her arm. Hard. No way was he going to let her run off in hot pursuit.

"Max," Theodosia cried. "He killed Drew Knight!"

Max continued to hold her tight, but Theodosia's eyes implored him to let her go.

"Okay, okay," Max relented. "But *we* have to be careful!"

"Call the police!" Theodosia yelled to Drayton and Timothy as she glanced back over her shoulder. "Get hold of Tidwell . . . and Sheriff Anson, too!"

Drayton nodded unhappily as Theodosia and Max took off running.

Turner had crashed through the crowd on the dance floor and left a mess in his wake; two men and one poor woman in a long white dress were muttering angrily as they picked themselves up off the floor.

Theodosia and Max careened to the door of the ballroom and pushed their way through, spinning out into the nearly empty hallway. Just up ahead they could hear Turner's feet pounding down the marble stairs. He had a head start on them, but just maybe . . . if they really booked it . . .

Skittering down the wide stairway, Theodosia and Max descended into the plush hotel lobby. They pulled up short for a few seconds, glancing at the check-in desk, the concierge's desk, the front door, and an acre of leather sofas and potted plants, trying to figure out which way Turner might have gone.

"Which way?" said Max. "Any guesses?"

"You head out the front way, I'll go out the back!" said Theodosia.

"Right," said Max. "But be careful! Please be careful!"

Theodosia trotted into the lobby, trying to decide if Turner had dashed out the back door or had maybe hopped an elevator to one of the upper floors as a clever dodge.

Then she heard it. A loud voice, angry and clearly upset, shouting, "Hey, man, are you crazy? What do you think you're doing!"

Theodosia pivoted and sprinted to her right, down a long corridor lined with shops. Up ahead of her, several pieces of expensive luggage lay strewn on the plush carpet. The bellman's brass cart had also been upended and the angry bellman was muttering fiercely and shaking his fist.

Aha! Turner had definitely come this way!

Theodosia chased down the hallway and spun around a corner, just in time to see Turner disappear through a heavy brass and wooden door into Cerise, the hotel's upscale French restaurant.

Like a hunter after its quarry, Theodosia followed Turner into Cerise. She abruptly brushed past the host's stand, then bumped and pushed her way through a bevy of tuxedo-clad servers.

"Pardon, madame!" the dapper-looking host called after her as she slewed around a corner, hot on Turner's trail.

Theodosia never broke stride. She dashed past table after table of dinner patrons, who seemed shocked to witness a footrace in what was normally a very sedate and posh restaurant.

Up ahead, Turner glanced back, saw her coming, and spun past a table. Then, just when he thought he was in the clear, he collided head-on with a waiter who was preparing salads tableside for a party of four. The enormous glass bowl teetered precariously, then toppled to the floor, spilling its contents of mixed baby field greens. A half-dozen crystal cruettes, filled with colored vinaigrettes, smashed to the floor also.

Theodosia continued after Turner, almost slipped on a piece of ten-dollar arugula, and caught sight of him again as he pushed with desperate force through a swinging door into the kitchen.

Hot on his trail, Theodosia followed right into the kitchen after him. Angry, raised voices—some jabbering in French, others in Spanish—told her that Turner had indeed come this way.

Theodosia ran past a stove where enormous kettles of beef bouillon and French onion soup simmered. Then past an enormous open-flame broiler, where tasty cuts of steak and chops sizzled and popped. Several men and two women in stained white chef's garb stood dumbfounded as she rushed by. A waiter—most of his face and part of his shirt covered in crème fraîche—struggled to get to his feet after what, Theodosia suspected, had been yet another collision with the crazed and panicked Turner.

Through the stifling heat, steam, and sheer pandemonium, Theodosia saw Turner up ahead. Arms akimbo, he skidded on the slick tile floor and yelped loudly as he took a nasty fall to one knee. Then, just as quickly, he pulled himself up and bolted for the emergency exit. As he smacked into the bar across the door, an alarm went off. Loud, buzzing, incredibly annoying.

As the door started to swing closed, Theodosia also hit it hard and pushed her way through after him.

Out in the back alley, the stench of garbage rose heavily in her nose.

Awful.

Theodosia looked right, then left, and saw Turner sprinting down the narrow alley, kicking up his heels as he went.

Turner glanced back at her over his shoulder, a look of panic straining his face. Then his arm shot out and he began tipping over garbage cans as he ran.

Like an Olympic hurdler, Theodosia sprinted after him, leapt over a battered tin can, sprinted some more, and made another flying leap.

"Stop!" Theodosia cried out to him.

Turner didn't stop. Instead, he barreled his way out into the crowded street into a critical mass of art vendors and food trucks, and hundreds of strolling art lovers.

Theodosia emerged from the alley a few seconds later. She pulled up short and gulped a mouthful of air, wondering exactly which way Turner had gone. Up and down Church Street, the carnival atmosphere prevailed. With crowds of people, bright lights, and strolling musicians— and no one had a clue as to what was going on!

With the sky just beginning to turn a purplish-black, Theodosia glanced to her left and was stunned to see Max hobbling toward her. He looked red-faced and exhausted.

"Did you see Turner?" she asked. "Which way did he go?"

"That way!" Max cried, pointing and gesturing frantically. "I ran the opposite direction, finally doubled back, and just caught a peek of him as he came out of the alley and headed up the street." He gasped and suddenly bent over. "But I can't . . ." He was completely spent, totally out of breath.

But Theodosia wasn't finished by a long shot. She'd spent the last few years keeping pace with her long-legged canine, Earl Grey, running through White Point Gardens, slaloming down back alleys and skipping across dark back-yards. She was surefooted and in condition, her muscles taut and well trained. She could run full out for the better part of twenty minutes. Could do an hour if it was just a lope. So she knew, deep in her steadily pumping heart, in every fiber of her being, that she could run down this killer!

She pushed off after him.

Turner, who was already halfway down the block, was starting to struggle. He was staggering and weaving his way through the art fair, maybe fifty or sixty strides ahead of Theodosia. Obviously tired and winded, he suddenly cut through a booth displaying framed color photographs, dodged past the Zorba's Gyros food truck, and almost ran smack-dab into a tent that was filled with ceramic mugs and bowls.

Turner pulled up short by a kettle corn stand, trying to catch his breath. As he peeled off his black jacket, the bet-ter to blend in, his head swiveled wildly and he searched frantically for an escape.

I've got him now, thought Theodosia. Turner was losing ground and he knew it. Every time he stopped to grab a breath or risked a backward glance, his face looked gaunter and more pinched with panic.

Where would Turner run to? Theodosia wondered. Maybe try to run a couple more blocks and then cut over to Gateway Walk? If he did, they'd have him! With all the hedges and wrought-iron fences, he'd be completely bottled up! Drayton had undoubtedly called 911, and the Charleston Police had probably scrambled squad cars. If they hadn't, Max would certainly put them on alert. So all she had to do was stay on Turner's tail and . . .

What on earth? What's he doing?

Turner suddenly dashed toward the back door of a large red food truck. The red-and-yellow sign painted on the truck's side said, BOWSER'S HOT DOGS.

Turner yanked the back door open and scrambled inside. He was obviously met with some resistance, because, without warning, an enormous tray of hot dog buns came flying out, followed by a shower of red that looked like blood but was really a crimson spray of catsup. Then the sputtering proprietor in a mustard-spattered apron came tumbling out.

Oh no! If Turner drives that truck out of here, we'll never catch him!

There was more clatter inside and then a loud revving sound as the food truck's engine roared to life.

Theodosia sprinted for the back door of the food truck just as she heard a massive grinding of gears. The door flapped open and she could hear Turner swearing inside as he shifted wildly, still trying to find the proper gear.

And just as the truck pulled away with a sharp jerk, Theodosia got one foot on the back bumper and grabbed hold of the back door.

With a burst of speed, Bowser's Hot Dogs caromed down Church Street with Theodosia hanging on for dear life!

Pedestrians stopped in their tracks, mouths agape, as they watched the truck wobble down the street. And once the truck reached cruising speed, the speakers on top began cranking out the glaring notes of "Pop! Goes the Weasel."

Turner powered his way down Church Street, relentlessly hitting parked cars, sideswiping oncoming cars, and almost nicking a horse-drawn jitney. And all the while, Theodosia was holding on for dear life, trying to pull herself into the truck.

Squealing brakes heralded a series of five orange construction cones that flew past Theodosia's head. Then, with one mighty effort, knowing this was it, she pulled herself inside.

Lurching to and fro in the swaying truck, trying to steady herself on a rubber mat, Theodosia fought to catch her breath. She knew she had to somehow get Turner to stop this food truck. To pull over to the curb before he killed someone.

But how to do that?

Theodosia's eyes searched the interior of the truck, looking for some sort of weapon. She saw cupboards; a flat grill crusted with grease; aluminum bins filled with pickles, raw onions, and chopped olives; and a cooler heaped with hot dogs. But none of it had any stopping power.

Frantic now, Theodosia ripped open one of the cupboards. And saw a large metal skillet hanging from a hook.

Okaaaaay. This might do the trick!

Grabbing the skillet in her right hand, Theodosia steadied herself with her other hand as she tried to move slowly, quietly, toward the front of the truck.

If Turner knew she was on board, he gave no indication at all. Instead, he seemed more intent on dodging pedestrians and loudly gunning the engine.

And still there were no sirens. Theodosia thought it bizarre that no police cars had shown up to give chase. That no one had reported seeing a woman in a black formal dress clinging to the back of a speeding food truck. Although probably, she decided, the entire scene would be shown on YouTube by tomorrow—the entire chase gone viral!

Keeping low, moving quietly, she crept forward, the rubber mat cushioning her steps and deadening the sound.

Finally creeping up to just behind the driver's seat, Theodosia paused and drew a deep breath. Then, raising the skillet above her head, she cried, "This joyride is over!" and slammed the skillet down on top of Turner's head.

Bong!

Turner's entire body reacted as if he'd been shot through with a jolt of electricity. His shoulders hunched forward and his hands flew off the steering wheel. Then his head lolled sideways, his eyes rolled back in his head, and his right leg stiffened hard against the accelerator.

Oops!

"Not quite as planned," Theodosia muttered. She lurched to grab the steering wheel just as the food truck blew through a red light. Thinking fast, she kicked Turner's leg out of the way and shoved his unconscious body up against the driver's side door. Then she tromped down hard on the brake pedal—and hoped for the best.

Tires screeched, pedestrians screamed and scattered, and oncoming cars honked their horns. Theodosia swerved dangerously as some of the speed began to bleed off, but they were still barreling directly toward another food truck, which had a giant ice cream cone painted on its side.

Oh no! We're on a collision course! We're going to smack right into that stupid truck and end up with hot dog–flavored ice cream!

And then, as if providence had dropped it there just for her express purpose, Theodosia saw a lamp pole looming directly in front of her.

Yes!

She jerked the wheel again and steered the food truck directly at it. And then held on for dear life as they struck hard.

Clank!

There was an agonizing screech of metal as the truck shuddered like a dying dinosaur. Then the lamp pole groaned and rocked over at an awkward angle. Theodosia lost her footing completely, was thrown one way and then the other. And then she toppled over backward onto the cushioned floor!

Boom!

"Oh!" she cried.

And then . . . nothing. No more motion, no more collisions.

But at least they had come to a stop!

Breathing hard, blinking wildly, Theodosia couldn't believe her wild ride was finally over. Her hair was frizzed and twined like a crazed Medusa and her dress was an absolute disaster. Groaning, knowing she'd sustained a number of bumps and bruises, Theodosia picked herself up and staggered her way through the food truck. Past the still-sizzling grill, stepping gingerly over an oil slick of onions. Just as she kicked open the back door and hobbled out, the speaker spit out one last shaky bar of "Pop! Goes the Weasel" and died.

The owner of the ice cream truck, a swarthy-looking man with wild eyes and frizzed-out hair, came running up to her, waving his arms and screaming. "You crazy lady!" he shouted. "You almost hit me, you know that? You almost hit me!" He was chattering like mad and hopping up and down from the shot of adrenaline his body had doled out to him.

Theodosia raised a hand and waved him off tiredly. "But I *didn't* hit you. Your truck's just fine. *You're* fine."

It took the ice cream guy a few moments before he realized that he and his truck really had survived. He drew a shaky breath, seemed to relax a bit, and wiped the back of his hand across his mouth. Then he squinted at Theodosia and said, "So you want a rocky road or what?"

26

❧

It took an entire cadre of police officers and a terse call from Detective Tidwell to finally mop up the damages. It was going to take a lot more time and energy to mop up all the spilled food. The "path of destruction," as Drayton called it, went on for almost five full blocks.

But even though Andrew Turner had been apprehended, the evening wasn't quite over. Theodosia, Drayton, Max, and Timothy had quietly retreated to the Indigo Tea Shop. Drayton and Timothy had abandoned the Art Crawl Ball when Theodosia and Max had taken up chase and then been privy to some of the action for a block or so. Now Theodosia and Drayton had thrown open the doors to the tea shop so they could all gather together, discuss the bizarre circumstances, and try to recover from the excitement.

"I've got chamomile and Dimbulla," said Drayton. He was standing behind the counter brewing tea.

"You don't have to go to all that trouble, Drayton," said Max.

"But I want to," said Drayton. "Keeps me busy, gives me something to do. Otherwise I'd be all nervous and kerfluey."

"We wouldn't want that," said Theodosia. She looked down at her long dress, which was basically ruined. It was spattered with grease and what appeared to be a nice paisley pattern of ketchup and mustard. The bottom of the hem was completely frayed, as if it had been clawed by a dozen crazed wombats. What would Delaine think? Was the skirt returnable? Worse yet, Delaine would probably go crazy when she found out that her date was an accused killer! So now she had that to deal with!

A heavy knock on the front door brought their excited chatter to a screeching halt.

"Who could that be?" asked Max.

"Customers?" said Drayton as he stepped to the door. "Well . . . only one way to find out." He pulled the door open.

Sheriff Anson stood in the doorway and stared in as if he were peering into a rabbit hole. Then he reached up, swiped his Smokey Bear hat off his head, and said, "Detective Tidwell told me I'd probably find you people here."

"Come on in," sang Drayton. "Come in and join the party."

"Some party," said Max.

"Would you care for a cup of tea, Sheriff?" Theodosia asked.

"Tea?" said the sheriff. He said the word as if he were referencing strychnine.

"You might enjoy it," said Drayton. He poured out a cup and handed it to Sheriff Anson. "Perfectly steeped."

Sheriff Anson set down the duffel bag he was holding and took a tentative sip. "Not bad," he said.

"No," said Drayton. "The words you were looking for are 'it's good.'"

"You have some news for us, Sheriff?" Theodosia asked. She figured the good sheriff must have shown up here for a reason.

Sheriff Anson nodded and stepped forward. "First things first. Andrew Turner just gave us a full confession—about killing Drew Knight, turning on the pesticide sprayer at the winery, and stashing the gun in Van Deusen's car. One of my deputies also took Pandora Knight into custody. She swears that she had nothing to do with the murder of Drew Knight. And that she never suspected Andrew Turner as the killer."

"But she was in on the counterfeiting scheme," said Theodosia. "She had to be."

Sheriff Anson nodded. "Yes, she completely owned up to that. She said that Turner approached her with a scheme to produce counterfeit wines when his art gallery started to go down the drain. And then they both pitched it to Tanaka."

"Or vice versa," said Theodosia.

"Perhaps we'll never know who was the instigator," said Timothy Neville.

"Anyway," Anson continued, "Pandora claims she jumped at the whole sorry scheme because she was desperate for money, too."

"But she *had* money," said Drayton.

"She wanted more," said Theodosia.

Max shook his head. "Do you believe her?"

Sheriff Anson tapped his thumb against his broad chest. "If you're asking me if I think Pandora was eager to get in on the counterfeit wine scam, yes I do. But I don't think she's any sort of killer."

"I believe that, too," said Theodosia. "In the end, Pandora and Jordan came together over the death of Drew. I think Pandora may be a world-class schemer, but I don't think she's a killer."

Theodosia vividly recalled the scene she'd witnessed at Magnolia Cemetery between Pandora and Turner. Pandora had said something to the effect of, "You wouldn't, would you?" And Turner had replied, "Of course not."

Theodosia now realized that they hadn't been talking about Drew's artwork as Turner had suggested. Pandora had been asking him if he'd killed Drew. Pandora had simply been too trusting of Turner. And way too greedy, too.

"Compared to Andrew Turner," said Max, "Pandora turned out to be the lesser of two evils."

"The lesser of two evils is still evil," said Theodosia.

Drayton nodded. "You're quite correct." He held up a blue-and-white teapot and asked, "Who else would like a nice cup of tea?"

"I was hoping for something a little stronger," said Max. "This evening seems to call for a nightcap of sorts."

"Interesting you should mention that," said Sheriff Anson. He reached into the duffel bag that was puddled on the floor beside him and pulled out a bottle of wine.

"Let me see that," said Max. He peered at the label. "Ho! Château Latour!"

"Another fake!" snorted Drayton. "Haven't we had enough of that for one night?"

"Don't be so hasty," said Sheriff Anson. "This particular bottle came from the back room of The Turner Gallery. Where, by the way, we found stacks and stacks of counterfeit labels."

"So . . . maybe this wine is for real?" said Max.

"Like I always say," said Theodosia, "there's only one way to find out."

A corkscrew was hastily produced and the cork was popped. Theodosia set out wineglasses and the wine was carefully poured.

Drayton swirled the wine in his glass and was the first to take a small sip. He frowned and wrinkled his nose, considering the wine. "Actually this is . . . rather nice. Timothy? Would you mind rendering your expert opinion?"

Timothy stuck his nose deep into the glass and inhaled. Then he tipped his glass back and took a taste.

"Well?" said Max.

Timothy's eyes seemed to sparkle. "Hmm, this is really quite good. It desperately needs to breathe, of course, but after a fair amount of aeration, this wine might actually prove to be quite remarkable."

Sheriff Anson chuckled. "I certainly hope so. Because I'm pretty sure this is the bottle they used as a model for the counterfeit labels."

"You mean to tell me it really is real?" said Theodosia.

"Absolutely," said Sheriff Anson.

Max pulled Theodosia into his arms and gave her a hug. "It's the real deal," he whispered. "Just like you."

"A toast, then," said Timothy.

Drayton raised his glass of wine and gave a sly smile. "To a mystery solved!"

They all clinked glasses together as they echoed his words: "To a mystery solved!"

The Indigo Tea Shop

Chilled Mango Summer Soup

2 mangos, peeled, seeded, and diced
¼ cup sugar
1 lemon, zested and juiced
1½ cups cream (or half-and-half)

PLACE mangos, sugar, lemon juice, lemon zest, and cream into a blender or food processor. Cover and whip until smooth and creamy. Serve chilled. Yield: 4 servings.

Vegetable Medley Tea Sandwiches

1 small cucumber, peeled, seeded, and diced
½ red bell pepper, diced small
¼ cup diced green onions
1 Tbsp. minced fresh parsley
1 (8 oz.) package cream cheese, softened

1 Tbsp. mayonnaise
salt to taste
16 thin cocktail rye bread slices

COMBINE all ingredients (except bread) in a bowl and mix thoroughly. Spread mixture on half of the bread slices, then top with remaining slices. Cut sandwiches in half diagonally. Yield: 16 sandwiches.

Strawberry Jammy Scones

6 cups flour
1 cup sugar
¼ cup baking powder
¼ tsp. salt
3 sticks butter, chilled
1½ cups milk
1 cup strawberry jam

PREHEAT oven to 425 degrees. In a large bowl, combine flour, sugar, baking powder, and salt. Cut butter into small cubes and add to the mixture. Use a pastry cutter or knives to incorporate the butter into flour mixture until it's nice and crumbly. Pour in milk and stir until dough forms a ball. If it's too dry, add a little bit more milk. Place dough on lightly floured surface and gently pat out into a 10-by-12-inch rectangle that is about ¼-inch thick. Spread strawberry jam over half the dough. Fold dough over to make a 5-by-12-inch rectangle. Cut dough into 8 triangles and gently pinch the edges closed. Bake on a greased baking sheet for 12 to 15 minutes, until scones are a light golden brown. Yield: 8 scones.

Haley's French Toast Casseroles

4 oz. cream cheese, room temperature
4 eggs
⅔ cup milk
⅓ cup orange juice
¼ cup maple syrup
½ tsp. freshly grated orange peel
3 cups bread crumbs (about 4 or 5 slices)

HEAT oven to 350 degrees. Whisk cream cheese in bowl until smooth. Add eggs, one at a time, whisking after each addition. Stir in milk, orange juice, maple syrup, and orange peel until mixture is well blended. Divide bread crumbs among 4 greased 10-oz. ramekins or custard cups. Pour egg mixture over bread, making sure mixture is equal in all 4 ramekins. Place ramekins on baking sheet and bake in center of oven for about 30 minutes. French toast casseroles are done when they puff and a silver knife comes out clean. Yield: 4 servings.

Apricot Scones

2 cups all-purpose flour
⅓ cup sugar
1 Tbsp. baking powder

¼ tsp. salt
5 Tbsp. cold butter, diced up
1 cup heavy cream
1 cup chopped dried apricots

PREHEAT oven to 375 degrees. In a bowl, combine flour, sugar, baking powder, and salt. Cut in butter with fork or pastry blender until crumbly. Stir in cream, then add apricots. Knead dough 5 or 6 times on a lightly floured surface until dough forms a ball. Roll dough into a circle about ½-inch thick. Cut into approximately 16 triangles. Places scones on greased baking sheet, sprinkle a little extra sugar on top, and bake for 16 to 20 minutes. Yield: 16 scones.

Blue Cheese and Grape Tea Sandwiches

4 slices pumpernickel bread
1 piece blue cheese, softened
bunch of red grapes, seedless, sliced thin

TRIM crusts off bread, then cut into quarters. Gently spread softened blue cheese on each piece of bread. Top with sliced red grapes. Yield: 16 sandwiches.

Baked Crab Rangoon

1 package cream cheese (16 oz.), softened
1 can crabmeat, drained and crumbled

2 green onions, chopped
2 tsp. Worcestershire sauce
½ tsp. soy sauce
1 package wonton skins

PREHEAT oven to 425 degrees. Combine first 5 ingredients in a bowl and mix until well blended. Lay out wonton skins. Place 1 teaspoon of crab mixture in the center of each wonton. Moisten the edges of the wonton with water, then fold in half to form a triangle. Pull two of the edges in slightly and pinch to seal. Arrange rangoons on a greased cookie sheet and bake for 12 to 14 minutes or until golden brown. Serve with your favorite sweet and sour sauce.

Ladybug Tea Sandwiches

6 slices white bread
cream cheese
18 cherry tomatoes
18 parsley leaves
18 black olives, pitted

USING cookie cutter, cut 3 rounds of bread out of each slice of bread. Spread rounds with cream cheese. Slice cherry tomatoes in half and arrange as wings on top of each round. Place a leaf of parsley under tomatoes so it looks like each ladybug is sitting on it. Slice olives in half. Reserve 18 halves. Slice the remaining halves into small bits. Place an olive half in front of wings to form the ladybug's head. Place the small bits on the tomato wings to create the ladybug's spots. Yield: 18 small (and very cute!) sandwiches.

Drayton's Coconut Iced Tea

2 cups boiling water
2 teabags jasmine or other fruity tea
1 Tbsp. honey
1 cup unsweetened coconut milk
lemon wedges

BREW tea by pouring boiling water over tea bags. Let steep for about 3 minutes. Pull out tea bags and stir in honey and coconut milk. Let cool to room temperature. Serve over crushed ice with a wedge of lemon. Yield: 2 servings.

Almond Joy Scones

2 cups flour
¼ cup sugar
2 tsp. baking powder
½ tsp. salt
1 stick butter, cold and cut into small pieces
¾ cup sweetened, shredded coconut
¾ cup sliced, toasted almonds
¾ cup chocolate bits, milk chocolate or semisweet
¾ cup heavy cream
1 large egg

PREHEAT oven to 400 degrees. Mix together flour, sugar, baking powder, and salt in a large mixing bowl. Using a pastry cutter or knives, cut in the butter until mixture is coarse and crumbly. In a separate bowl, combine cream and egg. Add wet mixture to dry mixture until just combined (dough will still look crumbly) and then mix in chocolate bits. Place dough on lightly floured surface and pat out gently until dough is about 1-inch thick. Using a cookie cutter, cut out 12 to 14 scones. If you'd like, you can cut them in wedges, too. Place on greased baking sheet and baked for 16 to 18 minutes, until golden brown. For best baking, rotate cooking sheet in the oven halfway through. Note: These are great breakfast or dessert scones! Yield: 12 to 14 scones.

Ricotta–Orange Tea Sandwiches

    1 package fresh ricotta cheese
    6 slices white or whole wheat bread
    1 jar orange marmalade

SPREAD ricotta cheese on 3 slices of bread. Gently spread orange marmalade on top of that. Top with remaining slices of bread. Cut off crusts, then cut into squares. Yield: 12 sandwiches.

Church Street Quiche

    2 cups milk
    4 eggs

¾ cup biscuit baking mix
¼ cup butter, softened
1 cup Parmesan cheese, grated
1 (10 oz.) package chopped broccoli, thawed and drained
1 cup cubed cooked ham
8 oz. Cheddar cheese, shredded

PREHEAT oven to 375 degrees. Lightly grease a 10-inch quiche dish. In large bowl, beat together milk, eggs, baking mix, butter, and Parmesan cheese. Batter will remain somewhat lumpy. Stir in broccoli, ham, and Cheddar cheese. Pour into quiche dish. Bake for 50 minutes, until eggs are set and top is golden brown. Yield: 4 servings.

Fast Bake Crabmeat Casserole

1 cup milk
1 package cheese spread (8 oz.), chopped into bits
½ cup butter, softened
1 jar pimentos (4 oz.), drained
1½ cups egg noodles, cooked
1 can crabmeat (6 oz.), drained
¼ cup dry breadcrumbs

PREHEAT oven to 350 degrees. Combine all ingredients together in a bowl except for breadcrumbs. Transfer crab mixture to a greased 2-quart casserole dish. Sprinkle with breadcrumbs. Bake uncovered for 30 minutes. Yield: 4 servings.

TEA TIME TIPS FROM
Laura Childs

Ladybug Tea Party

Have fun and go a little crazy when you decorate for your ladybug tea party! Think ladybug invitations, red napkins and place mats, and red balloons with black polka dots. You can also buy ready-made ladybugs in craft stores for décor and tie red-and-white polka dot ribbon on the backs of your chairs and the handles of your teacups. Start your first course with coconut scones, then serve ladybug tea sandwiches that you create from the directions in this book. Cheddar cheese and apple chutney tea sandwiches would also be lovely. For dessert, a cake store should be able to provide you with ladybug cake pops. And chocolates with ladybug-design foil wrappers are available in many candy stores.

Big Hat Tea

If all your guests are wearing hats, this tea is going to be a little bit more formal. So break out your linen tablecloth, crystal glasses, sterling silver, and nicest china. Start your high tea in high gear with ginger-pear scones and mounds of Devonshire cream. Croissants stuffed with crab salad would make a great second course, and you could also serve baked mushroom and onion tarts. Tea cakes are always a treat for dessert, and your tea flavors might include spiced plum and an Earl Grey floral. For goodness' sake, don't forget the fresh flowers and background music!

White Chocolate Tea

Dark chocolate is delicious, but white chocolate is a treat all its own! Start with white chocolate chip scones, then enjoy a smoked salmon and cream cheese tea sandwich or chicken salad with cranberries and walnuts. For sweets, consider strawberries dipped in white chocolate, cookies with white chocolate frosting, and white chocolate brownies. Flavored teas such as vanilla-caramel or mint tea would complement all your choices beautifully.

Pet-Friendly Tea

Did you know that dogs love taking tea? Oh, yes, they do. Especially when they're served special dog cookies and treats. Serve the people at your tea party an egg salad tea sandwich on pumpkin bread. Goat cheese with sundried tomatoes also makes for a tasty tea sandwich. And a small can of dog food spread on dog crackers is a lovely second course for dogs. Skip the sweets (you know why!) and focus on the tea. Maybe a cranberry-orange tea for the humans and Machu's Blend for your canine friends. This is a special herbal dog tea that you can order from Californiateahouse .com. It promotes healthy skin, lowers stress, and aids in digestion.

Store Bought in a Hurry Tea

Yes, of course, you're busy. But that's no excuse for not inviting your friends in for tea. Start with chicken salad that you buy at the deli. Spread it on cinnamon-raisin bread, top with another slice, and cut off the crusts. Now cut it into quarters. See how easy that was? Maybe you could even manage some cream cheese and sliced cucumber sandwiches. If you don't have a cutter to make tea sandwich rounds, use a juice glass. For dessert, buy a plain white cake and sprinkle it with edible flower petals. This bit of creativity takes your cake from simply store-bought to showstopper! And you are definitely permitted to cut corners and use teabags. Now send out those e-mail invites and have some fun!

Mother–Daughter Tea

Make this is a special tea and serve all the things that moms—and little girls—really love. Start with maraschino cherry scones and dabs of Devonshire cream (or whipped cream for the little ones). Move on to tea sandwiches with tuna salad and ham salad filling. You can also do peanut butter and raisin tea sandwiches or peanut butter and jelly. Desserts might include sugar cookies or lemon bars. Moms might like orange spice or English toffee flavored teas, while little girls are often happy with apple juice or a cup of milk. And remember, dolls and teddy bears have a standing invitation!

Father's Day Tea

Dads enjoy a tea party, too. Especially when you serve mini burgers (think sliders), triangle tea sandwiches filled with roast beef and brown mustard, or tea sandwiches with chicken salad and chutney. Your desserts might include brownie bites and chocolate cake. Some heartier Dad-style teas might include a rich Ceylon tea, or you could even try a spiced chai. And if Dad's not a tea drinker, remember there are a number of tea-infused vodkas on the market! A vodka-tea-tonic anyone?

TEA RESOURCES

TEA PUBLICATIONS

Tea Magazine—Quarterly magazine about tea as a beverage and its cultural significance in the arts and society. (teamag.com)

TeaTime—Luscious magazine profiling tea and tea lore. Filled with glossy photos and wonderful recipes. (teatimemagazine .com)

Southern Lady—From the publishers of *TeaTime* with a focus on people and places in the South as well as wonderful tea time recipes. (southernladymagazine.com)

The Tea House Times—Go to teahousetimes.com for subscription information and dozens of links to tea shops, purveyors of tea, gift shops, and tea events.

Victoria—Articles and pictorials on homes, home design, gardens, and tea. (victoriamag.com)

The Gilded Lily—Publication from the Ladies Tea Guild. (glily.com)

Tea in Texas—Highlighting Texas tea rooms and tea events. (teaintexas.com)

Tea Talk Magazine—Covers tea news and tea shops in Britain. (teatalkmagazine.co.uk)

Fresh Cup Magazine—For tea and coffee professionals. (freshcup .com)

Tea & Coffee—Trade journal for the tea and coffee industry. (teaandcoffee.net)

Bruce Richardson—This author has written several definitive books on tea (elmwoodinn.com/books)

Jane Pettigrew—This author has written thirteen books on the varied aspects of tea and its history and culture. (janepetti grew.com/books)

A *Tea Reader*—by Katrina Avila Munichiello, an anthology of tea stories and reflections.

AMERICAN TEA PLANTATIONS

Charleston Tea Plantation—The oldest and largest tea plantation in the United States. Order their fine black tea or schedule a visit online. (bigelowtea.com)

Fairhope Tea Plantation—Tea produced in Fairhope, Alabama, can be purchased though the Church Mouse gift shop. (thechurch mouse.com)

Sakuma Brothers Farm—This tea garden just outside Burlington, Washington, has been growing white and green tea for more than a dozen years. (sakumamarket.com)

Big Island Tea—Organic artisan tea from Hawaii. (bigislandtea.com)

Mauna Kea Tea—Organic green and oolong tea from Hawaii's Big Island. (maunakeatea.com)

Onomea Tea—Nine-acre tea estate near Hilo, Hawaii. (onomeatea .com)

TEA WEBSITES AND INTERESTING BLOGS

Teamap.com—Directory of hundreds of tea shops in the U.S. and Canada.

GreatTearoomsofAmerica.com—Excellent tea shop guide.

Afternoontea.co.uk—Guide to tearooms in the UK.

Cookingwithideas.typepad.com—Recipes and book reviews for the Bibliochef.

Cuppatea4sheri.blogspot.com—Amazing recipes.

Seedrack.com—Order camellia sinensis seeds and grow your own tea!

Friendshiptea.net—Tea shop reviews, recipes, and more.

RTbookreviews.com—Wonderful romance and mystery book review site.

Adelightsomlife.com—Tea, gardening, and cottage crafts.

Theladiestea.com—Networking platform for women.

Jennybakes.com—Fabulous recipes from a real make-it-from-scratch baker.

Teanmystery.com—Tea shop, books, gifts, and gift baskets.

Lattedavotion.wordpress.com—Coffee, tea, and book reviews.

Southernwritersmagazine.com—Inspiration, writing advice, and author interviews of Southern writers.

Allteapots.com—Teapots from around the world.

Fireflyvodka.com—South Carolina purveyors of Sweet Tea Vodka, Raspberry Tea Vodka, Peach Tea Vodka, and more. Just visiting this website is a trip in itself!

Teasquared.blogspot.com—Fun, well-written blog about tea, tea shops, and tea musings.

Bernideensteatimeblog.blogspot.com—Tea, baking, decorations, and gardening.

Tealoversroom.com—California tea rooms, Teacasts, links.

Teapages.blogspot.com—All things tea.

Possibili-teas.net—Tea consultants with a terrific monthly newsletter.

Relevanttealeaf.blogspot.com—All about tea.

Baking.about.com—Carroll Pellegrinelli writes a terrific baking blog complete with recipes and photo instructions.

Stephcupoftea.blogspot.com—Blog on tea, food, and inspiration.

Teawithfriends.blogspot.com—Lovely blog on tea, friendship, and tea accoutrements.

Sharonsgardenofbookreviews.blogspot—Terrific book reviews by an entertainment journalist.

Teaescapade.wordpress.com—Enjoyable tea blog.

Bellaonline.com/site/tea—Features and forums on tea.

Lattesandlife.com—Witty musings on life.

Napkinfoldingguide.com—Photo illustrations of twenty-seven different (and sometimes elaborate) napkin folds.

Worldteaexpo.com—This premier business-to-business trade show features more than three hundred tea suppliers, vendors, and tea innovators.

Sweetgrassbaskets.net—One of several websites where you can buy sweetgrass baskets direct from the artists.

Goldendelighthoney.com—Carolina honey to sweeten your tea.

Johnandkiras.com—Hand-painted ladybug chocolates and bees.

FatCatScones.com—Frozen ready-to-bake scones.

KingArthurFlour.com—One of the best flours for baking. This is what many professional pastry chefs use.

Teagw.com—Visit this website and click on Products to find dreamy tea pillows filled with jasmine, rose, lavender, and green tea.

Californiateahouse.com—Order Machu's Blend, a special herbal tea for dogs that promotes healthy skin, lowers stress, and aids digestion.

Vintageteaworks.com—This company offers six unique wine-flavored tea blends that celebrate wine and respect the tea.

Downtonabbeycooks.com—A *Downton Abbey* blog with news and recipes. You can also order their book *Abbey Cooks*.

Auntannie.com—Crafting site that will teach you how to make your own petal envelopes, pillow boxes, gift bags, etc.

PURVEYORS OF FINE TEA
Adagio.com
Harney.com
Stashtea.com
Republicoftea.com
Teazaanti.com
Bigelowtea.com
Celestialseasonings.com
Goldenmoontea.com
Uptontea.com

VISITING CHARLESTON
Charleston.com—Travel and hotel guide.

Charlestoncvb.com—The official Charleston convention and visitor bureau.

Charlestontour.wordpress.com—Private tours of homes and gardens, some including lunch or tea.

Charlestonplace.com—Charleston Place Hotel serves an excellent afternoon tea, Thursday through Saturday, 1 to 3.

Culinarytoursofcharleston.com—Sample specialties from Charleston's local eateries, markets, and bakeries.

Charlestonteaco.com—This small café on Ann Street sells loose leaf and iced teas and serves breakfast and lunch. They have even blended a special medicinal migraine tea.

Poogansporch.com—This restored Victorian house serves traditional lowcountry cuisine. Be sure to ask about Poogan!

Preservationsociety.org—Hosts Charleston's annual Fall Candlelight Tour.

Palmettocarriage.com—Horse-drawn carriage rides.

Charlestonharbortours.com—Boat tours and harbor cruises.

Ghostwalk.net—Stroll into Charleston's haunted history. Ask them about the "original" Theodosia!

CharlestonTours.net—Ghost tours plus tours of plantations and historic homes.

Turn the page for a preview of
Laura Childs's
next Tea Shop Mystery . . .

MING TEA MURDER

Available in hardcover May 2015
from Berkley Prime Crime!

Drums banging, sweet notes of a Chinese violin trembling in the air, the enormous red and gold dragon shook its great head and danced its way across the rotunda of the Gibbes Museum in Charleston, South Carolina. It was the opening night celebration for the reconstruction of a genuine eighteenth century Chinese teahouse, and the crème de la crème of society had turned out in full force for this most auspicious occasion.

And even though black tie events weren't exactly topmost in Theodosia Browning's comfort zone, there had been no easy way to refuse this particular invitation, especially when your handsome, hunky boyfriend was the museum's PR director. So here she was, applauding the music, mesmerized by the spectacle of the enormous dragon's gaping jaws as it snapped and slapped above the heads of the excited crowd.

Yes, the event was most impressive, Theodosia decided. Glowing red Chinese lanterns, stands of bamboo, elegant orchids, and miniature penjing trees, had transformed the cold, marble rotunda into an exotic Asian garden. And then there was the food. Serving tables were laden with tempting bites of shrimp dumplings, honey-glazed pork buns, chicken satay, and miniature crispy duck rolls. Delicious!

Of course, the real treasure was the Chinese teahouse itself, purchased and deconstructed in Shanghai, then rebuilt board-by-board inside the museum. The blue-tiled, exotically peaked roof, gleaming cypress walls, and intricately carved sandalwood screens seemed tailor-made for an emperor and his courtesans.

"I'm anxious to take a look inside," Theodosia told Max, who was gazing about proudly if not a little distractedly.

"We pulled it off," said Max. "I can't believe we actually pulled it off." He sounded surprised that his PR efforts had yielded such a turnout.

"Of course, you did," Theodosia told him. "Because nobody would pass up an opportunity to enjoy a fancy celebration like this." *Except . . . maybe me?*

Theodosia had a smile that could light up a tea room—and often did, since she was the proprietor of the Indigo Tea Shop on nearby Church Street. But tonight she'd been smiling so exuberantly that her face felt like it was about ready to crack. She'd flitted about on Max's arm, chatting and rubbing shoulders with Charleston's old guard, most of them big buck donors who were thrilled that their money had made it possible to import this masterpiece of a tea house.

But Theodosia was also counting the seconds to midnight.

Because when the clock struck the proverbial witching hour, she planned to cut and run like Cinderella. She'd kick off her pinchy black satin heels, climb into her pumpkin coach, which, in this case, was her venerable six-year-old Jeep, and head home to her cozy little cottage where her dog, Earl Grey, awaited her.

Shaking her head, forcing another smile, because Max

was saying something to her again, she leaned toward him and said, "Excuse me?"

"I need to schmooze a couple more board members," said Max. "You'll be okay?"

"I'll be perfect," said Theodosia.

"Go check out the photo booth," Max urged. "While I huddle with Edgar Webster, one of our illustrious donors." He grinned. "Maybe take a selfie." As a fun perk for the guests, Max had convinced the museum director to let him bring in a photo booth. And just as he'd predicted, there'd been a constant parade of guests in and out of the booth all night long. Everyone was seemingly thrilled with the notion of immortalizing themselves in photos, even if they were the small black and white variety.

"I'll do that," Theodosia told him. "That'll be fun." As she turned to push her way through the crowd, she caught sight of herself in a fragment of mirror. And as always, the image gave her pause.

Is that really me with that mass of auburn hair framing my face and blue eyes looking so expectant? Hmm, I don't look half bad for being in my mid-thirties.

She'd swooped a hint of blusher on the apples of her cheeks, smudged on the bare minimum of mascara. But with her confident bearing, winning smile, and fair Southern belle skin, she looked almost like a noblewoman who might have been portrayed in some delectable English painting. Perhaps something James Constable might have done.

"You're looking very lovely tonight," said a voice behind her.

Theodosia whirled about to find Drayton, her dear friend and tea master, smiling at her.

"If not a bit mischievous," continued Drayton.

Theodosia smiled and gave an offhand wave. "Ah, I think I might be a tad underdressed." She'd worn a simple black cocktail dress, an armful of colorful bead bracelets, and heels, while most of the other women were glitzed and glammed in the latest runway creations from Dior and Oscar de la Renta.

"Nonsense," said Drayton. "An LBD is always perfectly appropriate." Drayton was sixtyish, tall, and debonair. Tonight his gray hair was slicked back straight and he wore a slim-cut tuxedo with his trademark bowtie. He was the buttoned-up old guard to Theodosia's more playful boho cool.

"Did you get a gander at all the jewels these women are wearing?" Theodosia asked him. "I mean, a cat burglar would have a field day here."

Drayton's bushy brows rose in twin arcs. "Please don't interject a criminal element into the occasion. Even if it is only imaginary."

"Okay, then I'll just compliment you on all your lovely penjing, because they certainly add to the Asian atmosphere." Penjing were basically Chinese bonsai, miniature trees that had been cut, trimmed, and wired so they could exist in small, moss-encrusted ceramic pots. Drayton, a master at creating windblown-style trees and miniature forests, had lent the museum a dozen of his trees. Most had spectacularly twisted trunks and leaves that were smaller than a lady's pinky nail.

"They do look nice, don't they? Particularly my Chinese elm." Drayton prided himself on his composure and modesty, but he also appreciated a compliment now and then.

"You've been inside the teahouse?" said Theodosia. They both had to take a step back since the crowd was pressing so hard around them.

"It's a marvel," exclaimed Drayton. "I took the liberty of exploring while all that Chinese dragon business was going on." He paused and smiled. "You should run over and take a quick peak, too. You'll love it."

"I'm going to," said Theodosia. "But first I promised Max I'd check out his photo booth." She looked around, saw that

Max was backed up against a wall, talking to a rather red-faced man, a board member by the name of Edgar Webster. Neither of them looked happy.

"*Photo* booth?" spat out Drayton. Clearly he wasn't a fan. "What is this fixation everyone has today with memorializing themselves? And then posting every single silly photograph on . . ." Drayton made a face. "On the *Internet*?"

"Come on," Theodosia cajoled. "It's not as bad as all that."

"I'm just not sure a photo booth is apropos for an event such as this."

"Still, it's fun. And everyone seems to love it."

"You see," said Drayton, "that's why I'm not everyone." Drayton was a self-proclaimed Luddite who mistrusted smart phones, DVDs, and CDs. In fact, he was an old-fashioned, vinyl record kind of guy.

"But you're perfect just the way you are," Theodosia assured him. She glanced around again, but Max and Webster had apparently moved on.

"Oh my," said Drayton. As he gazed into the crowd his placid expression suddenly changed to one of horror.

"What?" Then Theodosia caught sight of the small, blond woman who was speedballing toward them on clacking kitten heels.

"I'm going to let *you* handle this encounter," said Drayton as he quickly slipped away.

"You look like you're having a *marvelous* time," cooed Charlotte Webster. She slalomed to a stop in front of Theodosia and grinned like the Cheshire cat, practically upending her glass of champagne in the process. Charlotte was the bubbly socialite who presided over the Broad Street Garden Club, was a sometime customer at Theodosia's Indigo Tea Shop, and was married to Edgar Webster.

"It's a thrilling night," Theodosia told Charlotte, mustering yet another smile. Since Charlotte's husband, a prominent businessman and philanthropist, had put up the largest chunk of money to import the teahouse, she pretty much had to make nice with his wife.

"I was just chatting with Percy Capers," said Charlotte. She fluttered a pudgy hand and adjusted her necklace, a string of sparkling diamonds with a large yellow diamond as the center stone. "You know, the museum's curator of Asian art?"

Theodosia nodded. She'd met Capers a couple of times.

"Anyway, Mr. Capers was regaling me with horror stories about importing this lovely teahouse. Shipping it across the Pacific, shepherding it through customs, misplacing some of the actual parts. Why, do you know there are no *nails* whatsoever in the construction? That the entire thing is held together with dozens of wooden pegs?"

"I've heard that."

"Is that the craziest thing ever?" said Charlotte. "Wooden pegs?"

"I guess that's how they built them two hundred years ago," said Theodosia.

"Two hundred years? That's how old that thing is?" said Charlotte. She took a quick glug of champagne. "Well, I certainly hope we got our money's worth then." She giggled loudly, patted Theodosia on the arm, and toddled off.

Charlotte was a real character, Theodosia thought to herself. And then, because she really didn't want to be unkind, decided that the Websters, as civic-minded underwriters of the teahouse, really had done a wonderful thing.

As Theodosia slipped past one of the food tables, she accepted a miniature egg roll from a black-uniformed waiter. Then, when another waiter held out a tray filled with champagne glasses, she took a glass. As she sipped and surveyed the crowd, she was struck again by how fancy and formal everyone looked. Of course, many of the guests, board members as well as donors, were friends and neighbors who lived in the nearby historic district. There was one of the Ravenels conspiring with a Clayton and a Tisdale. And Mr. Pinckney was talking to a large man with a rather pronounced Texas bray.

The pounding of drums suddenly started up again, loud and hard, and Theodosia turned to see what was going on now. Oops, it was dragon time again. The Chinese dragon was humping its way through the crown once more, tossing its head from side to side, its dragon beard fluttering with every move.

Theodosia had witnessed a dragon parade in San Francisco's Chinatown once, when she'd been roaming up and down Grant Street, popping into tea shops, looking for unusual varieties and blends. But seeing this guy up close and personal was a lot more fun. And, from the enthusiasm generated by the crowd, they obviously thought so, too.

Edging her way through a clutch of suitably enthralled guests, Theodosia headed for the photo booth. Maybe she could slip in and take a quick photo right now. She wasn't all that hot to pose, but it would make Max happy. Give him a small souvenir of tonight's museum triumph.

Dodging around an enormous celadon pot filled with leafy bamboo plants, Theodosia darted past a red Chinese lantern supported by a heavy wooden post. Over here, in an alcove off the rotunda where the photo booth was located, it was a little darker, a little quieter.

Perfect.

Theodosia rounded a stone lion-dog statue, heading for the photo booth. The drums were pounding furiously now, the erhu, or Chinese violin, pouring out high, pleading notes. Finishing the last sip of champagne, she set her glass down on a small rosewood table and turned toward the photo booth.

Was it still occupied? she wondered. Or could she dart in for a quick photo?

"Hello?" Theodosia called out, giving a couple sharp knocks on the shiny, bright yellow exterior. She didn't want to go crashing in and photo-bomb someone. That would be just plain rude.

"Is someone in there?" she called again.

When there was no reply, Theodosia took a step forward. And just before her hand parted the flimsy black curtain, the toe of her strappy black stiletto slid into a patch of something sticky.

Oh no, she groaned. All she needed was to ruin her best pair of shoes because some exuberant guest had spilled a glop of sweet and sour sauce.

Theodosia glanced down, expecting to see sauce, fragments of an exploded pork bun, or a puddle of champagne. After all, this art opening had turned into a fairly raucous party.

Only what she saw instead was a small, dark puddle.

A spilled drink?

No, Theodosia decided. Champagne or tea would be much more translucent.

As she pulled her foot back and stared at the floor again, taking a longer, harder look, her heart began to flutter. Then it began to dance a little jitterbug. Because whatever was on the floor was decidedly dark and sticky.

No, it couldn't be. Could it?

Slowly, tentatively, her heart in her throat, Theodosia reached forward and slowly parted the curtains. And saw . . . nothing.

It was pitch black inside the photo booth. Lights out.

Somehow that didn't feel right to her. What was going on? She pushed the curtains a little farther apart.

And that's when she saw him. A large man, sprawled on a narrow wooden bench, bent all the way forward so his forehead pressed tightly against the front panel of the booth. His eyes were closed and he looked like he was passed out cold.

"Excuse me," said Theodosia. "Sir?" Her mouth felt dry,

her breathing was fast and thready. "Are you okay, sir?" She paused. "Do you need help?"

No answer.

Theodosia glanced backwards, looking for a museum guard, one of the museum staff, anyone who might be able to lend a hand.

But everyone had their backs to her. They were still cheering and clapping like mad as the musicians played wildly and the Chinese dragon continued his energetic prance.

Tentatively now, Theodosia touched a finger to the side of the man's throat. To where she figured a pulse point might be.

She felt . . . nothing. In fact, he felt cool. Practically lifeless.

A loud pounding sounded inside Theodosia's head and she could feel the tiny hairs on the back of her neck prickle and rise.

No . . . please no.

And, as her eyes gradually adjusted to the darkness inside the photo booth, as her mind slowly wrapped itself around what might have just happened, that's when she saw the first telltale evidence of foul play. Just above where her fingertip had come into contact with the man's throat, a trail of dark sticky liquid dribbled from his ear!

Blood? Has to be.

Theodosia snatched her hand away and backed out of the photo booth as fast as humanly possible. Then she screamed as loud as she could, her voice rising in volume as it mingled with the urgent, shrill notes of the erhu.

AND A QUICK NOTE
ON A DIFFERENT KIND OF BOOK
THAT'S IN THE WORKS FROM LAURA CHILDS:

Living a Tea Shop Life

Drinking Tea, Finding Balance, and Reclaiming
Your Creative Spirit.

With more than one hundred recipes and tea time tips!

Coming May 2015 from
New York Times Bestselling Author

LAURA CHILDS

MING TEA
MURDER

Normally Theodosia wouldn't attend a black-tie affair
for all the tea in China. But she can hardly say no to her
hunky, handsome boyfriend, Max, who directs public relations for the Gibbes Museum in Charleston. Max has
organized an amazing gala opening for an exhibit of a
genuine eighteenth-century Chinese teahouse, and the
crème de la crème of Charleston society is invited.

But on the night of the gala, Theodosia makes a grim
discovery—the body of museum donor Edgar Webster.
Now she must examine the life of the fallen philanthropist and find out who really wanted him to pay up...

laurachilds.com
penguin.com

M1581T1014

The Tea Shop Mysteries by
New York Times Bestselling Author
Laura Childs

DEATH BY DARJEELING
GUNPOWDER GREEN
SHADES OF EARL GREY
THE ENGLISH BREAKFAST MURDER
THE JASMINE MOON MURDER
CHAMOMILE MOURNING
BLOOD ORANGE BREWING
DRAGONWELL DEAD
THE SILVER NEEDLE MURDER
OOLONG DEAD
THE TEABERRY STRANGLER
SCONES & BONES
AGONY OF THE LEAVES
SWEET TEA REVENGE
STEEPED IN EVIL

"A delightful series."
—*The Mystery Reader*

"Murder suits [Laura Childs] to a Tea."
—*St. Paul Pioneer Press*

laurachilds.com
penguin.com

M314AS0913